D0914778

ADVANCE PRAISE FOR
THE HIDDEN CODE

THE HIDDEN CODE

P. J. HOOVER

CBAY Books
Dallas, Texas

The Hidden Code

For Sophie, for pointing out I was the perfect person to write this story

CHAPTER 1

"YOU SHOULD GO WITH ME TODAY," I SAY TO LUCAS as I slip into the booth across from him. He's dressed in black jeans and a T-shirt and has chalk covering his dark arms and hands. Scattered all over the table are his chalks, erasers, and brushes. Hanging on the wall behind us at Java Coffee is this morning's work of art, a giant decorated chalkboard complete with amazing pictures of donuts and drinks, including a cappuccino like the one that is currently letting off steam in front of me.

"A lecture at Harvard, Hannah? Really?" Lucas says, trying unsuccessfully to wipe the chalk off his hands. "Why would I want to spend my summer going to school? I do that all year."

"It's one day," I say, tucking the bangs I'm growing out into the knit hat that's supposed to hold them off my face. They're still too short to reach the two ponytails I always wear. "Only a few hours actually. And Uncle Randall's giving it."

"It's still school," Lucas says. "And nothing you say is going to convince me otherwise. Anyway, I got tons of work. You know that."

I do know that. Lucas busted his butt and lined up twenty different chalkboard and window decorating gigs for the next month straight, for all sorts of places around Boston, not just coffee shops.

"Speaking of which, did you see this article?" Lucas asks, shoving his cell phone in my face.

I scan the headline. *Giant Pharma CEO faces expulsion from board. Bankruptcy possible.*

"Amino Corp?" I say, skimming the article. "Like that should surprise anyone. That'd be awesome if they went down." I blow my again-escaped bangs out of my face.

"What do you mean?"

That's right. Lucas doesn't read online science journals like I do.

"I mean that they're the worst. Their reputation is trash. They do all sorts of illegal tests on people in third world countries without their consent. And some people even think they released that gas in Indonesia earlier this year to test some new drug they're working on."

Lucas raises his eyebrows. "Seriously?"

I shrug. "If rumors can be believed. But this is kind of proof, isn't it? A scammy company is bound to get in trouble eventually. Why do you care though? You don't like science."

"No, I don't like science," Lucas says. "But I do like getting paid. And they're one of the places I'm scheduled for next week.

They have two coffee shops, and they're paying my full rate for both. They better not cancel on me." He sets the phone back on the table, getting chalk all over the screen. Then he starts to pack up his supplies.

"Maybe they'll pay you in coffee," I say.

Lucas scowls. "I don't want coffee. I want cash."

I try one last time. "If you come to the lecture with me ..."

Lucas puts up a hand to stop me. "I don't want cash that bad, Hannah."

I know that Lucas isn't going to budge. He'd way rather spend the day drawing than listening to a lecture on linguistics.

Lucas drives me to Harvard in his ancient Camry. It used to be tan, but the sun and snow have faded it to where it now looks more like old camel hide instead. He weaves through campus until he gets as close to the lecture hall as possible.

"Have fun without me," Lucas says.

I straighten my knit hat once more and tighten my ponytails, pulling them over my shoulders so they hang down in front.

"It's only three hours," I say. "Not even a whole day. It's still not too late ..."

"Nope," Lucas says, then to punctuate the matter he sticks his Camry into reverse and waves.

I'm ten minutes early, but when I walk into the lecture hall, it's packed. There are only maybe a hundred seats in the entire room, and they sell out basically in the first five minutes after registration opens. Uncle Randall sees me and waves and points to a single seat up front that's still empty. I kind of don't want anyone to know I'm related to him, so I grab a seat in the back row instead. Not two seconds later, a guy about my age walks into the lecture hall and sits in the empty seat. He's got shaggy blond hair with sideburns, a gray hoodie, jeans, and dirty work boots, like he's going to hit up the nearest construction site after the lecture and build a few houses.

Uncle Randall is hooking up his computer to the projector and doing mic checks, blowing into the microphone so loudly that it nearly shatters my eardrums because the room isn't that big. Blessedly, my cappuccino has cooled off enough to drink. While I'm waiting, the guy who took my seat up front turns around and scans the room, and when his eyes find mine, they hold there for a moment. Confusion crosses his face. A weird feeling runs through me, like I should know this guy. But I've never seen him before. So I look away and act like I don't see him.

Uncle Randall gets everything working and finally dims the lights. A handful of younger kids make spooky ghost sounds but then settle down once Uncle Randall clears his throat. He clicks the slide, and a giant tower appears.

"We start with the Tower of Babel," he says, and from there he goes on to talk about the myth surrounding the tower, how all the languages of Earth are said to have sprung from that moment in time. It can't be true, but it makes for a good story to explain why there are so many different languages on Earth.

Some of what we cover isn't new to me. Linguistics is Uncle

4

Randall's specialty. We talk about it all the time at home, and he's always putting together mysterious linguistics scavenger hunts for me. But everyone in the lecture hall, me included, is shocked when Uncle Randall shows the Ice Age map and asks where Boston is. After five wrong guesses, Uncle Randall clicks to the next slide.

"During the Ice Age, Boston was one mile under the ice," Uncle Randall says.

With the Boston winters we've had the last couple years, I think maybe the Ice Age is coming again.

"That's a lot of ice," some girl with a pink buzz cut in the third row says. "Didn't that cause a mess when it melted?"

Uncle Randall clicks to the next slide. It shows the entire world map but with much of it covered by water.

"Enter the Great Flood," Uncle Randall says with a flourish. "The single most destructive linguistics event in the history of our world. Nearly every language created to that point, every symbol, every letter, was wiped out to the extent that very little remains from before the Great Flood for us to study."

"But isn't the Flood like the Tower of Babel?" some Asian guy a couple rows ahead of me asks. "Aren't they both just myths?"

"Yes, for the Tower of Babel," Uncle Randall says. "Or at least that's a widely held popular belief. As for the Great Flood, nearly every civilization on Earth has some account of it. From the Sumerians and the Chinese to the Aztecs, all talk of a time when water flooded the earth, wiping out plants, animals, and people."

"And everything got destroyed?" the guy up front who'd looked at me earlier asks.

Uncle Randall smiles, like he's expected this question, but then he notices who's asked it. A weird moment passes where Uncle Randall looks at the kid but doesn't say anything, almost like he knows him. Then he blinks a few times and clicks to the next slide.

"Exactly what I was going to get to next," Uncle Randall says. "There are some linguistic artifacts that try to recreate what was lost." He goes on to talk about the Rosetta Stone, the Fuente Magna, the Dead Sea Scrolls. I've heard about these before. Seen pictures and documentaries about them. But then he clicks to a slide that has a picture of something I can't name.

"And then there's this beauty," Uncle Randall says. "Let me introduce you all to what is referred to as the Deluge Segment."

The slide shows a limestone colored circular piece of rock on a red backdrop with rough edges and symbols engraved all over it. There's a ruler next to it, showing us that it's only about a foot in diameter, but since the picture is head-on, I can't tell how thick it is. The picture is in color but pretty grainy, like it was taken back in the old days.

"The Deluge Segment is one of the oldest known linguistic archaeological finds ever. This piece was found by Lewis and Clark on their explorations across America, though based on the precise type of Precambrian stone the artifact is made from, there is no way that the segment originated here in America. Harvard acquired it in 1866, and for years it was on display here at the Peabody Museum."

The guy who took my seat leans forward, angling his head like he's trying to read the markings on the stone. "But not anymore?"

"Not anymore," Uncle Randall says. "It was sold to a private owner back in the eighties."

"Who?" the guy asks.

Uncle Randall narrows his eyes. "I don't know."

It's a pretty blunt response, and I immediately know why. Uncle Randall is old school. He thinks that artifacts like this should be available to everyone for studying. A private owner means that people like him can't study it anymore. We've been donating a ton of the stuff that our ancestors pilfered over the ages to museums.

"What does it say?" someone asks.

Uncle Randall zooms in so we can see the symbols up close although they still look pretty blurry. "Many of the symbols are similar to symbols we recognize from ancient civilizations, but as of yet this piece hasn't been deciphered. And now, out of the hands of experts, it probably never will be. The piece remains a mystery."

He clicks to the next slide and goes on to talk about changes in linguistics once the Roman Empire came along. Then it's on to language in the Americas. He's about to launch into what he calls his *Master Chart of Alphabets* when a girl walks into the room. She has on a navy blue Harvard polo shirt and tan pants, so I'm guessing she works here.

"Sorry," she says, waving at the group. "Just a message for Dr. Easton." She walks onstage and hands Uncle Randall a large manila envelope. Then she leaves the way she came. He opens the large envelope and upends it. A small yellowed envelope falls out, into his hand. Uncle Randall studies the envelope for a moment, then traces a finger over the front of it. His eyes are wide, and he looks right at me.

My heart races, but I have no idea why. It's just a piece of mail. Nothing special. Except Uncle Randall's face tells me that it's something more.

He tucks the envelope into the pocket of his jacket, but his hands are shaking. No one else probably notices, but also no one knows him better than me.

"Now where were we?" he says, clicking to the next slide.

We were at the linguistics lecture, that's where. But my mind isn't there anymore. It's spinning because I need to know what's in the envelope.

CHAPTER 2

I TRY TO FIND OUT WHAT'S IN THE ENVELOPE ALL week, but Uncle Randall doesn't mention it and doesn't leave it sitting around for me to find. I bring it up twice at dinner, but he changes the subject. So during the day, when he's at work, I scour Easton Estate. Our house was built in another age, for another time. There are twenty-seven bedrooms, as many baths, three kitchens—though I can't for the life of me imagine why anyone would need three kitchens—a ballroom that my parents converted to a lab twenty years ago, and two guest houses on the property, though no one has lived in them since Uncle Randall moved back into the main house after my parents died. I look everywhere. The envelope is nowhere.

Saturday rolls around, which happens to be my birthday. Uncle Randall tried to throw me a big party for my sixteenth birthday, but the only celebration I wanted was to have Lucas come over for dinner and to hang out and watch cheesy movies on the *Lifetime Network*. A few minutes after six, he pulls up and blows the horn just to let us know he's arrived. It sounds like a bullfrog dying.

"When are you getting your permit, Hannah?" Uncle Randall asks, cringing at the sound of Lucas's horn. The lines in his forehead crease. Uncle Randall's not old, only around forty-five, but over the last few years, I've noticed a lot more of his forehead showing. My grandfather never went bald, so genetics tells me that there's a good chance Uncle Randall never will either.

"I'm signing up on Monday," I say. For the last eleven years, anytime he couldn't drive me himself, Uncle Randall has insisted on having our driver Devin take me everywhere, refusing to let me take public transportation. The small fact that Lucas has been able to take me places these last six months has been a major relief. Getting my own license will be even better. Even though Devin is pretty chill, being chauffeured around town is like having a permanent babysitter.

For my birthday, Chef Lilly, who's been with our family forever, makes all my favorites, including vegetarian meatballs, butternut squash soup, and truffle layer cake. By the end of the sixth course, I want to undo the top button of my jeans.

"Did you show Lucas the Georgia O'Keeffe yet?" Uncle Randall says as Lucas is finishing up his third piece of layer cake.

"You do not have a Georgia O'Keeffe," Lucas says, shoving the last bite into his mouth. He stands awkwardly as he tries to figure out what to do with his dessert plate. One of our maids, Sylvia, spots him and swipes it from his hands before he can take a step.

"We just got it," I say, trying to act like it's no big deal. Lucas is convinced he's somehow related to Georgia O'Keeffe though there are no records to prove it. I've been trying to do a DNA test, which would be no problem if I could actually get some of Georgia O'Keeffe's DNA. Hence the painting. I spent a god-awful amount of money on it. I'm praying there are hairs or something caught under the paint.

"Show me now, woman," he says.

I laugh, and we head off into the game room where I've hung the thing. We stop in the ballroom-turned-lab to pick up my sugar gliders, Castor and Pollux, who, now that it's night, are awake and active. Castor sits on my left shoulder, tucked under one of my ponytails, and Pollux jumps to the top of my head, like it's some sort of game.

I show Lucas the painting, and he reaches his hand out, closing his eyes and holding his fingers inches away from the canvas, like somehow he can feel the image. Artists are strange.

"So I guess you like it," I say when he's finally finished worshipping the painting.

"Just a little," Lucas says.

"I was going to give it to you," I say.

Lucas's eyes open wide. "There is no way you can—"

I put up a hand to stop him. "Don't worry. Uncle Randall says we have to give it to a museum." It was the only way Uncle Randall allowed me to buy it.

Relief seems to flow through Lucas. "Good. Because there is no way I could even afford the insurance on that thing. And you can't be giving me stuff like that. It's ..."

"... awesome?" I suggest.

"Yeah, something like that. Oh, but speaking of presents, I got you one."

"I said no presents, remember?"

"How about you buy me a print of the Georgia O'Keeffe, and we call it even?"

"Deal."

He hands me a small box, maybe only five inches high by seven inches wide. It's obvious that he wrapped it using whatever he could find around his house, which in this case happens to be the last Chemistry test that he took.

"You got a C?"

"I'm not you, Hannah. Remember? I wasn't born with the Periodic Table implanted in my head."

"The Periodic Table is almost like a work of art," I say. "You'd like it if you gave it a chance."

"It's had its chance," Lucas says. "And I've determined that it sucks."

"Don't diss the Periodic Table," I say.

He puts up a hand. "No disrespect meant."

I tear the paper, ripping it in half so the subpar Chemistry test becomes nothing but a memory. Inside is a picture of an eye. But not just any eye. It's my left eye, green with two dots of brown mixed in like freckles, one on the bottom and one on the left. There are eyelashes and even my eyebrow, complete with the scar running through it where I cut myself when

I was three. It's printed on metal and surrounded by a black metal frame.

"This is the coolest thing I've ever seen," I say.

"It's a digital painting," Lucas says.

"It is not!"

"Would I lie?"

I hold it closer, looking for anything that looks computer generated. "You did this on the computer? How is that even possible?"

Lucas tries not to look proud, but he can't hide his grin. "I've been going through a ton of tutorials. Traditional art is great, but I figured since you gave me the computer, I might as well expand my skills."

I brush my finger over the image. "I'd say you're off to a good start."

"You should see some of the other stuff I'm working on," Lucas says. "It's unbelievable what you can do with a computer. Some of those software packages are crazy awesome."

I angle my head at him and wait.

"I know," Lucas says. "This is where you say 'I told you so.'"

"I told you so." I've been nagging Lucas to get started with digital art since the beginning of high school. He used the "we can't afford a computer" excuse so many times that I was sure if I heard it one more time, I would scream.

Uncle Randall pops his head into the game room. "Did you find it?" He has a huge stack of papers tucked under his arm. Given that he's a workaholic, my guess is that his plans for the rest of the evening involve work. But I swear that on top of the stack is the letter he got delivered during the lecture. The yellowed envelope is hard to miss.

"Find what?" I ask, trying to act like I don't want to run over and grab the envelope right now.

"Your present, of course."

Present? It's like he and Lucas teamed up to completely go against my wishes.

"I thought we said—"

Uncle Randall holds a hand up. "It's something I've been waiting to give you. Something that's rightfully yours. I left it in Egypt." Without another word, he leaves the room.

To anyone else, leaving a present in Egypt might sound like a ridiculous thing to do. For Uncle Randall, it's just another day at Easton Estate.

Egypt at Easton Estate is a room near the south-most corner, just off the ballroom, filled with archaeological treasures that would make the curator of the Field Museum in Chicago consider burglary. I shine my cell phone in front of us as Lucas and I walk into the room because there's no switch on the wall like most of the other rooms in the estate. Instead there's a chain attached to a giant chandelier that spans five feet across. I pull the chain, and the room comes to life.

Ahead of us is a golden throne rumored to have belonged to the Pharaoh Thutmose II from the Eighteenth Dynasty. One of my ancestors had gone on a dig around the time of Napoleon and brought it back along with whatever else he could take when he

14

excavated the tomb. It's crazy to think about now, but back in the day, Egypt was like the Wild West as far as tomb robbery went.

The walls of Egypt are painted with murals of detailed columns, palm trees, and the twisting Nile River, and the floor boards are stained black like onyx. On every shelf, niche, and pedestal sits some random Canopic jar or head bust. But the prize piece of the room is the sarcophagus rumored to have belonged to Pharaoh Ramesses VIII. The inscriptions on the sarcophagus suggest that the pharaoh had murdered his two older brothers in order to take the throne, and because of that, a curse had been placed on his mummy.

Lucas steps close so he can whisper. He's always been freaked out by the curse. "You and Uncle Randall really want to get rid of all this stuff, Hannah?"

"It shouldn't be here in the first place," I say. We've been looking for the perfect museum for the last two years. If all goes according to plan, this entire room will be cleaned out and on display to the public within the year.

"But it is here," Lucas says.

"That doesn't make it right. It should be in a museum." I'm not knocking my great-ancestor, but stripping a country of its archaeology is totally not cool.

"You know Egyptian art—" Lucas starts.

I place a hand over his mouth to stop him. Given the chance, Lucas will descend into a twenty minute long dissertation on art across the ages.

Where the two arms of the sarcophagus meet is almost like

a shelf. Sitting on top of it is a wrapped present with a small card attached. The card has a bunch of symbols scrolled all over it, which, to the untrained eye, might look like gibberish. I recognize them as my name in ancient Sumerian. Oh, the fun of having a linguistics professor as an uncle.

Castor and Pollux both jump to the top of the sarcophagus and peer down at me, like they're daring me to tell them to stop. I don't think that, after all this time, two sugar gliders are going to do much damage. But then Castor jumps to a pedestal next to the wall with a Canopic jar sitting on top of it. He climbs to the top of the jar. Even though he hardly weighs a thing, it's still enough to make the Canopic jar wobble.

Lucas and I both jump forward as the jar starts to topple. It balances almost perfectly, at an angle, for half a second, then it tips over and falls straight to the wood floor, shattering into a million pieces.

"Oh my god," Lucas says. "Uncle Randall is going to kill you. That thing had to be worth millions."

This is my exact thought, too. Uncle Randall is going to completely freak out. Except then I notice the folded piece of paper that's been hidden inside the Canopic jar. It's now under a pile of shattered clay.

"You see this?" I say, pulling it from the rubble.

Castor jumps back to my shoulder and peers over as I stare at the paper. It's rice paper, the kind used to make grave rubbings, and it's folded in fourths. My breath catches as I see what's written on the outside.

My mom. She put this here the year before I was born. I don't think it's been touched since.

"Dude, that's your—" Lucas starts.

"I know," I say and unfold the paper, smoothing it out.

It's a rubbing of some kind of artifact covered in all sorts of symbols and letters. It only takes me a moment to realize how similar it is to the artifact Uncle Randall had shown earlier in the week at his linguistics lecture. The Deluge Segment. It looks about the same size, same shape. It could be the same piece, or one similar. Which is weird. Uncle Randall had said the Harvard piece got sold to a private collector back in the eighties. If it were the same piece, then how would Mom have been able to make a rubbing of it in 2002?

"That's really cool," Lucas says. "What do you think it is?"

I shake my head. "Not sure." And I tell him about the lecture and the picture Uncle Randall had shown.

"So maybe it's similar to the Harvard piece but different," Lucas says. "That wouldn't be all that unusual. Look at all the tablets the Sumerians carved."

"True," I say.

"You should show your uncle."

I fold the paper back into fourths. I should show Uncle Randall, but I also don't want to. Mom put this here, maybe for me to find. And it feels like my own mystery that I want to solve.

"I will," I say. "But not yet."

CHAPTER 3

I MANAGE TO FIND A BROOM AND DUSTPAN, AND Lucas and I clean up the shattered Canopic jar in Egypt. We collect the broken shards and hide them inside the sarcophagus. But what else are we going to do? Get my glue gun out and try to stick it all back together? It's too far gone. Hopefully Uncle Randall won't notice that it's missing. Just to make sure, we pick out a different Canopic jar and place it on the pedestal instead. Then I grab the present from the sarcophagus, turn out the light, and we leave the room.

Back in the game room, I open the present. It's an old maroon leather photo album. I flip it open. Right there on the first page is a picture of two people with Harvard Yard in the background.

"It's my parents," I say, pointing to the picture. They look so young, almost like teenagers. Dad has his arm around Mom, and they're grinning like crazy.

"You look so much like your mom," Lucas says, leaning over my shoulder. "Except, my god, look at that hair. It's huge!"

He's right. Mom's hair is permed into spiral curls, and she has bangs as thick as a horse's mane.

"She was a lot prettier than I am," I say.

"Your opinion, Hannah," Lucas says. "Not fact."

He always gets me with the fact thing.

I almost turn to the next page, but out of nowhere, a huge lump forms in my throat. My parents. This photo album. My birthday. It's all too much. Instead I flip it closed. I try not to think about my parents too much. I don't allow the thoughts to creep into my mind. But when they get past my defenses, when something like this photo album ends up in my hands, I can't stop them. Maybe that's why Uncle Randall waited so long to give it to me.

I wipe a tear from my eye with the edge of my sleeve, hoping Lucas doesn't notice. I don't want him to feel bad for me. My parents have been gone a long time. But it's my sixteenth birthday. They should be here.

"You can look at it later," Lucas says, handing me a tissue.

So much for subtlety.

I wipe my eyes with the tissue and cast him a grateful smile. "Yeah, sounds like a good idea."

Then I walk him to the front door and head to bed.

I sleep until ten on Sunday. When I stumble down to the kitchen for coffee, Uncle Randall is sitting at the island working on his computer.

"You didn't wake me," I say as I pour beans into the coffee maker, adding an extra tablespoon so it'll be stronger than normal. Even though I slept late, I'm still exhausted. I'd crawled in bed around midnight but hadn't fallen asleep until after three because my mind tossed through every thought it possibly could. My parents. The rubbing hidden away by Mom. Uncle Randall's letter. The photo album.

"I didn't want to disturb you." He cuts a slice from a loaf of banana bread Chef Lilly must've made before I woke up.

I laugh. "You wouldn't have. I was awake most of the night."

He narrows his eyes. "The photo album?"

"Yeah," I say. I'd flipped through more of it this morning, but each picture was like ripping open a wound that would never heal. Part of me wishes that he'd never given it to me, and part of me can't believe he waited this long.

"They would have wanted you to have it," Uncle Randall says.

Of course they would have. That's the thing.

"Why'd you wait so long to give it to me? They've been dead for almost eleven years." I'm trying to keep the anger out of my voice, but now that I'm more awake from the coffee, the frustration is setting in.

"I didn't want to upset you," Uncle Randall says. "You'd adjusted so well. I'd adjusted so well."

"Who cares? You should have given it to me years ago."

"I realize that now," Uncle Randall says. "I realized it every day. And yet I let so much time go by. It's been eleven years since they disappeared—"

"You mean since they died."

"Since they disappeared," he says. Then he lifts his laptop. Under it is the envelope he got delivered during the lecture.

My heart speeds up. "What is that? Who's it from?"

Uncle Randall smooths his fingers along the edge of the envelope, looking from it to me then back to it again. Then he takes a deep breath.

"Hannah, there is nothing I want more in this world than for your mother to be alive."

I can't respond. I nod slowly then take a sip of my coffee. I'm afraid if I speak, I'll lose every bit of control I've mastered over the last eleven years. But on this, Uncle Randall and I are of the exact same mind.

"I got this the other day," he says.

"During the lecture," I manage.

He nods.

"Who's it from?"

Uncle Randall presses the envelope between his hands. "It's from your mother."

My vision clouds. My heart pounds.

"She's alive? They're alive?" My face warms and the rest of the world vanishes around me. If there is any chance …

"I don't know," Uncle Randall says, and he slides the envelope over to me.

There's no return address and no mailing address. Only the name Randall Easton on the front, in cursive. Inside is a folded piece of paper with a date at the top. It's from eleven years ago.

"It must have been written before they went missing," Uncle Randall says. "I don't know why I got it only now."

I dare my eyes to drift beyond the date, to the words written there.

Hey there Randall,

I'm sure you're wondering where we went, and I wish I could tell you. I honestly do. But I know you understand us not telling you because you were part of the decision to keep it secret. That decision was supposed to be final, but now, with what's happened with Caden, the risk of it falling into the wrong hands is too great. If the Olivers bring it back, even for such a worthy cause, it will never be safe.

Our hearts grieve for Caden and his family, but even one life can't outweigh the threat of it being found. You know this. You understand. I know you do.

They're looking for it, and so we have to destroy it. There's no other choice. If for some reason, we don't make it back, please don't come looking for us. Forget about it. Pretend it never existed. Go on with your life. Take care of Hannah.

Please let Hannah know how much we love her and miss her. Tell her that we'll be home soon.

I love you,
Laura

"What did they destroy?" I ask. My hands shake as I hold the letter. I want to keep reading it over and over again. *Please let Hannah know how much we love her and miss her. Tell her that we'll be home soon.* Except they never came home. I never saw them again. And this letter never made it either, at least not until now.

"I don't know," Uncle Randall says.

I glare at him. "They say right here that you were part of the decision to keep it secret. What was it?"

He fixes his eyes on me. "Nothing."

He's lying. Even an idiot would know that.

"Tell me," I say.

It's almost like I can see the battle going on inside Uncle Randall's head. He wants to tell me. I know he does. But he knows that he shouldn't. And I think that maybe if I ask the right questions, I can get him to slip up and give more information away.

"It's nothing."

"How dangerous could whatever it is be?" I ask. "Seriously? Is it like some kind of nuclear bomb?"

"It's not a bomb," Uncle Randall says. "But it's dangerous enough that they were willing to give up everything they loved to destroy it."

Everything like me.

No, I can't focus on that right now. That's not important. What is important is getting facts.

"Who are the Olivers? Who is Caden?" I've never heard the names in my life.

Uncle Randall reaches for the photo album I've brought down with me and opens it to the first photo, the one of my parents in front of Harvard Yard. Harvard is where they met. They started dating their first year as undergrads and got married just after graduating with their PhDs. Uncle Randall smiles at each photo as if seeing Mom brings back wonderful memories for him that maybe he's hidden away, too.

"Laura was so pretty," he says. "But she never showed any interest in dating until she met your dad. I remember when she introduced me to him. It was the first time I'd seen her passionate about anything besides science. She was so much like you that way, driven by a need to understand the world around her. Wanting to change the world."

"You miss her," I say, tempering my anger.

"Every single day."

Uncle Randall and I have that in common.

He turns to the middle of the album. There's another picture of my parents, and next to them is a couple who look about the same age. The woman has long blond hair, spiral permed as badly as Mom's, and the man's wearing a Red Sox hat so I can't see a lot of his face.

"These are the Olivers," Uncle Randall says. "Stephen and Amy. Amy was your mom's best friend through college and after. They were all students together in the biology department at Harvard. All undergraduates together. Then graduate school. And when they graduated, your parents started their own lab, here. You know that. The Olivers went to work for a company called Amino Corp."

I suck in a breath. "Amino Corp?" They're the ones getting all the bad press recently. Their CEO is probably going to get canned.

Uncle Randall nods. "It was a good job, and they were all top of their field."

Good job or not, I can't believe anyone would work for that company.

"What about the Olivers?" As I flip through the album, each picture I see shows the two couples together, at ball games, at restaurants, at Easton Estate. "Where are they now?"

Uncle Randall turns to the very last page of the album. The final picture shows my parents standing with me between them and the Olivers next to them on either side of two small boys that look about the same age as me, probably about four years old.

"Just before you were born, Amy Oliver gave birth to twins. Ethan and Caden. You played together all the time when you were younger. Do you remember anything about them?"

I dig through my childhood memories. Most of them involve my parents telling me about the world around me. They used all sorts of big words I didn't know, and I'd ask about each one. Molecular Degeneration. Bioluminescence. Now, thinking about it, I realize that they did it on purpose. They never spoke down to me because they wanted me to learn. I also remember many times without my parents. They'd be working or having people over for dinner. And me, being Princess of Easton Estate—or so I liked to imagine myself—would be left to entertain whatever kids got dragged along. We'd run around the halls, shrieking and playing hide and seek. In my memories, I sometimes imagined that there were two boys that looked the same, but since I never really remembered their names or faces, I figured that maybe they were imaginary friends or something.

"Kind of?" I say.

"You were pretty young," Uncle Randall says. "When the twins turned five, Caden got really sick. They ran tests, and he was diagnosed with a rare form of leukemia."

"He died?" I barely whisper.

Uncle Randall nods. "He was only five. And it was especially awful since so much of what your parents and the Olivers did was research cures for diseases and study genetics of what causes diseases in the first place."

It's ironic in the worst possible way.

"What ever happened to the Olivers?" I ask. "Do you ever see them?"

"I haven't seen Amy and Stephen," Uncle Randall says. "I looked them up online not too long ago. Stephen still works at Amino Corp. Amy Oliver works in forensics for the FBI. But Ethan I've seen very recently."

"Really? Where?"

"The other day. At my lecture," Uncle Randall says. "He was there, sitting in the front row."

He has to be talking about the guy who'd looked at me. I didn't recognize him, but maybe he recognized me. It would explain why he'd looked at me so strangely.

"That's Ethan Oliver?" I say, squinting at the little boy in the picture.

"Well, he has grown up, same as you," Uncle Randall says.

"Did you talk to him?" I say.

"I thought about it," Uncle Randall says. "But I couldn't bring myself to do it. I didn't want to bring up bad memories."

"Bad memories?" I pry. Whatever he's talking about must have something to do with this letter.

"Your parents and the Olivers had a falling out," Uncle Randall says.

"About what?"

Uncle Randall stares into his cup of coffee, like he's hoping maybe the answer to my question is in there. I count the seconds of silence, willing him to tell me what's going on. Finally he looks at me.

"Hannah, I need you to give me a couple days, okay?"

"Why?"

"Because I'm asking you to," he says. "A couple days. Let me make some calls. Let me try to figure out where this letter came from. That's all I ask."

"Why can't you tell me now?"

Uncle Randall grits his teeth, but seriously? I've waited eleven years, and now he's asking me to wait longer.

"I just need you to be patient, okay? Just a couple days."

I don't want to give him another second, but I also want answers.

"You have to tell me what's going on," I say.

"I will … in a couple days."

I ball my fists up to hold in my frustration. "Okay, fine, but answer me one thing."

"What?"

I take the last sip of my coffee, mostly to stall, then I summon up my courage. I have to address this now even though doing so opens the sealed lid on my emotions far more than I want to. "Do you think they're still alive?"

"Well, that's a little difficult to—" he starts.

"The truth," I say. "What do *you* think?"

Uncle Randall stares at the letter, sitting on the table between us. "What do I think?"

"Yeah, what do you think?"

He waits there for a solid minute. Then he says, "Maybe. I don't know. I mean I really think they could be. I really want them to be. I really think there's hope."

There's hope. The words echo around me. Uncle Randall wants to believe it's possible. I do, too, more than anything. The lid holding back my deepest wish vanishes, and instantly a desire buried so deeply inside of me that I've almost learned to ignore it explodes to the surface of my brain. My parents could still be alive. Like really alive. They could be out there, now, waiting for me. And if my parents are still alive—if there is any chance—then I am going to find them.

CHAPTER 4

THERE'S NO WAY I'M WAITING A COUPLE DAYS FOR ANY more answers. The next day, when Uncle Randall goes to work, I head out to his old guest house on the property and find boxes of old photos. I drag them into the house, pour myself a giant cup of coffee, and scour them.

In these photos is an entire life I knew nothing about. My parents. The Olivers. Uncle Randall. In foreign countries. In labs and libraries. In churches.

I flip through the photos, studying them, looking for clues. I have to search the Internet for lots of the landmarks in the pictures to even know what countries they've visited. There are the pyramids of Egypt. The Ishtar Gate in Babylon. The Colosseum in Rome. The Hagia Sophia in Turkey. Machu Picchu in Peru. I set the Peru photo aside and move on to the next one, but my brain stops me. I reach for the Peru photo again.

Dad, Uncle Randall, Mr. Oliver, and some guy I've never seen before stand in front of the ancient city with the mountains behind them. In Mr. Oliver's hands is a stone artifact just like the Deluge Segment. But by the time this photo was taken, Harvard didn't own the piece anymore, so it can't be the same one.

I smooth out the rubbing I have and compare the symbols. The quality of the Peru picture is horrible, and I can't make out fine details, but by the way the markings are placed, I can tell that the one in the photo is definitely not the same as my rubbing. It could be the Harvard stone, I guess, but I don't remember what the markings on it looked like. I have to get another look at the artifact Uncle Randall showed in his lecture.

That evening Uncle Randall eats dinner in his home office. He's avoiding me. I'm sure of it. But after dinner, I knock on his office door and go inside. He's sitting at his desk, laptop open. An untouched plate of food sits off to the side.

"Hannah, what's up?" he says.

What's up? It's a ridiculous question.

"Can I have a copy of that slide you showed in your lecture?" I ask, trying to sound super casual. "The one of the Deluge Segment?"

His eyes widen the smallest amount. "Why?"

I shrug, acting like it's no big deal. "I just thought it was interesting. I was telling Lucas about it, and he wanted to see the markings. You know how he is about ancient art."

Uncle Randall's shoulders relax. "Oh, sure. Let me find it."

I walk all the way into the office and scoot around so I'm behind the desk with him. It's covered in papers with all sorts of ancient symbols and notes scrawled on them. I swear that there's some kind of sketch on his desk of exactly what I'm asking about except there are three circular artifacts sketched out, not one.

"What's that?" I ask, pointing at the sketch.

He covers it with papers. "Nothing. Just something I'm working on."

"What?"

"It's nothing, Hannah."

It's not nothing. He's being way too secretive about it. It only makes me want to see it that much more. A completely irrational part of me almost grabs the sketch and runs.

"Does it have anything to do with my parents?" I ask. Uncle Randall already isn't the best at multitasking. It's not like he'd just go back to his everyday research projects when there's a chance my parents are alive.

Uncle Randall rests his elbows on the stack of paper. "It's something I'm looking into. But like I said yesterday, you need to give me a little time."

What I need to do is to sneak in here when he's asleep and take a look at it myself.

"Sure. No problem. So you have that picture?"

He minimizes a few windows, one of which looks like an address book, and brings up a fresh Internet browser. A handful of clicks later, and he pulls up the presentation and flips through the slides. Then he turns the laptop to me.

"This one?" he says.

I lean close. "Yeah, that's it. Can you email it to me?" I don't want to take the time to study it now.

"Sure." He saves the picture and attaches it to an email, then clicks send.

"Anything else?"

"Do you know who it sold to?" I ask.

"No idea," Uncle Randall says. "A private owner. That's all they told me."

He does that thing where he specifically doesn't look at me as he answers, and I know he's lying.

He completely knows. He just doesn't want to tell me. But it doesn't make sense why he wouldn't want to tell me.

A plan begins to form in my mind.

"Can you look it up at Harvard?" I ask.

He fixes his eyes on me. "Why, Hannah?"

I almost tell him about the rubbing. I'm so close, because with the sketch on his desk, he must know more about it. And somehow it's related to my parents. Maybe even to their disappearance. But I bite my tongue.

"No reason. Just curious, I guess."

"Well, you'll have to stay curious."

Twenty seconds go by, and neither of us says a word. Finally, I break the silence.

"Too bad," I say. "It would be cool to see it in real life."

Uncle Randall clears his throat. "You know, I'm really busy ..."

"Yeah, I was just leaving," I say. Then I smile and leave the room. If the piece got sold, even to a private buyer, there have to be records about the sale. I can't imagine they have them locked away in some vault. All I have to do is look them up.

I compare the picture Uncle Randall sent me to the rubbing, but the image quality is even worse than the Peru picture. I can't tell if it's the same stone or a different one. My only option is getting a look at the Harvard piece. But first I have to figure out who bought it.

Tuesday morning, I wait until Uncle Randall leaves for work. Except I never hear his bedroom door open. I peek out and knock on his door.

No answer.

I head downstairs because he must have left without me hearing. He's not in the kitchen having coffee. He's not in his office.

"Have you seen my uncle?" I ask Madeline, one of our maids, as she's walking by with her daily checklist. She kind of keeps track of all the other people who work around our house.

"Dr. Easton?" she says.

I nod.

"He left for a trip," Madeline says. "He said he'd be back within the week."

A trip? Within the week! Is she seriously kidding? Uncle Randall took off without telling me?

"Oh, okay." I try to act like I'm not furious, but as soon as she's out of sight, I text him.

Where are you? I text. I actually want to write, **Where the hell are you?**, but I stop myself.

Business trip. I should be back this weekend, he texts back.

I squeeze my phone so hard, I'm afraid the screen will crack. But today was supposed to be the day he'd give me more answers, not take off to god knows where.

Are you kidding? I text.

A minute passes. Then he responds. **More when I get back.**

Whatever, I text back. At least without him here, I'll have plenty of time to snoop around his office.

I refill my coffee and head to my lab. I play around with Sonic, my hedgehog, because he gets lonely if I leave him alone too long. Then I peek in on Castor and Pollux, but they're fast asleep. I also head out back to check on our giant tortoise, King Tort. He's basking in the Boston sun, happy to be out of his tortoise house for the day. All together, we have over thirty animals here at Easton Estate. We hire professional animal keepers, and Harvard actually uses some of them for research into animal behavior, so my only responsibilities are the sugar gliders and Sonic. But I still grab a couple carrots and hand-feed King Tort. Then I rub his neck for a few minutes and head back inside.

The first thing I do is look on the Internet. I search on *Deluge Segment*, but nothing comes up. Not a single thing. I try putting it in quotations and everything. The only explanation I have for that is that its real name is something else and the

Deluge Segment is just what Uncle Randall calls it. But without knowing its real name, as much as I want to find information on the Internet, I'm out of luck.

So I pick up the phone and call Harvard. Specifically the Peabody Museum where the artifact used to be kept.

"Hello. Peabody Museum," the girl who answers the phone says.

"Hi. I was hoping you could help me get some information."

"Sure," she says. "What department?"

I shrug even though she can't see me. "Records, I guess."

"Sure. Let me connect you."

I'm put on hold and then after maybe a minute a guy picks up.

"Records department. How can I help you?"

"Hi," I say. "I was hoping to get some information about an artifact you guys used to have there. I think it's called the Deluge Segment."

The guy laughs. "You're the second person today to call and ask about it."

A chill runs through me. There's no reason why anyone else would be interested in the Deluge Segment. This can't be a co-incidence. Except Uncle Randall did show it in his lecture a week ago, and everyone who signed up for the lecture is bound to be interested in stuff like this. Still, the thought rests un-easy with me.

"That's weird," I say, trying to play it off like it's no big deal.

"Yeah, popular artifact. Anyway, I don't remember the de-tails. Let me pull up the file."

I cross my fingers as I hear him typing.

"Here it is," he says. "But just to warn you, we don't have much on it."

"I don't need much," I say. "Well, I mean, if you have a high resolution picture of it, that would be awesome."

The guy laughs. "The picture we have looks like it was taken fifty years ago."

Crud. It has to be the same one Uncle Randall has.

"Oh well," I say. "What I really need is to know who bought it."

I hear him clicking. "Yeah, we have the bill of sale as the third page of the file. It was signed by a person named John Bingham. Does that help?"

It sounds familiar, but I can't place it.

"Does it say anything else?" I ask.

"I think so. Let me zoom in." he says. "Yeah, there are a few letters next to his name. CEO. And below that it says Amino Corp."

It all comes together. Amino Corp, the pharmaceutical giant. John Bingham must have been the CEO back in the eighties, but why would a pharmaceutical company want to buy an ancient relic? That part doesn't make sense. They do drug research, not archaeological excavating. But it can't be coincidence that the Olivers worked at Amino Corp and that Mr. Oliver was in a picture with a piece of the Deluge Segment. It all has to fit together somehow, yet I'm not sure how.

"That's perfect," I say. "Does it say anything else?"

The guy whistles. "Only that it sold for twelve million dollars."

That is some serious cash, especially back in the eighties. Amino Corp must have wanted the piece pretty badly to pay that for it.

"Thanks," I say.

"I can email you a copy if you want," the guy says.

I do want that, but I also don't want to give him my email. The last thing I need is Uncle Randall somehow figuring out I was snooping around.

"That's okay," I say. "Thanks again."

I hang up and dial Lucas's number. He picks up on the fourth ring.

"What's up, Hannah Banana?" Lucas asks.

"Not much," I say, smiling at the nickname. "When did you say you have the gig at Amino Corp?"

"Friday," Lucas says. "Why?"

Why? Because it's the perfect opportunity to get inside Amino Corp. Because I have to figure out what's going on. Because this could get me one step closer to finding my parents. There are so many answers to his question.

"I was hoping to be your assistant," I say.

CHAPTER 5

ONCE I GET OFF THE PHONE, I HEAD INTO UNCLE Randall's office. I look through the papers on his desk. Cluttered doesn't even begin to describe it, but I check each page. There are all sorts of symbols and translations from every language known to mankind and even something that looks like a Sudoku puzzle with symbols instead of numbers. But whatever sketch he was looking at last night is nowhere to be found. He must've taken it with him. I look in the drawers, too, just to make sure, but if it's around, I can't find it. I try to replace all the papers as messy as when I found them, then I leave the office.

The next day I check again, just in case I missed anything. Then I spend some time trying to decipher the symbols on the rubbing I found in the Canopic jar. It's like Uncle Randall said about the Deluge Segment. Some of the symbols are familiar, but most of them just feel incomplete. I also get as much information as I can on Amino Corp and the layout of their headquarters from what I can find online. It's a combination of floor plans, advertisements, and public photos from holiday parties that people have posted on their Facebook pages. Hopefully it's enough.

Friday morning finally rolls around, and I meet Lucas at Java Coffee.

"Tell me again why I have an assistant for the day?" Lucas says.

I've been reluctant to give him all the details because I haven't wanted him to tell me that I can't come along. But now that it's finally Friday, I give him the plan.

"You want me to get you through security so you can snoop around?" Lucas says. "How is that being my assistant?"

I shrug. "I can carry some chalk sets in for you if you want."

"No, I don't want," Lucas says. "And I also don't want you to get me fired."

"I'm not going to get you fired."

"What if you get caught?"

"I won't get caught," I say.

"But what if you do?"

Getting caught isn't an option.

"I won't. No one will even notice me," I say. "Anyway, I've done some research on Amino Corp. This isn't the only artifact they have."

My research turned up quite a few things. John Bingham, the CEO who'd bought the Deluge Segment back in the eighties, is the father of the current CEO, Doctor Peter Bingham. Both father and son have a huge interest in artifacts and have set up a private viewing gallery for parties that's open to employees by request. I'm sure I can talk my way in. All I need is two minutes to take a picture of the Deluge Segment.

"I'm not sneaking around with you. You know that, right?"

"You can be my lookout," I say. "We'll keep the phone line open. All you have to do is let me know if someone's coming."

He seems to consider this. "And I don't have to go anywhere I'm not supposed to?"

"Nope," I say. "It'll take five minutes, tops."

"Five minutes," Lucas says. "That's all you get."

"That's all I need."

"Hmmm ...," Lucas says.

"So that's a yes?"

"Fine, yes."

And so it's set.

Lucas drives us to Amino Corp. They're located downtown, with a parking garage underneath. It's employee parking only, and Lucas refuses to talk to the security guard. I don't mind. I'd rather not be on some parking garage camera just in case something goes horribly wrong.

Nothing will go horribly wrong.

I tell myself this over and over as he drives around looking for street parking. It takes forever, and finally he shoves his Camry into a questionable half-spot next to a dumpster.

"You better not make me late, woman," Lucas says.

I try to open my door, but with the dumpster, there's not

enough room, so instead I crawl over the front seat and get out on the driver's side.

"Me make you late!" I say. "You know, next time I'll have Devin take us."

"No way." Lucas has a strict "no chauffer" policy.

We walk the two blocks to the front entrance of Amino Corp. Lucas opens the door and lets me go in first. Beyond the first door is a second one, secured with a swipe card. Lucas presses a buzzer next to it.

"Hey, my name is Lucas O'Keeffe. I'm here to do art in the coffee shops." He's completely awkward when he talks, like he's nervous.

Wait. He probably is nervous. This art stuff is his dream. And there is no way I'm going to get him in trouble.

"Come on in," whoever is talking into the intercom says, and the door clicks.

Inside is another world. All I've heard about Amino Corp is the bad stuff. The unregulated tests in third world countries, the unsanctioned animal testing, the accidental gas releases that might not have been accidents. But this …

First off, along the entire back wall are artifacts behind glass cases, like a museum. The CEO and his interest in antiquities isn't an exaggeration. Just what's in the lobby alone must be worth tens of millions.

Lucas elbows me and nods toward them. I scan them quickly but don't see anything that looks like the Deluge Segment. It must be back in the private gallery. My heart speeds up at the possibility of seeing it.

We walk to a receptionist's desk, and she gives us visitor badges.

"You have access to anywhere with a yellow carpet," she says, pointing at the ground under our feet. "Anything else is off limits. But don't worry too much. If you aren't supposed to be somewhere, you shouldn't be able to enter."

That's just perfect. Maybe I can snag a badge from some unsuspecting employee when they aren't looking.

Maybe I can end up in jail. Because it must be illegal to sneak around some giant pharmaceutical corporation. Amino Corp would probably have me arrested.

Okay, this is getting completely ridiculous. All I want to do is take a couple pictures of some artifact. It's not anything to do with their research or drugs. Everything is going to be fine.

"You okay, Hannah?" Lucas shakes me from my thoughts. We're already a few steps away from the receptionist. I turn back to see her watching me like I'm crazy.

"Fine," I say. "Which way's the coffee shop?"

He points down the path ahead of us. "Follow the yellow brick road."

I smack him on the arm. "*Wizard of Oz*? Really?"

"Sure," Lucas says. "Somewhere over the rainbow."

I need to stop the dorky references before they get out of hand.

"Okay, here's the plan. You get set up. I help you. Then we say we're going to the bathroom."

"The bathroom? They probably have one in the coffee shop," Lucas says. "That'll never work."

I smile. "I'll tell them that I need some privacy. You know … for that time of the month. That always works."

Lucas cringes, like the mere thought of this excuse gives him the heebeegeebees. "Always?"

"Always."

It turns out that Amino Corp has the best coffee shop in the world. They offer Lucas and me free drinks, so I get a cappuccino. Lucas only wants water. I take a sip and then set it down.

"You guys don't have a bathroom, do you?"

"Sure," the guy barista says. "Right back there?"

I look toward the café bathroom and grimace. "Oh uh …"

"Is there a problem?" he asks.

"Well," I say. "It's just that I have this embarrassing … Okay, I don't really like to talk about it, but is there one with a little more privacy?"

I swear the guy takes a step back, like maybe he's afraid he'll catch whatever I have. Which is nothing, just for the record.

"Oh, sure," he says. "If you go back out in the hallway and turn right, you'll see them halfway down on the left." Then he turns away and makes himself really busy grinding beans.

"Good lord, Hannah, you are so embarrassing."

"Yeah, I know. Now come on."

Lucas sets his art supplies down near the chalkboard and we head back out of the café, down the hall. Sure enough, there are the bathrooms.

I slip in my Bluetooth earpiece. "Okay, you wait here. If you see something, let me know. I'll be back in five minutes."

I hope. According to the Internet, the gallery is here on the first floor, toward the back of the building. It can't be that hard to find.

I wind my way down the hallways, from the yellow carpet and on to the blue. And there, when I'm nearly to the back, are two fancy double doors. Beyond them is a large room, lit with dim lights, and along the edges of the room are all sorts of artifacts. I know this, not because the doors are made of glass, but because they're already wide open.

I stop and press myself against the wall then call Lucas on my cell phone. "Have you seen anyone come in?" I whisper to Lucas through the earpiece.

"Not yet," Lucas says, way too loud.

"You need to talk softer," I whisper.

"Is this better?" he whispers, so quietly that I can barely hear him.

"A little louder than that."

"How about this?" he says, a bit louder.

"Perfect," I say. "It's just that the doors are open."

"Be careful, Hannah," he says.

I nod in reply even though he can't hear me.

I stand there, pressed against the wall for a solid minute, listening for anything, but it's as silent as a vacuum tube. Then I edge forward on the blue carpet, so softly that I don't even hear my own footfalls. A couple more steps and I'm peering through

44

the door. I don't see anyone, so I step in and scan the room. And there, on the back wall, behind a glass case, is the Deluge Segment, exactly what I'm looking for. The only problem is that someone's standing directly in front of it.

CHAPTER 6

I SUCK IN A BREATH OF SURPRISE. THE PERSON standing in front of the Deluge Segment snaps their head around in my direction.

The gallery is dim and covered in shadows, with only the display cases lit, but I can tell that it's a guy, maybe six feet tall or so, wearing a hoodie.

"What are you doing here?" I whisper. With that outfit, he sure as heck doesn't work at Amino Corp. Maybe he's a maintenance person, except he's kind of young for that.

"What are you doing here?" he says, with a harsh edge in his voice that is way meaner than I think he needs to be. As far as I can tell, he has no more right to be here than I do.

"Who are you talking to?" Lucas's voice pipes in through my earpiece.

"Hang on a second," I say back to him. I walk closer so I can get a better look at the Deluge Segment. It's beyond weird that this guy is looking at the exact thing I came to see. Unless he was the one who called Harvard to ask about it.

"Hang on for what?" the guy says.

"Hannah, who is that?" Lucas says.

"Never mind," I say. "Just give me a minute."

"I'm coming in there," Lucas says.

"No," I say.

"Look, I don't know who you're talking to, but you need to explain yourself pretty fast or—" the guy says. Besides the hoodie, he's got on dark jeans and work boots.

I've seen those boots before. I try to place them in my mind.

"Or what?" I say. "You'll report me? You don't work here."

He holds up a badge. Crud. Maybe he does work here. I am so busted.

"Hannah," Lucas says.

"Not now, Lucas." I push the tiny button on the earpiece to turn off the Bluetooth.

"Who's Lucas?" the guy says.

"Lucas is none of your business," I say. "Who are you?"

"Who are you?" he counters.

I don't answer because no way am I giving this guy my name.

I step forward, closer to where he is, closer to the artifact. "Look, I just want to get a picture." I hold up my cell phone. "One picture. No harm or anything. Then I'm out of here."

I notice he's gripping a cell phone, too, and it's on the camera screen.

He narrows his eyes at me. And with that, I recognize him. This is the guy who'd come to Uncle Randall's lecture. Ethan

Oliver, the son of my parents' ex-best friends.

My heart nearly stops. According to Uncle Randall, we used to play together when we were little kids. Does he remember? Does he have any clue who I am? And if he doesn't know who I am, should I tell him? He'd looked at me during the lecture, but that doesn't mean anything.

"Why do you want a picture?" Ethan Oliver asks.

"Archaeology is a hobby," I say kind of lamely. But I hadn't expected anyone else to be here.

"You look familiar," Ethan says.

"Do I?" Silently I curse the fact that I am the only girl I know who wears two ponytails and a knit hat every day. But even still, that doesn't mean he knows who I am.

"Yeah, I saw you at Doctor Easton's lecture last week," Ethan says. "You were sitting in the back."

"Good memory," I say, deciding not to mention that Doctor Easton is in fact my Uncle Randall. "That's why I'm here. The picture he showed in the presentation. This is the piece. Is that why you're here, too?"

It makes perfect sense. He'd seen it in the lecture. Gotten interested. And come to check it out. But that doesn't explain the badge.

"Yeah, exactly," Ethan says, but the quick way he answers makes me think this is not quite the full truth.

"How'd you get a badge?" I ask. Not that I'm complaining. His badge solved the problem of me trying to get inside this room.

He shrugs. "My dad works here."

That's right. I knew that. But I don't tell him that I knew that.

"Convenient." I push the small button on the earpiece, turning it back on. Lucas is probably freaking out. "You there?" I whisper.

"Who are you talking to?" Ethan says. "That Lucas person?"

I ignore him.

"Who is that, Hannah?" Lucas says.

"It's no one," I say. "What's happening out there?"

"That's what I've been trying to tell you," Lucas says. "Someone is coming your way. I had to head back to the coffee shop. You're on your own."

Crud. It's bad enough that Ethan is here. The last thing I need is someone else discovering me.

I hold up my phone again, swapping from the phone to the camera screen. "Do you mind if I take a picture?" With him standing in front of it, I can't get a good image.

"You didn't say please," Ethan says.

"May I please take a picture?"

Ethan flashes a smile that is almost worth the anxiety that I'm feeling. "Well, since you asked so nicely ..." He steps to the side.

I move directly in front of the Deluge Segment and snap the picture. But the flash is on, and it reflects off the glass. I fumble with the buttons and turn off the flash, then take another one. It will have to be good enough.

"Hannah, hurry," Lucas says. "Two security people just walked past the coffee shop, heading your way. You need to get out of there."

"I gotta go," I say.

"Are you talking to me or Lucas?" Ethan says.

"Someone is coming," I say.

For a brief moment, Ethan and I are of one mind. We both take off running for the door. I dash out first, then him. He pulls the doors closed just as two security guards round the corner. Ethan tucks his dad's badge into the pocket of his jeans.

"Do you guys know where the bathroom is?" I ask, trying to look like I'm ready to pee my pants.

They don't smile.

"This is a restricted area," one guard says.

"Yeah, I was just visiting my dad," Ethan says, and he walks off. They let him. Anger seethes inside me. This is so not fair.

"I was just going to the bathroom," I say.

"You need to come with us," one of the guards says.

What I need to do is get out of here, but I can't just make a run for it. Fine. I'll talk my way out of this.

They lead me back to the yellow carpet, to a conference room not far from the coffee shop. Lucas stares at me as I walk by.

Inside the conference room, I'm greeted by a man in a blue dress shirt and khaki pants. His hair is graying but smoothed back. I've seen this man before, on the news, being interviewed during protests about questionable testing ethics. I've also seen him most recently in the news articles and interviews about Amino Corp going bankrupt. This is none other than Doctor Peter Bingham, president and CEO of Amino Corp.

CHAPTER 7

"Hannah Hawkins, if I'm not mistaken?" Doctor Bingham says.

The president of Amino Corp knows my name? I don't find this comforting.

I tuck my cell phone into my pocket. "You're Doctor Bingham aren't you? I've seen you on the news."

"Not the best news recently, I'm afraid," he says. "But it will all be resolved. I'm sure of it."

According to the news, they're going to either can Doctor Bingham, or the entire company is going to tank. He's pretty upbeat for either of these options.

"What am I doing here?" I ask.

He opens his hands wide. "Why don't you tell me?"

My heart speeds up, but I force my face to stay calm. "Well, I'm here helping my friend in the coffee shop. And I was trying to find a bathroom. But then your guards brought me here. I really need to get back to the coffee shop."

"How's your uncle doing?" Doctor Bingham asks.

I have no clue why he would care.

"Fine," I say. "Why? Do you know him?"

"Oh, we go way back," Doctor Bingham says. "Did you know that he worked for me for a while?"

"My uncle worked at Amino Corp?" Uncle Randall had never mentioned that.

"Just as a consultant."

"Doing what?" Maybe I shouldn't be prolonging the conversation, but curiosity gets the better of me. Uncle Randall is a linguist, not a scientist, and as far as I know, the two fields don't have much in common.

Doctor Bingham's smile never falters. "Projects here and there."

It's so obvious that he's being intentionally vague. I don't want to give him the satisfaction of knowing that I'm curious or that it matters. My jaw is clenched. My muscles are tight. I need to get out of here.

"Can I go?" I ask.

He puts up a hand to stop me. "Do you remember an artifact from around Easton Estate?"

My heartbeat quickens.

I put on a silly grin. "We have lots of artifacts around Easton Estate. We have an entire room of Egyptian stuff. Even a sarcophagus."

He holds his hands about a foot apart and makes a circular motion with them. "About this big across and round. With symbols carved into it."

Oh my god. He is seriously asking about the Deluge Segment. But not the piece he has here. Which means that there must be multiple pieces. He's asking about the piece that Mom made the rubbing of.

I shake my head. "It doesn't sound familiar."

"You're sure?" he says. He's trying to hold his face calm, but the muscle below his left eye twitches the smallest amount.

"Yeah, I'm sure."

"Do you think there are any pictures of it?" he asks.

Okay, this is just plain weird. Why would he care about this piece now?

"Not that I've ever seen," I say.

Doctor Bingham lets a smile fall onto his face. "Too bad. Tell you what, Hannah. If you happen to find anything like that around Easton Estate, will you let me know?" He hands me a business card. It's green with gold metallic lettering on it.

"Um, yeah, sure," I say aloud, but inside, all I want to do is scream. Something big is going on. Something way out of my control.

I stand. "Can I go now?"

Doctor Bingham stands and walks to the door, opening it for me. "Of course. Thank you for taking the time to talk to me. Oh, and say hello to your uncle for me. Please tell him that if he ever wants a job ..."

No way am I telling Uncle Randall any of that. I'd rather be destitute than have him work for a company like Amino Corp.

I step out into the hallway and act like I'm lost. "Which way is the coffee shop?"

Doctor Bingham points to the left. "That way. Don't get lost again."

My skin crawls as I walk away, almost like I can feel his eyes on my back. But I don't turn to check. Instead, I go right to the coffee shop. Lucas is halfway done with the chalkboard when I get there. His eyes widen when he sees me.

"Hannah, you're alive."

I tuck the business card into my pocket and hold up my phone. "Mission accomplished."

Barely, I think. That had been too close.

As Lucas finishes up, I tell him everything that happened, including meeting both Ethan Oliver and Doctor Bingham.

"You didn't mention my name?" he says.

I shake my head. "I didn't mention your name."

"And why was this Ethan guy looking at the thing? That's a little strange. Do you think his dad knows?"

I think about the way Ethan had run out of the room and the way he'd hidden the badge from the guards. "I doubt it. He didn't want to get caught any more than I did."

But why would he care about the Deluge Segment that much in the first place? Simple linguistics interest isn't enough to sneak around giant pharma. There has to be more to Ethan Oliver's interest.

"I don't know, Lucas." I study the picture, but I don't remember the other ones enough to know if it's the same as the picture from Peru. I'll have to compare it when I get home.

It's after six when Lucas finishes both coffee shops and drops me back at Easton Estate. Uncle Randall still isn't back from his trip yet. I stop by the kitchen to grab a protein bar and a bottle of iced tea, then head right for my lab. First, I release Castor and Pollux from their habitat. They scramble up onto my shoulders and pull at my ponytails. I feed the sugar gliders and Sonic, take a bite of the protein bar, and then pull up the photo on my phone.

I take the rubbing that Mom had hidden away and place it next to the phone. Side by side I can see how similar they are. I didn't measure the Amino Corp piece, but from what I remember, they're about the same size, about twelve inches across and circular. Both artifacts have a pattern of five notches near the edge which are similar but not exact. I don't think they're in the same place. Covering both artifacts are symbols and markings. These aren't exactly the same either. These are definitely different pieces of the Deluge Segment.

I snag the photo of Dad, Mr. Oliver, Uncle Randall, and the other guy in Peru from the box of photos and compare the piece in the photo with the other two pieces. The one in the Peru photo also has the five notches along the edges like these two, but even with the horrible quality of the photo, I can tell they aren't the same. None of the markings look exact. There has to be a third piece of the artifact, just like in the sketch Uncle Randall had been drawing.

Ethan Oliver had been interested in the piece, both during

the lecture and at Amino Corp. He'd taken a picture today, just like I had. And his dad is in the Peru picture holding the thing. If there is a third piece, which I'd wager next month's allowance on, then I'm willing to bet there is an excellent chance that the Olivers are in possession of it. I need to see it.

CHAPTER 8

I'M DYING TO ASK UNCLE RANDALL ABOUT DOCTOR Bingham and Amino Corp, but on Saturday morning, he's still not home. I can't imagine what kind of work he'd do for Amino Corp, or even more importantly, why he hadn't said anything about it when we talked on Sunday. It seems like key information that he had consulted for them. But I also don't want to tip him off about my sneaking into the company headquarters.

I finish my breakfast and make my plans for the day. A quick check online is all it takes. I locate Ethan Oliver's address in zero point four nine seconds according to the stats on my search engine. I have no clue how people used to survive without computers. I dress in dark jeans, black boots, and a black long-sleeved shirt. It's too warm today for a sweater and too chilly for a T-shirt. I add a small amount of color to my outfit by slipping an army green knit hat over my ponytails, and then I set out.

I argue with Devin for five minutes straight. He wants to drive me. I want to ride my bike. Devin wins because Uncle Randall pays him to drive me around.

The address for the Olivers is deep in the heart of downtown Boston, in one of the new apartment buildings just north of Kings Chapel, only about a fifteen minute drive. The bellman is a bit reluctant to let me head up the elevator until I tell him my name, making sure to include the Easton part. Everyone knows about Easton Estate. Everyone also knows about my parents. When their deaths were reported, it made national news. From what I was told, Uncle Randall did a pretty good job keeping us out of the media spotlight, but for a solid three months, theories abounded as to what had actually happened to them.

I take the elevator to the seventeenth floor and ring the bell for apartment D.

A woman I recognize from the photos as Mrs. Oliver answers the door. I've been looking at them so much, it's almost like I know her. I have to remind myself that we haven't met, or at least haven't seen each other for many years. Her hair is shorter now, just framing her face, and the spiral curls are gone.

The second she sees me—recognizes me—her face falters.

"Oh, hello," she says.

"Hi, Mrs. Oliver. My name is Hannah Hawkins. I believe my parents used to be friends of yours." I've practiced this line all morning.

"Hannah. Yes, of course." She stands there, unmoving.

"I was actually here to see your son, Ethan," I say. "We met

58

at my uncle's lecture last week at Harvard."

Understanding seems to dawn in her eyes, as if this single convenient excuse might explain everything. "Oh, of course. Please, come in." She steps to the side, allowing me to pass.

I enter the apartment, but once I'm fully inside and she closes the door, awkwardness ensues. She's way flustered, so I nudge her along.

"So Ethan ...," I say.

"Right, Ethan," Mrs. Oliver says. "I think he's in his room. I'll go get him if you want to wait in the living room."

"Thanks. That would be great." I'm hoping that maybe he's not quite ready for visitors, which will give me a little time to look around and see if the artifact is here. I follow her out of the entryway to a room with two chairs, a red sofa, and a coffee table.

"Go ahead and sit down," she says. "I'll get Ethan for you." Without another word, she's out of the room and heading toward the back of the apartment.

The second she is out of sight, I'm on my feet, scanning the place. I scour the built-in bookshelves, looking behind books, seeing if maybe it's hidden somewhere. I peer back the way I came, wondering if I have time to actually go searching. But I stop my search when the sound of voices drifts across the air to me.

"What is she doing here, Ethan?" Mrs. Oliver says in what she must think is a whisper but has that husky undertone that makes it almost louder than if she'd been talking normally.

"I have no clue, Mom," Ethan says. "I don't even know her."

"She said she met you."

"She did. I mean, I did. We met once. Talked once. I never even told her my name though."

"Then why is she here? You must be forgetting something."

I notice that he's not mentioning where we talked, meaning his parents must not know about his little trip to Amino Corp.

"I'm not forgetting anything," he says.

"You need to get rid of her," his mom says. "If your father gets home and she's still here, he's going to be upset."

"He'll be fine," Ethan asks.

"He won't be fine, Ethan. Trust me. You think you've seen your father angry before, but you've seen nothing. It won't be pretty. See what she wants, and then get her out of here."

I hurry to my chair because I'm pretty sure that this is my hint to get back to where I'm supposed to be. I'm sitting down just as Ethan Oliver walks into the room.

He, unlike me, has not had the morning to prepare for our encounter. He's got ripped jeans on, a rumpled T-shirt, and his blond hair and sideburns are total bedhead. The work boots are nowhere to be seen.

I paste on a happy, bubbly smile. "Hi, Ethan. Did you have a good rest of your day yesterday?"

His mom watches us from the hallway, and he scowls at my words, further confirming that she didn't know. He can sort that out later on his own.

"Fine, Hannah, thanks so much for asking." The sarcasm

drips from his voice.

So he does know my name.

"I was worried about you when you disappeared so quickly," I say because I can't stop myself. This is far too much fun.

"Yeah, I'm sure you were." He crosses the room and sits on the sofa opposite the chair I'm sitting in.

His mom finally disappears from view and—I'm hoping—from earshot.

"So, I'm not saying this isn't a nice surprise," Ethan says, "but why are you here? How do you even know where I live?"

"I'm guessing that you know where I live, don't you?"

"Of course," Ethan says. "Everyone in Boston knows where you live."

I lower my voice as my conversation takes a turn I don't expect. Words slip from my mouth that I haven't planned. "I've seen you there, in pictures, when you were younger. We used to play together."

His face softens, and he lowers his voice. "I remember running around the halls. Playing hide and seek in some Egyptian looking thing."

"Our sarcophagus," I say. "We still have it."

"And there were huge gardens out back with a hedge maze. My mom never let us go in the maze without her. She was sure we'd get lost."

"You remember all that?"

He nods. "It was fun. You, me, and Caden. We were like the Three Musketeers."

"I wish I remembered more," I say. Not only about that, but about my parents. It's almost like I've been cheated out of the only five years I had with them because I was too young.

Ethan and I both seem to snap out of whatever trance we've fallen into.

"Why did you want the picture of the artifact?" I ask him.

"No reason. I just did."

"I don't believe you," I say. "There has to be some reason."

He shakes his head, and then his eyes move to the hallway where his mom has popped back into view.

"Ethan, your father is on his way home from his run," she says. "Maybe it's time for your guest to be leaving."

"Yeah, right," Ethan says. "Hannah, you need to go."

I can't imagine why it matters if I'm here when his dad gets home, but they're both being so weird about it. That said, I still haven't found what I'm looking for.

"Yeah, no problem," I say. "Do you mind if I use the bathroom really fast?"

"Of course not," Mrs. Oliver says, and she points down the hallway, in the direction from where she's come.

"I'll only be a second," I say, and I duck in the bathroom. But as soon as I hear their voices again, I peek out, making sure they aren't watching me. I tiptoe from the bathroom and continue down the hall, looking in each room I come to, seeing if there is any sign of the third artifact. But each room I look in, it's not there. I'm running out of time. I can only pretend to be in the bathroom for so long.

I'm about to give up because at least three minutes have passed. I peek in one final door, almost at the end of the hall. My efforts are rewarded. This must be the Oliver's library because it's filled with all sorts of books. Inset in the giant bookshelves is a glass display case, and in that display case is the third artifact, identical in shape and size to the Deluge Segment. This is what I've come for.

I grab my phone from my pocket and turn on the camera. My finger hovers over the shutter as I wait for it to focus.

"You need to leave, Hannah. Seriously," Ethan says from behind me, causing me to jerk around and miss the shot. And now it's too late because he's standing there watching me, like he knew what I was trying to do all along.

I have no clue what I'm supposed to do now. It's not like I am going to break into the Olivers' house at night and try to steal the thing.

"I was just looking for the bathroom," I say.

"Yeah, right. Come on, or my mom's going to freak."

"Let me just wash my hands," I say. "I'll meet you—"

"Now, Hannah," Ethan says.

I raise my camera to quickly take a picture since I'm already busted, but he grabs my hand and drags me out of the room.

When we get to the front door, Mrs. Oliver stands there holding the handle. She pulls the door open, like she doesn't want to waste one second getting rid of me.

"Okay, well, thanks for letting me drop by," I say.

"Not to be rude, but it's best if you don't come back," Mrs.

Oliver says.

So much for a warm invite or hopes of rekindling the friendship between our families.

"Don't worry. I won't." I step toward the door.

"Hannah?" Mrs. Oliver says.

I turn back. "Yes?"

She steps toward me and catches me in a hug. "It's so wonderful to see you. You've grown up into such a beautiful girl, and I'm so sorry that things had to work out like they did."

My brain has no idea how to respond. There are so many pieces of this puzzle flying around me, and I'm trying to catch on to them and fit them back together. To decipher this mystery that happened in my past. "Thank you, Mrs. Oliver," I manage.

She releases me from the hug and gives me a final smile. "Now you really need to go."

I nod and leave, and no sooner do I step out the apartment door, they close and lock it behind me. And though part of me wants to wait around and see Mr. Oliver, too, and maybe gauge his reaction when he sees me, another part of me cautions that this is not such a good idea. That maybe there is a very good reason why Ethan and his mom want me out of the apartment before he gets home.

CHAPTER 9

UNCLE RANDALL IS HOME WHEN I GET THERE. BUT IF I thought for any reason he was going to jump into telling me what was going on, I am completely wrong.

"Tell me about Amino Corp," he says.

Crud. Somehow he's found out.

"What do you mean?" I ask because before I admit to guilt, I am going to get as much information as I can.

"You went there," Uncle Randall says.

I take a deep breath. There is nothing wrong with going there. I was there for a valid reason. And maybe he doesn't know I got caught in a restricted area.

"Lucas had a gig," I say. "Painting the coffee shops."

Uncle Randall's face is deadpan. He knows more.

"And I went looking around while I was there?" It comes out more like a question. I didn't technically do anything wrong.

Okay, fine, I did. But I didn't do anything bad.

"Anything else to that story?" Uncle Randall says.

What does he know? About the artifact? About me talking to the CEO?

"Anything like what?" I ask.

"Getting caught by security for being in restricted areas?" Uncle Randall says. "Does that sound familiar?"

"How did you know that?" I ask.

"Because they called me," Uncle Randall says. "And I don't particularly like getting phone calls about you being in trouble."

"I got lost," I say. "What's the big deal?"

"The big deal is that you got lost in Amino Corp," Uncle Randall says. "Those aren't the kind of people you want to mess around with."

"And you know that because you used to work for them?" I say, but the second the words leave my mouth, I want to take them back.

I count as the seconds go by. One. Two. Three.

Uncle Randall raises an eyebrow.

"You used to work for them. You forgot to tell me that."

"I consulted for them," Uncle Randall says. "But only for a short period of time. And how do you know about that anyway?"

I cross my arms. "I know that because, yeah, I did get caught. And they took me to a conference room where I had a nice chat with Doctor Bingham, you know, the CEO of Amino Corp. He said that he knew you. That you did some work for him."

"You talked with Peter Bingham?" Uncle Randall seems genuinely surprised by this information. And best of all, he seems distracted from the fact that I got caught.

"Yep."

"What did he say?"

I hold back, not telling him about how Doctor Bingham asked about the Deluge Segment. Or about how Amino Corp has a Deluge Segment, though I'm willing to bet Uncle Randall already knows that.

"Nothing really. He told me how he knew you."

Uncle Randall clutches the handle of his coffee cup so hard I'm afraid he'll break it off. Finally he says, "You're grounded for the week."

"Are you kidding?" I say. "You run off for a week with no explanation and then you come back and start parenting me?"

"I'm your guardian," Uncle Randall says.

"I don't care," I say. "You're not my mom or dad. And I don't have to listen to you tell me what to do."

Without another word, I stomp off, climbing the grand staircase of Easton Estate and retreating to my rooms. I don't come down the rest of the evening.

I wake the next morning and spend about an hour lying in bed, trying to figure out how I'm going to get another look at the third piece of the Deluge Segment. I'm sure as heck not going back to the Olivers' house. The photo I took is worthless. It's nothing but a blurred stretched image of half of a face—I'm guessing Ethan's face—along with a door frame. The piece of the artifact is nowhere in sight. But after the hour, I know I have to face Uncle Randall. There is no avoiding it.

I throw my dirty work clothes on and head downstairs. Uncle Randall is already busy watering the plants. I silently join him, hoping he'll maybe forget about the whole discussion from the day before. He doesn't say a word. I guess this means he hasn't forgotten.

During the week, Uncle Randall has Horticulture students from Harvard come in to take care of the indoor plants, but at least once a month, Uncle Randall insists we take care of them ourselves. He claims there's no better way to learn. Taking care of the plants may sound like a simple job, but our Sunday routine takes the better part of three hours. I invite Lucas over to help, and he says he'll come over later after he finishes spring cleanup around the house for his mom. I wish I could hire someone to do the stuff for him and that he could come over instead, but he tells me that would be "Totally not cool, Hannah. Totally not cool."

Uncle Randall is especially particular about his new carnivorous plants, and he finally uses them as a way to break the layer of ice between us.

"I'm worried they aren't catching flies," he says, handing me a fly swatter. "So what you need to do is find a fly buzzing around, swat it, and then pick it up carefully, with just the tips of your fingernails by its wing so you don't squish it, and then place it in the leaves of the Venus Fly-Traps."

"No problem," I say, taking the fly swatter. "I should be able to find a fly around here."

"Not one," Uncle Randall says. "Based on the number of plants we have, I'm guessing we'll need around ten."

"You're kidding, right?" I've watered plants with Uncle Randall many times before, but this is the first time he's actually asked me to hand feed the plants. Of course the carnivorous plants are a relatively new addition.

He points to himself. "Does this face look like it's kidding?"

It doesn't. It also doesn't look like it's angry any longer, and I don't want to refresh his memory, so I begin scanning the greenhouse for flies.

I'm four flies in, wishing for a plague of insects to descend upon us, when Madeline, one of our maids, comes into the greenhouse.

"Sorry to bother you, Mr. Easton, but Miss Hawkins has a guest."

"Lucas is here?" I say. He must've finished his chores early, but it's weird that she didn't send him back. Besides my uncle, me, and the staff who work for us, Lucas knows Easton Estate better than anyone.

"Not Mr. O'Keeffe," Madeline says. "The gentleman introduced himself as Ethan Oliver."

Uncle Randall angles his head so he can see me and raises his eyebrows, waiting for an explanation.

"I met him this week, just really quickly," I say.

He waits for more.

"And I may or may not have gone by his apartment yesterday, but there's a really good explanation for that."

"I'm sure there is," Uncle Randall says.

"Should I send him in?" Madeline says, deftly avoiding the conflict between us.

Uncle Randall looks to me for the answer. Ethan did say he was here to see me.

"Yes, please. You can send him to my lab." I haven't fed Sonic yet. And Castor and Pollux are going to be frantic that I ignored them last night.

"Absolutely, Miss Hawkins," Madeline says, and she leaves the room.

I'm covered in mud and water. I haven't showered. I am hardly ready for guests. If it were Lucas, it would be no big deal. But I look like crap. Still, it's not like I have time to go take a shower and change clothes. Ethan will just have to deal with me the way I am.

"Why is he here, Hannah?" Uncle Randall asks.

I shrug, trying to play it off. "Guess I'll go find out." And I leave Uncle Randall to the remainder of the plants.

Ethan is looking into Sonic's habitat when I enter the room.

"You want to hold him?" I ask.

He turns at my words, and okay, I'm not sure why I haven't put this together before now, but Ethan Oliver is completely hot. He's brushed his blond hair, and he has these blue eyes that remind me of turquoise. Today he's got a black T-shirt on, showing off his arm muscles, which are cut and buff, and kind of make me want to touch them. Holy smokes. How have I not noticed this before now? Maybe I was too busy looking at the dirty construction boots he wears. I should have made time to shower.

"What?" Ethan says.

"Sonic," I say, walking over to join him at the hedge-hog's habitat.

"Are you supposed to?" Ethan asks.

"Sure, he loves it," I say, setting the flyswatter on top of the habitat because I realize I've carried it with me, which must really complete my fabulous ensemble.

"It doesn't hurt?"

I open the door of the habitat and reach for Sonic. His spines go out, but I smooth them and pick him up so they don't poke into me.

"You have to be careful when you first pick him up," I say. "But then he relaxes."

Sonic has not yet relaxed, but I figure Ethan can deal with it. I hold Sonic out, and Ethan takes him, surprising me by not getting poked even once. And within thirty seconds, Sonic actually relaxes to the point of curling into a ball.

"That means he likes you," I say, trying not to notice how relaxed Ethan looks holding the hedgehog. How nice he looks. Animals have that effect of people. Well, at least the relaxation part. Ethan is looking nice all on his own.

I wipe the thought from my mind because how ridiculous am I being anyway? I distract myself by heading over to Castor and Pollux's habitat. They're sleeping, but when they hear me rattle the door of their habitat, they wake and peer from their hammocks.

"Did you guys miss me?" I ask, reaching for the sugar gliders. They love me so much that they basically melt into my hands like putty.

"You like animals?" Ethan says.

"More than people," I say. "Except for my uncle. And my best friend. But otherwise, I think that animals are the best companions. They're loyal and true. They don't ignore you unless they have a really good reason. They like to snuggle." Almost like they are putting on a show, Castor and Pollux climb down my arm and slip into the pockets of the apron I wear.

"Nice apron, by the way," Ethan says. "You didn't have to dress up for me or anything."

My face flushes with heat. "It's not like I knew you were coming over."

"Like I didn't know you were coming over yesterday," Ethan says. "So I guess that makes us even."

When he puts it that way, it does seem to even out, but I see no need to agree with him verbally.

"So you have a brain collection," Ethan says, nodding his head toward the shelf where there are eight glass jars, each holding a different kind of animal brain.

"Sort of," I say. "It's for an experiment I'm doing."

"Uh huh. And ...," Ethan says, waiting for more.

"And did you know mammals are the only creatures with wrinkles in their brains? It's because we needed extra surface area for processing. Unlike mammals, if you look at the brain of your average bird, it's super smooth, meaning it has less gray matter and less ability to process information, hence the term 'bird brain.'" I want to put my hand over my mouth because I'm babbling at this point.

"A brain collection is weird," Ethan says.

This kind of summarizes why I've never had a boyfriend and most of the girls at school don't want to be friends with me. My interests are not the norm.

Madeline blessedly picks that moment to come into the lab. "Miss Hawkins, will you and your guest be wanting any refreshments?"

I'm not exactly used to having normal guests, I mean besides Lucas. Politeness says that I should offer Ethan something to eat or drink.

He's watching me. Waiting for my response. I decide to go for politeness.

"Do you want to stay for lunch?" I ask.

His face breaks into a smile. "Why I'd love to stay for lunch, Hannah."

My asking him to lunch has nothing to do with the fact that he's cute.

I turn back to Madeline. "Lunch would be wonderful."

"Perfect. It should be ready in a half hour," Madeline says, and she leaves the room.

A half hour! I guess I'd expected lunch to be ready now. That means I have a half hour of talking to Ethan before lunch is even ready. Then there's the time that lunch actually takes. But there's no backing out now.

"How do I put him down?" Ethan asks, holding out Sonic.

"You can kind of roll him onto the floor of his home," I say. "And then, if you don't mind, you can feed him. He takes the stuff on the shelf next to the brains. Just a scoop. You don't want him to overeat and get fat."

"That can happen?" Ethan says as he reaches for the food, making sure to avoid the brain jars completely.

"It happens to people," I say. "It can happen to animals."

"You seem a little obsessed with animals," Ethan says. He sets the food in Sonic's bowl, and the hedgehog scampers over to it and begins to eat.

"I've been studying them my entire life. I'm fascinated with their genetics. Seeing how they're all related to each other. Studying their mutations. You probably didn't notice, but Sonic only has four fingers on his front right paw instead of five. Mutations like that occur randomly, but if you try to breed for them, you can create new species."

"So you're creating a four fingered hedgehog species?" Ethan says, peering into the habitat, trying to get a look at Sonic's paw. The hedgehog is too preoccupied with eating to worry about Ethan.

"Not quite," I say. "That would take too long. But I do make really good notes in case anyone ever wants to continue my research."

"Your parents were into genetics also," Ethan says. "Both our parents were."

I nod, even as my mind tries to process this early childhood that is so not a part of my life.

"This is the first time you've been back here since you were little?" I ask. I can't see how Ethan could have been back here any other time, but maybe he has and I just didn't know.

He nods. "It's a little smaller than I remember."

I laugh. "You may be the first person I've ever heard call Easton Estate small."

"I never said it was small. Just smaller than I remember."

"That's because you were like three years old or something. Everything seems enormous when you're that little. I used to imagine the tortoises were giants, like dinosaurs, roaming the backyard."

"That's right!" Ethan says. "I remember the tortoises. I think I took a ride on one."

"King Tort," I say. "He's famous for having kids ride on his back. There are probably more pictures of little kids sitting on him than there are of Old North Church."

"Can I see him?" Ethan asks.

I almost say yes, caught up in the moment, but I hesitate. "Why are you here, Ethan? What do you want?"

Maybe it's rude to be so blunt, but I don't care.

"Why did you come by yesterday?" Ethan counters.

I open my mouth just a second too late. "I was—"

"Okay, stop," he says. "I know why you came by yesterday. Remember. I caught you trying to take a picture of it."

My stealth moves definitely need some improvement.

"I figured you must have a piece of the artifact," I say. "I wanted to take a picture of it. But you and your mom were trying to get rid of me so fast that I didn't have time. What was up with that? Why would it have been so bad if your dad had gotten home?"

"King Tort?" Ethan says, implying that maybe he'll answer my question if I let him see the giant tortoise.

"Fine." I lead him back out, through the greenhouses, and into the area outside where the tortoises are kept.

Ethan's eyes light up when he sees King Tort ambling around the grassy enclosure. The giant tortoise stops every few steps to nibble on the fresh grass that's poking up out of the ground.

"Okay, he's bigger than I remember," Ethan says.

"You can't sit on him," I say. King Tort may be strong, but he can't take a full grown guy sitting on top of him, especially one as swole as Ethan.

"There are smaller ones, too," Ethan says. "Will they get that big?"

Voldetort and Nefertorti have both made their way out of the heated tortoise house and are basking in the sun. "Yeah, but it will take a long time. You'll be an old man."

"They're really cool, Hannah," Ethan says.

The tortoises, above all else, seem to be the favorite of people who visit. It's like they really are prehistoric giants.

"So your dad," I say. "Why did I have to leave?"

Ethan runs a hand through his blond hair, breaking up the style. "My dad has a little bit of a temper. According to my mom, if he'd seen you, it would have set him off. He would have brooded for days."

"But why?" I say. "He doesn't even know me. Hasn't seen me for at least ten years, right?"

Ethan swallows before answering. "Yeah, but the thing is that my parents and your parents had this huge argument back when we were little. Back when my brother died." He looks away when he says it, like mentioning his brother brings up too many bad memories.

"Do you know what they argued about?"

"My parents blamed your parents," Ethan says.

"For your brother getting sick?" I say. "Uncle Randall told me that your brother got leukemia. How would that be my parents' fault?"

Ethan shakes his head. "They didn't blame your parents for Caden getting sick. They blamed your parents because he never got better. Because he eventually died."

I feel anger bubbling up inside. "And that's my parents' fault? How could anyone even think that? It's not like you just cure leukemia. It's not like my parents could have done anything about it."

"Yeah, Hannah, they could have."

The anger that's been brewing inside me pushes over. The letter from Mom pops into my mind. Could they have done something? But no. It's impossible.

"You have no idea what you're talking about," I say. "My parents are not responsible. That's the stupidest thing I've ever heard in my life. People get sick and die sometimes. That's reality. That's life. How did my parents have anything to do with that?"

"Because they didn't help Caden when they had the chance," Ethan says, and I see the anger growing on his face, too. "They were fine to let him die."

"My parents didn't have a cure," I say.

"They did. That's what my parents said," Ethan says. "And they refused to let my parents use it."

One second passes. Two. Ten seconds pass before I can formulate words.

"You're telling me that my parents had a cure for leukemia and they not only didn't use it to heal your brother but that they didn't use it to heal the other thousands of people who die from it each year? That's ridiculous. That was their life's work. What they'd always wanted to do. They wanted to cure diseases. I can promise you that if my parents had some cure, they would have shared it."

"You're wrong," Ethan says.

"And you're right?" I say. "Okay, fine. Why has no one else found this cure? If they had a cure, where is it?"

Ethan reaches into his back pocket and pulls out his phone. "I don't know where it is. I don't know what it is. But I'm almost certain that it has something to do with this."

He turns on the phone and holds it out in front of me. On the screen is a picture of the third piece of the Deluge Segment. The piece from his apartment.

CHAPTER 10

"HOW COULD THAT HAVE ANYTHING TO DO WITH YOUR brother? Or him getting sick?" I say. "You realize that makes no sense at all."

Ethan's hands are shaking, just the smallest amount, probably from anger. Or maybe he's nervous.

Maybe he's trying to find answers just like I am.

"I realize that it sounds crazy," Ethan says. "But I'm serious here. I'm not sure I understand exactly what I'm talking about, but everything my parents have ever said about the artifact in our house has made me believe that it's the case. My brother died because your parents wouldn't help him. It's why they stopped being friends. Why there is no way my dad could have seen you at our apartment because if he had, he would have flipped out completely."

I don't love the fact that some man I only knew as a child seems to hate me. It makes me feel like the suspect of a crime I didn't commit.

I reach for Ethan's phone, but he pulls it out of my reach.

"Fine," I say. "Let's just say you're right. Better yet, let's just put that aside for the moment. What does this thing even say? What is it really?"

"It's part of a puzzle," Ethan says. "From what my dad's said about it, there are three pieces: the one my parents have in our apartment, the one at Amino Corp, and the one you have."

I shake my head although my mind immediately goes to the rubbing I found. "We don't have an artifact."

Ethan twists up his lips. "Yeah, right. I've seen a picture of your parents holding it."

"Really?" I've scoured all the old photos of my parents and never seen them holding an artifact.

"Yeah, really. In an old photo album my parents have."

"We don't have an artifact."

"You're lying."

"I'm not."

"She's not," Uncle Randall says, walking from the greenhouses out to the back where Ethan and I stand. "It's true. They used to have the artifact. A piece of the Deluge Segment. You're right about that, Ethan. But they hid it shortly before your brother Caden died, and I have no idea where. I thought it was in South America, but I've been there for the last week, tracking down clues, and came up empty. It originally came from India, from the Indus River Valley, so that's next on my list."

So South America is where Uncle Randall ran off to. But why had the letter from Mom triggered him to do that?

"Why would they hide it in the first place?" I ask. The rubbing seems to taunt me from where I have it hidden under Sonic's cage.

Uncle Randall puts his hand out for Ethan's phone, and Ethan actually hands it over. Uncle Randall studies it, zooming in on the symbols and letters almost like a book that only he can read. After a couple minutes, he looks up.

"I'm pretty sure lunch is ready," Uncle Randall says. "Why don't we talk about it while we eat?"

I don't know what Madeline told Chef Lilly about our visitor, but she's gone all out on lunch, preparing the makings for lettuce wraps, both vegetarian and with steak.

"No, we don't normally have lunch like this," I say to Ethan before he can make some judgmental comment. I gathered from his downtown apartment that his family has money enough to live comfortably, but nothing like us.

"I wasn't judging." He actually seems sincere. Maybe he's not a complete jerk like his first impression had led me to believe. Well, and his second impression, too.

I'm one bite into my lettuce wrap when Lucas walks in.

I stand to greet him, but he's not looking at me. His eyes are locked on Ethan. And Ethan's eyes are locked on him.

"Hey, Lucas," I say because the room has immediately gotten chilly.

Uncle Randall stands and shakes Lucas's hand, finally getting his attention.

"Who's your guest?" Lucas asks once I'm able to give him

81

a hug hello.

Ethan stands also, so that we're all four now standing awkwardly around the lunch table.

"Ethan Oliver," Ethan says, extending his hand.

Lucas's eyes widen. He recognizes the name.

"I'm Lucas O'Keeffe."

"My best friend," I add, trying to break the tension.

Thankfully Chef Lilly picks that moment to walk in with a plate for Lucas and with dessert: freshly made carrot juice, scones, and fruit tarts.

"Perfect timing," Lucas says, and then we all sit back down.

If I thought the conversation was awkward before, that was nothing compared to now. Lucas proceeds to grill Ethan on everything from where he goes to school, if he plays sports, and what he had for dinner last night. Okay, the last one isn't true, but it feels that way as the conversation keeps droning on. And with every word, all I want to do is get on to the real topic of conversation.

"About the Deluge Segment," I say to Uncle Randall when he starts on his third fruit tart. "If my mom and dad had an artifact, why did they hide it?"

Uncle Randall spears a giant strawberry with his fork and shoves it in his mouth. He waits until he's finished chewing to answer. "Because they thought it was too dangerous."

"The Deluge Segment is dangerous?" I say, picking at a scone.

"Not by itself," Uncle Randall says. "But it's part of a bigger picture, something that could be more dangerous than anything Earth has ever known."

"What bigger picture?" Ethan says. "My parents never told me anything about that. All they said was that Hannah's parents ruined everything. That Caden is dead because of them."

"That's not true," I say. "And we're not talking about that right now, remember?"

Ethan glares at me but lets it go for now.

"Yeah, well all of a sudden, my dad's all interested in it again," Ethan says. "He keeps talking about trying to get a picture of the third piece. So I called Harvard to find out who it had been sold to after I saw it in the lecture the other day. That's what I was doing at Amino Corp. I was going to get the picture. But when I got home, I found out that he already had a picture of the Amino Corp piece. It wasn't the third piece he was looking for. Your piece was."

That clears up the mystery of who called Harvard asking about the Deluge Segment.

Uncle Randall's face pales. "So your father doesn't have all three pieces?"

Ethan shakes his head. "No. Only two. Why does it matter anyway? What is the Deluge Segment?"

Uncle Randall blows out a long breath almost in relief. "It's a promise of hope. And very likely a map, too."

"A map to what?" I ask. In this moment a spark ignites inside me. A hope of what this could be. An explanation as to why Uncle Randall ran off to South America looking for it.

Uncle Randall's tart sits unfinished in front of him as he stands. "Let's go to my office."

We follow him to his office. From inside his briefcase, he pulls out the sketch that I'd seen the other night and lays it out on his desk, pushing other stacks of papers out of the way to do so. It shows three pieces, all the same size, in a row.

"The Deluge Segment is made up of three pieces," he says, pointing at each one. "All different, and yet all part of the same instruction manual."

Ethan leans close. "The symbols look really familiar. Like this one means power, right?"

"You can read them?" I ask. I've seen similar markings before but certainly can't decode them.

Ethan's face reddens, almost like he's embarrassed. "Kind of. I've been studying languages for years. They look like stuff I've seen before."

Uncle Randall traces his finger in a circle around the outside of one of the pieces. "The ones around the edges I can read. I spent years decoding them. And you're right about the symbol. Together, these tell of a great power. A power to change the world."

"What power?" Lucas asks.

Uncle Randall reaches to the bookshelf on the wall behind his desk and pulls down a thick leather book. The spine is cracked, so only three letters of the title remain visible: IBL.

He sets it on top of his sketch and flips it open, to a picture of the Tree of Life. It's a Bible, an old one by the looks of it. He turns a handful more pages until he stops and holds it out so Lucas, Ethan, and I can see the picture on the page.

"You recognize this?" Uncle Randall says.

"Noah's Ark," I say. It doesn't take a Bible scholar to recognize Noah's Ark.

"You remember the story?" Uncle Randall says.

"I know the story," Lucas says. "God told Noah that there was going to be a flood that was going to wipe out life on Earth. He told Noah to build this giant boat and to collect two of every animal so he could save all the different types of animals. Then the flood came, wiping out life as we know it on Earth. But the Ark was okay, and when the flood was over, Noah released all the animals who went off and repopulated the animal world. Then Noah and his family repopulated the human world. The end."

"Glad you listened in Sunday school," Uncle Randall says.

Lucas shrugs. "My parents would be proud. Anyway, it's hard to miss the story of Noah's Ark, even when you're falling asleep."

Being fascinated by genetics and evolution, I always found the story to be complete baloney. Every animal on Earth fit in the boat? All the people on Earth are descendants of Noah? That means, if we look at all the species on Earth today, over five thousand species of mammals alone were placed on that ship. It's completely unrealistic. And let's not forget about birds and insects and how all these animals were fed and kept calm.

"You guys don't believe the story, do you?" I ask. Surely Ethan can't. His parents are geneticists. And I guess I've never really asked Lucas.

"No way," Lucas says. "But don't you dare tell my parents."

"What about you?" I ask Ethan.

He shakes his head. "It always felt a little farfetched."

"And yet," Uncle Randall says, holding up a finger to stop our words. "We know something happened. Nearly every civilization on Earth has a flood story. In Sumer, Ziudsura survived the flood. In Mesopotamia it was Utnapishtim. In Greece it was Deucalion, the son of Prometheus. In India it was Manu. The list goes on. And with so many stories, as with the physical evidence, things like the level of the Black Sea rising and evidence of an ancient tsunami in Africa and Asia, it is hard to dispute that the earth was flooded. That much of life could have been wiped out. And yet somehow, that life was rebuilt."

"So you believe in Noah's Ark," I say.

"Not in an exact sense," Uncle Randall says. "But when I was working with your parents on this, I spent a long time trying to understand the Deluge Segment. We had the piece here as long as I was alive, and I used to try to translate it when I was younger. Then we found the second piece, in Peru. I thought that's all there was to it. But that's when Amino Corp hired me to consult for them. They had the third piece, and that's when the answers really came together. It was a linguistic scholar's dream. I spent months consulting old tablets and scrolls, interpreting every symbol that I could. Hardest work I've ever done. It was a full year before I made even the slightest breakthrough."

Uncle Randall pushes the Bible aside and points at

one specific symbol on each of the three sketches. It's the same symbol.

"This right here is what really gave it away. The entire world opened up. And that's when I stopped working for Amino Corp."

"What is the symbol?" Ethan says. "I've seen it on our piece at home. I even asked my dad about it a couple times, but he always said that he didn't know."

"Oh, he knew," Uncle Randall said. "It was the symbol that hooked both of your parents. They were geneticists, and this changed everything."

I close my eyes so my brain can try to figure it out. It's a twisting symbol almost like an infinity sign except not connected at either end.

"What does it mean?" Ethan says.

"It's a symbol that refers to genetics. To the creation of life from the primordial soup. To DNA if you will."

That's why the symbol looks familiar. It's like a double helix DNA symbol.

"That's ridiculous," I say. "DNA wasn't even a thing until the mid-nineteen hundreds. There is no way that one of the oldest artifacts in existence talks about DNA."

Uncle Randall snaps his fingers, like I've nailed the point he's trying to make. "Exactly! That's why it stood out. The idea of life being created wasn't new. And the recipe for that life had to be somewhere. That's all DNA really is. A recipe for every living creature. It wasn't called DNA, but the idea was the same. It used to be understood. It was encoded. At least according to this artifact."

He pauses as he lets this sink in. I look to Lucas and Ethan. Ethan is completely engrossed in what Uncle Randall's saying, but Lucas seems fixed on the sketches.

Uncle Randall continues. "After I made the breakthrough, I was able to translate large portions of the segment." He taps one of the drawings. "My sketch doesn't do it justice, but the lines along here speak of an artifact, created by God, given to a protector before the Great Flood. It refers to the artifact as the Code of Enoch."

"Enoch was one of Noah's ancestors," Lucas says. "I learned that in Sunday school, too."

"Right," Uncle Randall says. "Father of Methuselah. Great-grandfather of Noah. Rumored to have lived for nearly four hundred years, which is nothing when you look at how long his offspring allegedly lived. Methuselah was said to have lived to nine hundred sixty-nine. Noah to nine hundred fifty. Many in the line after the Code of Enoch was delivered were said to have had extended lives, as if they had some secret. Something that was keeping them alive."

"Okay, so God gives Enoch some code," I say. "What does it do? Make people live forever? Like a fountain of youth?"

He continues to trace his finger along the sketch, almost as if he is reading it right now, translating it, though his eyes seem far away, like he's remembering a different time. "God delivered the Code of Enoch, and it was passed down to Noah who took it on the Ark with him. As to whether there were any more animals on the Ark than what Noah and his family needed to survive is irrelevant because when the flood was over, when the water receded, Noah used the Code of Enoch to recreate life on Earth."

"What are you saying?" I ask. My mind is spinning, and I don't want to jump to any conclusions.

"I'm saying that the Code of Enoch contained all the genetic information for every species on Earth. Every single recipe. Plants. Animals. Insects. Humans. Bacteria. It was all there, in the Code, along with instructions for how to use it, for how to make the power of the Code come to life. Noah used it to recreate the world, and then he hid it away. The Deluge Segment talks about being a map. Once the Code of Enoch was hidden, Noah instructed his family to hide the map so that no one would ever find him or the Code."

"So this really is a map?" Lucas asks.

"That's what we believed," Uncle Randall says. "But if it is, I was never able to fully decode it."

"But if the Code of Enoch really has the power to create life, why would it need to be hidden away?" Ethan asks.

"The Code of Enoch has the power to create life. It also has the power to cure diseases."

"Why my parents wanted it," Ethan says.

"Exactly," Uncle Randall says.

"Why is that bad then?" Ethan says. "Something like this could have saved Caden's life."

Uncle Randall nods, "True. We all wanted to find it, at least until we truly understood it. Then we realized how dangerous it was."

"But—" Ethan starts.

Uncle Randall puts up a hand. "It also contains the power to create diseases. To destroy species. To eliminate life on Earth as we know it. It's a power too treacherous to contain. And so Noah took the Code of Enoch and hid it away, and it has never been seen since."

"You never got close to reading the map?" Lucas asks.

"Close?" Uncle Randall says. "Sort of. One of my colleagues was also researching the Code. We traveled across the world to visit with him. But after talking to him, we all agreed—all of us—that we couldn't pursue the Code anymore. That it was too dangerous. So we destroyed the copies that we had and pretended that it didn't exist. And that was the end of that."

"Until Caden got sick," Ethan says.

Uncle Randall nods. "Until your brother got sick. Your parents wanted to find the Code of Enoch. They wanted to use it to cure your brother. Hannah's parents almost gave in. But then ..."

His voice trails off, even though there must be more to the story.

"Then what?" I don't know my parents, but helping their best friend's sick kid seems like a pretty worthy cause.

Uncle Randall looks to Ethan. "Then Ethan's father threatened them."

Ethan's face holds steady, but I can't imagine what's running through his mind.

"With what?" I ask, hardly in a whisper.

"He said that if they didn't help, he would tell Amino Corp everything. As you can imagine, a company like Amino Corp being in possession of this kind of artifact could change the world, and not only for the better. It was a risk that your parents were not willing to take, even if it meant that Caden would die."

Ethan balls his fists up. "They should have helped."

Uncle Randall fixes his eyes on Ethan. "Should they have? Should they really?"

Ethan doesn't say anything.

"Regardless, the time for that judgment has passed. That's when Hannah's parents told me that they were going to hide their piece of the map, and then they disappeared. Now I know, from the letter, that they went to destroy the Code itself. I never heard from them after that."

"So this map … it leads to my parents," I say, more certain about this than I have ever been about anything. "That's why you don't think they're dead. You think they found it. You think they're still alive."

Uncle Randall rubs his forehead with his hand. "I don't know what to think. I think maybe they weren't able to destroy it. But without the third piece, we have no way of tracking them."

I take a deep breath. This is it.

"If you had the third piece, would you go after them?" I ask Uncle Randall.

He fixes his eyes on me. "Absolutely."

I step back from the desk. "Wait here."

I try not to run as I make my way to my lab, but my heart

pounds in my chest. This is it. I have the final piece of the puzzle. With shaking hands, I grab the rubbing from under Sonic's habitat and run back to Uncle Randall's office. I'm completely out of breath when I get there.

I walk into the room, trying to keep my composure, but my mind is spinning.

"I found this," I say, and I lay it down on top of the sketch.

Uncle Randall sucks in a sharp breath. "Where did you get that?"

I force myself to hold back the tears that brim at the edges of my eyes as I speak. "Mom left it for me."

CHAPTER 11

LUCAS AND I EXPLAIN ABOUT THE CANOPIC JAR. UNCLE
Randall doesn't even flinch when we tell him how
Castor and Pollux knocked it over and shattered it. All he can
do is stare at the rubbing of the Deluge Segment in front of him.

"So this means we can find it," Ethan says. "Right?"

It's a little unexpected. I get that I want to find it. If my
parents are still alive, then this will lead me right to them. But
I don't understand why Ethan would care one way or the other.

Almost like Lucas can read my mind, he says, "Why do
you care?"

Instantly the room ices around us.

Ethan bites his lip. "Because … well, it's the right thing to
do to find it."

"Why?" Lucas says. "Didn't you hear the part about how
dangerous it is?"

Ethan glares at Lucas. "Of course I heard that. That's what
I'm saying. If it really does exist, and if we can find it, then that

means other people could find it, too."

I want to pretend it's not a valid point, except it really is. The thought of someone else finding this artifact makes my stomach twist into a knot.

Uncle Randall looks away from the rubbing to Ethan. "You said your dad had a renewed interest in it?"

Ethan nods.

"Why?"

Ethan swallows. "I don't know. He's just been talking about it a lot lately. Talking about finding the third piece. He's probably just curious."

I highly doubt it's just curiosity. He wanted to find the Code of Enoch before because of Caden. If he's interested in it again, then that means he wants to find it, for some reason. There's no other explanation for the interest.

I instantly want to snatch the piece off the table and tuck it away. What if Ethan takes a picture of it? Then his dad would have all three pieces. And given that his dad works for Amino Corp ... it's not hard to connect the dots.

"He wants it for the company," I say.

Ethan scowls at me. "He does not. If it's dangerous and if my dad found it, it's not like he'd hand it over to Amino Corp so they could destroy the world. And it's not like they would destroy the world. You guys are being really paranoid about this whole thing."

Maybe so, but every word out of Ethan's mouth is making me only more paranoid. I'm about to grill him some more when

94

Lucas picks up the rubbing. "Hannah, can I use your computer to scan this in?"

I look to Uncle Randall who nods. I trust Lucas with my life. Ethan? Not so much. I follow Lucas from the room toward my lab. Uncle Randall and Ethan trail behind. Uncle Randall asks Ethan something, but he whispers so I can't hear. I walk faster so I don't have to listen to them.

In my lab, Lucas sits at my computer and scans in the rubbing. Then he loads it up in Photoshop.

"Where'd you store the picture you took the other day when you busted into Amino Corp?" he asks.

"With an accomplice," Uncle Randall says.

"It was completely her fault," Lucas says. "I told her it was a bad idea from the start."

"A likely story," Uncle Randall says. But I can tell from the tone of his voice that's he's not mad anymore. He's too focused on what's here in front of us.

I point Lucas to the right directory, and he loads in the picture I took. He does a bunch of stuff that I definitely don't follow, merging the two images, making the background disappear, flipping them around. Pretty soon, the two images are the same size and layered on top of each other.

"We did stuff like this," Uncle Randall says. "The images didn't line up. The symbols didn't make sense."

"Maybe," Lucas says. "But did you try this?" With the cursor, he points to the five notches at the top of one of the pieces. "The ratio for these notches isn't random. You ever heard of the golden ratio?"

"Like seashells, right?" I say.

"Exactly," Lucas says. "You see it in art all the time, for as long as art's been around. If we use that ratio to line up the notches, rotate them just right ..." He rotates one of the images, leaving the other as is. Then he messes around with the opacity of the images and makes a few more adjustments. Instantly, the image comes to life, almost like the symbols are popping off the screen in a three dimensional display of art that may have never been seen before.

Uncle Randall sucks in a breath. Maybe I do to.

"The map," Uncle Randall says.

"Except it's not complete," Lucas says. "We still need the third piece."

Uncle Randall, Lucas, and I all look to Ethan. He takes a step back.

"What?"

"May we see it?" Uncle Randall asks.

"Um ...," Ethan says, but his hand reaches toward the phone in his pocket.

"Come on. You have a picture," I say, grabbing for the phone. Which is totally irrational. It's not like I'd be able to unlock his phone even if I wrestle him for it.

"It's just that—" he starts.

But I can't let this opportunity slip away. If there is a map and if there is some way to read it, then I need all the pieces of the map to do that.

"Please," I say. "You have to help me. This is my parents we're talking about. They've been gone for eleven years, and I'll never get those years back. But if there is any chance that they're still alive ..." My voice catches, and I can't go on. But this is everything to me. All I've ever dreamed of.

Ethan narrows his eyes at me like he wants to disagree, but then his eyes soften. He reaches for his pocket and pulls his phone out, unlocking the screen and passing it to Lucas.

Lucas downloads the image onto my computer and then brings it into Photoshop also. Then, with a couple more rotations and adjustments, the entire image comes together. It's like a real map, complete with hills and valleys and rivers. The image is in black and white, but with the adjustments that Lucas has made, color appears, highlighting everything, almost to the point where certain sections glow. The map is alive. The map is complete.

The map is going to lead me to my parents.

CHAPTER 12

"I CAN'T BELIEVE IT," UNCLE RANDALL SAYS. "WE TRIED everything to discover the map."

Lucas pushes back from the computer. "Well, you didn't have the advantage of layers and adjustments and opacities back in the old days, did you?"

Uncle Randall slowly shakes his head. "No, we didn't." Then he says, "I need to make a phone call," and leaves the room.

"Glad I got you into digital art," I say once Uncle Randall is gone.

"Who'd have thought?" Lucas says. "So what next?"

That's easy. "We follow the map. We find my parents."

"When?" Ethan says.

Lucas and I turn to him.

Ethan stares me down. "What? You think you're going without me? No freaking way. I contributed to this. I get to go."

"But—" I start.

"But nothing," Ethan says. "I'm going."

I shake my head. "This isn't about finding the Code of Enoch. This is about finding my parents. There is a really good chance that they're still alive."

A chance so good that even Uncle Randall believes it.

"Look, Hannah, I appreciate that," Ethan says. "And I get that you miss them. But I'm going to find the Code of Enoch. If I can find it, it could ..." His words trail off.

"It could what?" I ask.

"Nothing," he says. "It could just make a lot of things better at home. That's all."

"You can't be thinking that you're going to bring this thing back. Were you listening to Uncle Randall even the tiniest bit? Because I'm pretty sure that he mentioned this Code of Enoch being the equivalent of a nuclear bomb that could wipe out all of humanity."

Ethan crosses his arms. "Even if I did bring the stupid thing back and give it to my dad, it's not like he'd do anything bad with it. He's not that kind of person."

"I'm not saying that he is," I say. "But what if you brought it back—which you're not doing by the way—and someone took it from your dad. Some terrorist group or something. Then what?"

"That's not going to happen," Ethan says. "And it's irrelevant anyway. I gave you my piece of map, which means I have as much right to go on this adventure as you do. And if you don't take me, I'll go to the news. Is that what you want?"

My chest tightens. That is definitely not what I want. The

last thing we need is anyone knowing about the Code of Enoch. It's bad enough that Ethan knows.

"You wouldn't do that," I say, glaring at him.

"Do you want to test me?"

Crud. This is the worst. I ball up my hands in frustration. There is no way I'm going on some archaeological quest with Ethan Oliver. I hardly even know the guy. I don't trust him. I don't trust his intentions. But I also don't see much of a choice.

"This is really not cool," I say.

"Never said it was," Ethan says. "But it's reality. You can either bring me along, or the entire world can know about the Code of Enoch, and that will be on you. It's your choice."

Lucas steps forward. "This is blackmail. You realize that, right?"

Ethan crosses his arms and stares Lucas down.

"So?" Ethan says.

The whole situation makes me feel completely helpless. I don't want Ethan coming along. And I sure as heck don't want him telling his dad about this.

"One condition," I say.

"What?"

"You can't tell your parents anything."

Ethan's mouth drops open. "Are you kidding?"

"No, I'm not kidding. Not a single word."

If he doesn't tell them, then I'm sure I can convince him along the way to give up any dreams of bringing back the Code of Enoch, if we even find it.

And we will find it because we will find my parents.

"They're going to want to know where I'm going," Ethan says.

"Uncle Randall can figure that out," I say. "If you come along, it stays between the four of us."

Ethan glares at Lucas. "Is he coming, too?"

I smile at Lucas. "Of course."

"Hannah, you know I—"

I put up a hand to stop Lucas's words. He and I can talk about that later.

"Do we have a deal or not?" I ask.

Ethan blows out a long breath. "Fine. I agree. But only because you'll need someone along to keep you safe."

I let out a laugh devoid of humor. "What did you say?" I can't tell if Ethan is joking or not. He's got a funny little smirk on his face, like maybe he's trying to push my buttons.

Ethan shrugs. "You know. Someone to protect you on the journey."

At this I really do laugh. Lucas lets out a low whistle like he knows what's coming.

I smile at Ethan. "Just so we're clear on things, I'm not afraid of bugs or snakes or spiders. I camped in the wilderness with Green Peace for two weeks last year. I helped build libraries in Uganda. I climbed to the top of Mount Kilimanjaro. I can take care of myself. Got it?"

Ethan twists up his lips, again in a way where I can't tell if he's being serious or not. "If you say so. And just for the record, everything you just said, the same goes for me."

Small streams of relief begin to trickle through me. I can make this situation work.

"Well, except the Mount Kilimanjaro part," he says. "I never went mountain climbing."

I narrow my eyes at him.

"And the bugs part," Ethan says. "Bugs kind of freak me out."

I further narrow my eyes and shoot him a look of pretended annoyance because at this point, I'm pretty sure that he is joking. "Anything else?" I ask.

Ethan shakes his head. "No. I can take care of myself, too. I spent a month building houses for Habitat for Humanity last summer."

"Seriously?" Habitat for Humanity is an amazing organization. I've thought about volunteering for them lots of times.

"Yeah, seriously," Ethan says. "Why? What's wrong with that?"

"Nothing," I say. "It's pretty cool actually."

"So is building libraries in Uganda," he says. "I was thinking about doing that later this summer."

There's this weird silence that passes between us, almost like some kind of unknown camaraderie. Then Ethan's phone rings.

He looks at the screen, and the muscles around his mouth tighten.

"It's my dad. Don't say anything, okay?"

Lucas and I nod. It's almost like Ethan is scared of his dad.

"Hey, Dad," Ethan says.

I can't hear the other side of the conversation, only hear

that sound is coming out of the receiver.

"Nothing. I was just out with some friends."

Pause.

"At your work? No. Why?"

Crud. Maybe his dad found out Ethan had been using his badge at Amino Corp the other day.

Pause.

"You're sure? Maybe they made a mistake."

Pause. Then he looks right at me.

"No, I don't know her," Ethan says. "She was there? At Amino Corp?"

Whoa. That's not good. I don't know Mr. Oliver, but I also don't want him having anything to do with this whole thing. Not when my parents might be alive. Especially not if there was some argument between them.

Pause.

"I didn't see her. I just dropped by to say hi to you. That was all."

Pause.

"I told you. I'm just out with friends. I'll be home later."

Pause.

"No, I'm not coming home now," Ethan says.

Pause.

"Fine. I'll be home in fifteen minutes," Ethan says, and then he hangs up the phone.

I've been trying not to completely eavesdrop, but it doesn't take a genius to see that Ethan's entire demeanor has shifted.

The light in his eyes is gone, whatever small hint of a smile he wore before has evaporated, and his face is flushed red like he's embarrassed.

"What's up?" I say, trying to keep it light.

"I gotta go." Ethan won't look me in the eye as he answers.

"Your dad found out about the other day, didn't he?"

He nods. "The guards reported it. But ... well, you heard me. I won't tell him."

I'm not sure if I can believe him.

"You can't tell him, okay?" I say. "You really can't."

"I won't. I said I won't. Look, let's just talk about this tomorrow, okay?"

Ethan's face is bright red, from anger or embarrassment. Or maybe both. What kind of jerk is Mr. Oliver anyway?

"Tomorrow works," I say. "I'll see you then."

Lucas and I walk Ethan to the front door. Outside is a beat-up old green Bronco sitting in the circle drive. Normally I'd say something about it, but Ethan hasn't uttered a word since the conversation with his dad. So we say goodbye, and he leaves.

"I don't trust that guy," Lucas says the second the door is closed.

"He's fine," I say. "It'll be okay." Maybe I'm trying to convince myself.

We make our way back to the lab where Lucas prints out a picture of the complete Deluge Segment for me. Uncle Randall still hasn't come back. But I'm ready to get started right now.

"I'm serious, Hannah. I don't think he should go with you," Lucas says. "You only just met him, and you're going to go on some world adventure? That doesn't sound like a good idea."

I cross my arms. "Well, you're coming along."

"Yeah, right," Lucas says. "What if you find out you have to go to Siberia or something like that? And you have no idea how long you'll even be gone. There is no way my mom and dad are going to let something like that fly. Not to mention, I have to work."

"Maybe we'll find out that we have to go to Florida for a short weekend trip," I say, trying to give him hope.

"Oh, sure," Lucas says. "You think some genetic artifact that is so secret it isn't even in the Bible is hidden underneath Disney World?"

"I was thinking more of Key West," I say. "Sand. Sun. Drinks with umbrellas in them."

"You're just trying to make me feel better," Lucas says.

"Maybe."

"I appreciate it," Lucas says. "But the odds of it being in Florida are pretty slim."

I know he's right.

"Uncle Randall will be there." There's no way he wouldn't go. If anything, he'll try to leave me at home.

"He better be," Lucas says. "Anyway, I gotta head out also. I have one more job lined up for today. But I'll come by tomorrow after I finish my gigs."

Lucas is such an amazing friend. Not only is he always

there for me, if it hadn't been for him, we may never have de-coded the map.

"Thanks, Lucas. For everything." I give him a hug.

"Yeah, you're welcome," he says. "As a reward, I'm putting in an order for cheesecake tomorrow. With caramel drizzled on top. Oh, and whipped cream on the side. You remember that one time Chef Lilly made it?"

"Deal." I remember the cheesecake perfectly. Lucas and I had almost finished the entire thing ourselves.

I walk Lucas to the door and then check on Uncle Randall. He's on the phone almost the entire rest of the day. He's closed himself in his office, and the few times I peek in on him, he's drawing on the sketch while speaking in another language. One time I swear he's whispering, and I'm sure he says something along the lines of, "I miss our time together, too." I immediately walk away.

I don't know much about Uncle Randall's personal life. What little I do know is that Uncle Randall has never been married, but from what I've gathered from gossip around town, he was in love once. Some visiting professor who worked with him in linguistics for a year. One day she left and never came back. I never asked him about it. But I can't help but wonder if he's talking to her on the phone. Maybe she knows about the Code of Enoch. I'm tempted to ask, but I don't.

Finally, after dinner, he's off the phone.

"Where do we start?" I ask.

He lets out a long sigh. "That's what I'm trying to figure out."

"Why you've been on the phone the entire day?"

He nods.

"And do you have any leads?"

"Possibly," he says. "I'm going to fly to Turkey tomorrow."

My stomach drops. He can't possibly be considering going without me.

"Then I'm flying to Turkey also," I say. I don't know what's in Turkey, but if it gets me one step closer to my parents, then there is no way I'm being left behind.

Uncle Randall shakes his head. "You'll stay here. It's too dan—"

"No," I say, before he can finish. "No way. Do not even say it. I'm coming along no matter what. And if you even try to leave me here, then I swear I will follow you. You won't be able to stop me."

Uncle Randall purses his lips and studies me. "I would be able to stop you."

I fill my eyes with determination. "Are you sure?" I will find a way to Turkey no matter what I have to do.

Finally he shakes his head. "How do I always forget how stubborn you are?"

I shrug. "My charming personality deceives you?"

Uncle Randall laughs. "Yeah, something like that. Okay, tomorrow we'll go to Turkey."

Relief flows through me, but then I remember the added complication.

"Oh, yeah, there is one more thing," I say, and I tell him about Ethan.

"Absolutely not," Uncle Randall says. "Even if we thought we could trust Ethan—which we can't—his dad works at Amino Corp. He could feed back every bit of information he gets to his father who could in turn be giving it to Amino Corp. If they think anyone is looking for the Code, if they even get wind of it, they could start their own search."

A sick feeling fills my stomach. What if they already have? Doctor Bingham had seemed way too interested in the Deluge Segment. And then there's the whole thing with Ethan's dad taking up a new interest in it. That can't be coincidence. I know for sure they have access to two pieces. What if somehow they have the third? If they set out to find the Code now and my parents are still alive, it only increases the danger they're in.

This is so much bigger than I could have ever imagined. It makes my head spin.

"Doctor Bingham asked me about it," I say. "When I was at Amino Corp."

Uncle Randall's eyes widen. "What did he say?"

I tell him what I remember.

"And you told him nothing?" Uncle Randall says. "Not about the rubbing you found?"

I shake my head. "No way."

Uncle Randall slowly shakes his head. "I have a really bad feeling about this, Hannah. Why now? Why would he care?"

"I don't know," I say. "But Amino Corp has been in the news a lot recently. The last article I saw said that the Board of Directors was thinking about firing Doctor Bingham."

He puts a finger to his lip. "I've seen those articles also. And I think that somehow, this must be related."

Panic fills me. If someone like Doctor Bingham found the artifact, it would be horrible.

"Did you ever tell the authorities about any of this?" I ask. "The FBI? The CIA?" I had no clue who else you'd tell about an artifact with the power to destroy the world.

"Never," Uncle Randall says. "The fewer people that know about the Code the better."

"Yeah, I know. And that's why we have to take Ethan along. We can't risk him going to the news."

Uncle Randall frowns. "There must be another way."

I've gone over it in my head a million times, and if there is another way, I can't think of it.

"Fine, we take Ethan," Uncle Randall finally says. "We'll leave in two days. That'll give me time to figure out a way to bring him along."

That at least eliminates the threat of the news finding out. But that still leaves Doctor Bingham and Ethan's dad both being interested in it.

"The timing of all this …," I start.

"I know. It really leaves us with no other choice. We have to go after it before someone else does."

We are going to find my parents.

"My parents went to destroy it, right?" That's what the letter Mom had written to Uncle Randall said.

"That seems to have been their plan," Uncle Randall says.

"But we tried to destroy their piece of the map here and weren't able to. That's why they hid it. I have every reason to believe they wouldn't have been able to destroy the Code itself. And if it still can't be destroyed when we find it—when we find them—then we must ensure that it remains hidden forever."

I nod my agreement, still bubbling over that this is actually going to happen. We are actually going. "When we find it, we have a solid agreement. Our goal is to find my parents, but no matter what, we have to protect the Code."

"Agreed," Uncle Randall says. "Protect the Code. It can never fall into the wrong hands. No matter what the cost."

CHAPTER 13

Lucas finishes his gigs early the next day and comes over. Chef Lilly comes through and makes exactly what he requested.

"I think someone asked for cheesecake drizzled with caramel," Chef Lilly says, placing a giant slice in front of Lucas.

A huge grin pops onto his face. "Did I ever tell you how much I like you?" he asks.

Chef Lilly smiles and hands him a fork. "Only every time I make you dessert for lunch."

"Just don't tell my parents, okay? My mom gets really upset if I don't get enough vegetables."

"Deal," Chef Lilly says, then leaves the room.

Ethan shows up when Lucas is cutting his second piece. Uncle Randall has been at Harvard all morning, clearing his schedule. When Ethan walks in, I fill him in on what's happening.

"So tomorrow—" I start.

He sits at the table across from Lucas, next to me. "Don't I get a piece of cheesecake?"

I roll my eyes. "Do you want a piece of cheesecake?"

"Are you kidding? I always want cheesecake. Every time I come over. It's my favorite dessert in the entire world."

"Dude, me too," Lucas says, and he stops eating long enough to fist bump Ethan. I can't believe they're bonding over cheesecake.

I cut Ethan a huge slice because otherwise Lucas will eat the entire thing. Then I break down and cut myself a second slice, too.

"Anyway, about tomorrow …," I say. And I fill him in on our plans.

"Turkey?" Ethan mumbles with a mouthful of cheesecake. "You're leaving tomorrow?"

I finish chewing before I answer. "It was going to be today, but Uncle Randall had to take care of a few things."

He runs a hand through his blond hair, and I realize that maybe this is the perfect excuse. There is no way he'll actually be able to go. He may not even have a passport.

"Can we wait?" he finally says. I guess he's having the same doubts.

I'm about to give him the fifty reasons why we can't wait when Uncle Randall walks in.

"I took care of everything," he says, handing Ethan a folder. On the front of it is written LIBRARIES OF LOVE. "You've been signed up to build libraries in Uganda for the next month."

Ethan stares at the folder then looks to Uncle Randall.

"For real?" he says.

"For real for your parents," Uncle Randall says. "And for the record, I do not like lying to them at all. But in this situation, I don't see any other way around it."

So much for hopes of leaving Ethan behind.

"We leave tomorrow. Meet us at the airport." Then Uncle Randall cuts himself a slice of cheesecake and leaves the room.

Lucas leans back and pats his stomach, which isn't sticking out even the smallest amount. I don't know how he can eat so many desserts and never gain weight. "It's pretty amazing when you think about it," he says. "You might actually find your parents. That's like the coolest thing ever."

The lump in my throat is there before I can stop it, and I don't trust myself to speak. My parents might actually still be alive. Out there waiting for me. I imagine seeing Mom, running up to her, letting her hug me the way she used to do when I was only a child. It's a dream I've had forever, even though I knew it would never come true. Now, with the sliver of hope that it might happen, I feel like an avalanche of emotion could come toppling down on me if only I give it the tiniest of nudges.

"What would be cool would be if somehow my brother could come back to life," Ethan says, knocking me back to reality. "Now that would be cool."

A weird wave of guilt rolls over me. My parents are missing. Maybe dead. His twin brother did die. He probably has the same dreams about Caden, but the only difference now is that his dreams will never come true. And even though logically I know I shouldn't feel any guilt about this, I can't help it.

"I'm sorry," I say.

Ethan shrugs but doesn't say anything in response.

"Okay, Hannah," Lucas says. "I may not be able to physically be there, but you keep me up to date on everything. I can help, even if I'm not there. I don't care what time of day or night. You let me know if you need anything."

"You're not going?" Ethan says. I can't tell if he's surprised or if he's pushing Lucas's buttons. If the latter, then he totally succeeds.

"I have to work," Lucas says. "But I swear, if I hear one thing about you not being cool, I will find a way to fly to Turkey and kick your ass myself."

Ethan puts his hands up and leans back. "No worries, man. I swear."

"I mean it," Lucas says. "I already don't like this."

I rest a hand on his arm. "It's okay. Everything is going to be perfect."

I say this as much for myself as for Lucas. If he thinks he's nervous about what's ahead, he knows nothing. The butterflies in my stomach are having a full-on dance party. This is the moment I've been waiting for my entire life.

CHAPTER 14

ETHAN MEETS US AT THE AIRPORT THE NEXT MORNING. Instead of the worn work boots he's had on every other time I've seen him, today he has on gym shoes. I almost comment on it, but stop myself. I don't want him to think that I'm studying his appearance.

"You guys own a plane?" he asks once we meet up and Uncle Randall gets Devin to take us to the private terminal.

"We lease it," I say quickly. For some weird reason, I don't want Ethan thinking I'm some spoiled brat that jet sets around the world anytime I want to.

"Same thing," he says.

It's completely not the same thing. But I'm sure no matter what I say, it won't change his impression of me.

"Leasing is much more cost-effective," Uncle Randall says, and I kind of want to hug him.

Ethan shrugs. "Yeah, well, still, it must be nice to go anywhere you want anytime you want."

I will not react to his comments and start this trip off on the wrong foot. "Yeah, it is." I don't say another word. Maybe he gets the hint. Maybe he doesn't.

In the private terminal, Uncle Randall makes a detour for the coffee shop and returns five minutes later carrying three cups of coffee, a sight that pleases me beyond imagination.

"What did you tell your parents about the trip?" Uncle Randall asks Ethan as he hands him a coffee.

It's good to know that he's still suspicious of Ethan.

"That I was excited to build libraries," Ethan says, then hesitates for a second. "But I did set up a scheduled email for my parents. If I'm not back in a month, they'll get it. Otherwise, I'll cancel it once I get home."

Uncle Randall seems to consider this. "That's fine. They are your parents. If something does happen to us, they have a right to know."

What does Uncle Randall think will happen? Like the three of us will die?

Wait ... he must think that's a possibility. But no way am I going to believe that. We are going to find my parents and the Code of Enoch and keep it safe. That's how this whole adventure will end.

"Nothing is going to happen," I say. "Ethan should cancel the email."

"It's a month away," Ethan says.

"What if that's not long enough?" I say.

"It'll be fine, Hannah," Uncle Randall says. "Just let it go."

I wish Lucas was a hacker instead of an artist. Then he'd be able to break into Ethan's email and cancel it.

"Just make sure you remember to cancel it," I say to Ethan.

"Don't worry so much, Hannah," he says.

I wouldn't worry so much if he weren't along, but I bite my tongue and keep that thought to myself. Still, having him here sets my nerves on end.

We pass through private security and head to our gate. The coffee warms me and also helps give my hands something to do. I am beyond excited. I am going to find my parents. Bring them home. Reunite our family. But as we're walking, Ethan keeps looking back, almost like he's expecting to see someone.

"What are you looking for?" I ask after the third time he's done this. It's more than obvious.

"What do you mean?" he says.

"You keep looking over your shoulder, like this," I say, mimicking the motion. "Why?"

"I don't."

"You do."

"If I am," he says, "then maybe it's because I'm worried that you dropped something. Seriously, can't you do the buckle on your bag?"

The flap on my messenger bag bounces back and forth with each step I take.

"The buckle is a pain," I say. "And nothing's falling out."

"I don't need you losing the map," Ethan says.

"Uncle Randall has it," I say.

Lucas had printed the only copy and Uncle Randall insisted on being the one to hold it. Even Ethan agreed this would be okay. Then we'd deleted the file from my computer. As for the rubbing I'd found, I'd given it to Lucas who promised he would keep it with him at all times. Uncle Randall and I had talked about it and decided that we couldn't destroy it yet.

"Well, you might lose something else," Ethan says. "Like your passport. Or do rich people not need passports?"

"Everyone needs a passport," I snap. "And can we stop with the rich comments?"

"Enough," Uncle Randall says. "Look, I know this isn't the most ideal thing ever, but you two have to stop the squabbling. I feel like I'm with two small school children. Like he dumped his pears into your spaghetti, and now you're trying to steal his ice cream."

I stop walking. "Are you kidding? He's totally been the one who's instigated everything."

"I have not," Ethan says.

"See, that's what I'm talking about," Uncle Randall says. "This bickering can't go on. We have a ten hour flight ahead of us, and if you two can't get along, it will drive me crazy."

"But—" I start.

Uncle Randall puts up his hand.

It's infuriating how wrong he is. But I decide to ignore Ethan and see how that goes.

How that goes is unsuccessful. No sooner do we buckle in, Ethan turns to me and says, "I can't sleep on flights." He's sitting across the aisle from me. Uncle Randall is in back, working at a built-in desk.

"Sure you can," I say because I specifically didn't get a lot of sleep last night since I knew I had this flight today.

He shakes his head. "Nope. Never been able to."

"You could try again," I say. "Because this is a long flight. I'm going to be sleeping."

"Lucky you," Ethan says. And he starts in on a Sudoku puzzle.

I close my eyes, but he keeps tapping the end of his pencil on the table in front of him.

"Could you stop that?" I say after fifteen minutes, opening one eye.

He looks over at me. "Stop what?"

"Tapping your pencil. You haven't stopped since we took off."

Ethan looks at the pencil, like he's surprised to see it in his hand. "Oh, was I tapping it?"

"Yeah, you were."

He sets the pencil down. "How about we talk?"

"I'm tired." I close my eyes.

Next thing I know, I hear him unbuckling and coming over to sit next to me.

He taps me on the arm. "Hey."

I try to ignore him.

"Hey, Hannah," he says.

I pop one eye open. "What?"

He holds up his phone. "What's your favorite game?"

"I don't play games. They're a waste of time." I close my eye again.

He taps my arm. "Sure you do. I saw you playing something yesterday on your phone."

I open the eye again. "That wasn't a game."

"It looked like a game. What was it?"

"It was an evolution challenge," I say. "You pick which two species to breed to get specific DNA results. The closer you get and the fewer number of matings you need to make, the higher your score."

"So it is a game," Ethan says.

"It's not a game."

"Sounds like a game to me," he says. "What's it called?"

"*Evolution*," I say. "You can download it."

He finds the app and downloads it. "I bet I can get a higher score than you."

I close my eyes again, happy he's now occupied, but *Evolution* must not be his thing because no sooner are we out over the Atlantic, he's pestering me again.

"How about twenty questions?" he says.

"What about it?" My eyes are closed, but sleep has yet to come.

"We can play it," Ethan says.

"You're kidding?"

"I'll go first," he says. Apparently he's not kidding.

I let out a deep sigh, and give up the wonderful pipe dream I had about actually sleeping. "Fine," I say. "Animal, Vegetable, or Mineral?"

Twenty questions turns out to be way more fun than I would have thought. I guess his choice of school bus and manage to stump him on armadillo.

"Armadillos are weird anyway," Ethan says. "I'm not entirely sure that they really exist. They seem more like a myth, like the Chupacabra or something."

"Of course they exist," I say. "They're descendants of the giant sloth."

He scratches his head. "Yeah, those giant sloths are a bit sketchy, too. And how could something so little be descended from something so big anyway?"

"Haven't you studied genetics?" I ask.

"Not much," Ethan says. "Languages were more my thing."

"But your parents ... they're geneticists like mine. I'm sure you guys talk about it at home."

Ethan finishes the last of his Sprite (I insisted he not drink a Coke on the remote chance that he actually does fall asleep), and like magic, the flight attendant brings him a new one. From the way she hovers around him, I'm beginning to think that she has a crush on him. Maybe it's his eyes. Or his smile. That's probably it. His smile is pretty sweet, and he's been flashing it at her every time she's come over.

"Yeah, I'm not all that close to my parents," Ethan says. "I mean I'm close to my mom. We talk sometimes. But my dad ... we don't talk much. Actually not like ever."

"Why not?" I ask, and memories of the conversation I'd

overheard with his dad come back to me. I don't know Ethan very well, but he seemed like a different person while talking to his dad.

"He's always so disappointed in me," Ethan says. "It's like no matter what I do, it's never good enough. I think that's what turned me off to genetics in the first place. I'd try to act like I was interested in it, but all it would do is make my dad angry. I always figured he would have preferred if Caden had lived and I was the one who got sick."

My heart breaks a tiny bit in that moment as I picture Ethan as a young boy, growing up thinking that his dad wished he was dead.

"That can't possibly be true."

Ethan gives a small shrug. "It sure feels that way sometimes. But enough about that. I thought we were talking about giant sloths."

"Right," I say, not wanting to push him. I think the only reason he's being so talkative is because he's sleep deprived. "I can show you how they're all related sometime. There's a beautiful pattern that forms when you study animals and link them all together. It's a work of art that makes you believe in a master plan while still being able to believe in evolution."

"So you believe in evolution?" Ethan says.

"Of course," I say.

"But what about this Code of Enoch?" Ethan says, whispering the name. "Don't you believe in it?"

It's my turn to pause. "I don't know. It seems a little farfetched that the DNA code for the entire world is stored on some clay tablet. But my parents actually believed in it, and they're scientists. Your parents believed in it, too. They believed so much that it changed all of their lives. And I'll admit that I don't know what we're going to find when we get wherever we're going. I have no clue. But I can't let that stop me from trying."

Ethan doesn't say anything, and I think that maybe I've rambled on too much.

"Do you believe in it?" I ask.

"Maybe," Ethan says. "Maybe not. But I do believe that if I look for it—if there's a chance that I find it—my dad will never think I'm a loser again."

"He doesn't think you're a loser," I say.

"Yeah, he does," Ethan says. "But it's okay. I'll show him that I'm not."

I hate the dividing line this places between me and Ethan. I hate that I can never let him bring back the Code of Enoch if it does exist. But there's nothing I can say right now that will change his mind, so I don't say anything at all.

Ethan pulls a notebook from his backpack and begins to write letters. Symbols. The kind of thing Uncle Randall would do. I recognize some of them. Greek. Aramaic. Russian. Others look familiar, but I can't quite place them. But I don't interrupt Ethan to ask because based on the way he's not talking, I'm guessing that our conversation is over. So instead, after watching him for another five minutes, I close my eyes and finally drift off to sleep.

∞

I wake with my head on Ethan's shoulder. God, I hope I wasn't drooling. I sit up the second I realize what I'm doing.

"Sorry," I say.

"For?"

"For falling asleep on you."

"What about for the snoring? Are you sorry for that?" Ethan asks.

I roll my eyes. "I don't snore."

"How would you know? You're the one sleeping."

"Did you sleep at all?" I ask, hoping that he's lying about the snoring. He's gotten through half the blank pages in the journal and still seems to be going strong. In addition, there are a bunch of papers in front of him that I'm sure Uncle Randall gave him. Symbols and words that make my head hurt.

"No," Ethan says. "But your uncle gave me some stuff to study. It's actually really cool. Like all the symbols on the Deluge Segment are so close to others that I already know and yet different. It's got to be the most amazing archaeological find ever."

Genetics may not be his thing, but linguistics certainly is. I bet he and Uncle Randall could talk endlessly for days about it. Maybe he should have sat next to Uncle Randall during the flight.

The flight attendant is going around opening window screens, letting in the light. We've flown through the evening and into a brand new day.

Once we're off the plane and through customs, Uncle Randall hires a driver named Mert, and though Mert speaks English about as well as Sonic, my hedgehog, does, Uncle Randall speaks fifteen different languages fluently and has no problem communicating with him. They spend about ten minutes in an animated discussion while Ethan and I stand there looking stupid. What I really want is a cup of coffee, and like magic, the airport has a Starbucks.

Ethan takes his credit card out to pay for his coffee, but I pull his hand back. "Won't your parents know where you are if you charge something?"

He continues to hand it over to the barista. "It's not like they're going to check my charges."

I pull his hand back again. "I don't care. You can't use it."

"I'm not letting you pay for everything for me," Ethan says.

"Yeah, you are." I attempt to confiscate the credit card, but Ethan pulls it out of my reach.

"Fine. I won't use it." He shoves it back in his wallet. "But my parents aren't going to be checking up on me. I told my mom I'd call if I could but that cell service might suck."

"You have to let me know if you call home," I say.

"Why?"

Okay, fine. I'm not his babysitter. But still …

"Knowing will just make me feel better," I say.

"No promises," Ethan says.

I don't push it.

By the time we get back from coffee, Uncle Randall and

the driver, Mert, have come to some kind of agreement. I'm guessing much cash was passed to Mert because he has a giant smile on his face and nods incessantly. He grabs all three of our duffle bags and leads us outside and to a black van where he throws our bags into the back and opens the door. Once we're all set, Mert pulls out onto the streets of downtown Istanbul.

CHAPTER 15

OF ALL THE PLACES I'VE TRAVELED, I'VE NEVER BEEN to Istanbul. The city is the perfect mix of ancient and modern, with skyscrapers next to neighborhood cafés. I take a picture of the Hagia Sophia as we pass it and text it to Lucas. He'd go crazy in a place like this with all the art.

"The city was founded in 660 BCE," I tell Ethan because I stayed up a lot of the night before reading about it. He sits in the far back while Uncle Randall and I are in the middle seats.

"Maybe the official city of Byzantium," Ethan says. "But did you know they found relics here dating back to the seventh millennium BCE?"

I guess I wasn't the only one who stayed up reading about it.

"Wait, really?" I turn to Uncle Randall. "Is he right?"

Uncle Randall nods. "Deluge period artifacts. That's why we're here."

"You think the starting point could be right here in Istanbul?" I say. Uncle Randall had been kind of vague about why exactly we were coming to Turkey, only that it was to consult with an expert. I have no clue who that expert might be. As far as I know, no one else in the world knows about the Deluge Segment.

"Possibly," Uncle Randall says. "The fact that so many of the flood theories stem from this region can't be a coincidence. But that's what we're here to find out."

When I actually think about how long ago the Deluge really was, it blows my mind. They suspect that hundreds more species of mammals alone used to be alive back then. That over the last twelve thousand years, we've lost them. We've lost too many. And every day, new species are being threatened. I wonder, just wonder, if we do find this Code of Enoch, if I could use it to bring some of those species back. It would be an amazing leap forward for endangered species.

No, we can't do that, even though it would fall in line with everything I believe in. But that's not what this trip is about. The Code itself is not important. My parents are what's important. And yet the more I think about this Code of Enoch, the more I think about its possibilities, I'm tempted at everything that it could do. And if I'm having thoughts about the potential the Code could offer, so is Ethan. So is Uncle Randall. And so is anyone else who might be looking for it, like Amino Corp. We can't let them find it first.

Mert drives us to a hotel near the outskirts of town. With our money, I have no clue why Uncle Randall would pick this place. Unlike the modern awesomeness of so much of Istanbul, there are rat droppings near the front door, half the windows are missing at least one shutter, and graffiti has been sprayed on the sidewalk out front.

"What's it say?" I ask.

"'The ground has ears?'" Ethan translates, but he sounds unsure of himself and looks to Uncle Randall for confirmation.

"It's a way of warning caution," Uncle Randall says. "Be careful what you say. Anyone could be listening. It's an idiom."

"I didn't know you spoke Turkish," I say to Ethan.

"I'm learning," Ethan says. "Mostly self-taught online. But I didn't get to idioms yet."

Uncle Randall says something to him slowly, I'm guessing in Turkish, that I don't understand, and Ethan answers, and then the two of them laugh. I almost ask what they said, but I decide not to give them the satisfaction of knowing I want to know.

We check in to the hotel, and Uncle Randall says he wants to get some sleep. I don't buy it for a second. The minute I close the door to my hotel room, I crack it back open and peek out. Sure enough, he goes into his hotel room, drops his bag off, and leaves. I give it enough space so that he won't see me, and then I tiptoe out of my room and follow him.

Uncle Randall goes down to the lobby where he talks with the guy behind the desk who points toward the side of the hotel lobby opposite the stairs. Uncle Randall nods and then heads in that direction, walks into the hotel restaurant, and sits at the second table from the back on the right.

My phone buzzes. I curse under my breath and silence it.

It's a response text from Lucas from the pictures I sent him. He also asks what's going on. But I can't answer because just then someone walks over and sits down at the table with Uncle Randall.

It's hard to see the person's face because they have a wide scarf covering most of their head, but it is abundantly clear from the way the person walks and the shape of their hips that it's a woman. They don't do the familiar Turkish greeting of kisses on the sides of the cheeks or even a handshake. Uncle Randall doesn't even stand up. The woman wears jeans, a long sleeved black shirt that looks like it might be made of leather, and tall black boots.

I'm not close enough to hear what they're saying, but I don't want to move closer and risk Uncle Randall seeing me. For all I know, they could be speaking Turkish. They talk for a bit, back and forth. The woman acts upset for a moment, but then Uncle Randall says something that seems to calm her down. What calms her down even more is when Uncle Randall pulls out an envelope that he opens just enough for her to see what's inside. Based on the size and thickness, and the fact that this completely looks like some kind of black-market trade, I'm guessing it's a wad of money. The woman doesn't pull the contents out, but she does feel the thickness between her fingers. She nods and tucks the envelope away in her bag, pulling out instead a wrapped package.

She slides it over to Uncle Randall who lifts back the covering just a small amount, so he can see what's inside. If only I'd thought to position myself behind him where I could see, too.

That seems to be the end of their deal. The woman starts to stand up, but before she does, Uncle Randall reaches out and takes her hand in a way that looks completely endearing. Words pass between them that I can't hear, and then she gently pulls her hand away. She adjusts the scarf so even more of her face and head are covered and leaves the restaurant.

What was that all about? My head spins with the possibilities.

Uncle Randall scoops the package off the table, tucks it under his arms and walks out. I press myself behind the dying palm trees so he won't see me, and only when he's up the stairs and out of sight, do I dare to return to my room. It's only then that I return Lucas's text.

All fine here. Arrived in turkey. Lots of cool architecture. What's up there?

I have the thing you gave me safe. Thanks for the pics. I'm worried about you, Lucas texts.

Nothing to worry about. And thanks, I text back.

There's a long pause where Lucas doesn't type anything. It's late at night in Boston. I can't actually believe he's still awake.

Finally he texts back. Stay safe, Hannah. I don't trust Ethan.

It'll be fine. He's not so bad, I text.

Lucas doesn't respond. I wait five minutes, then ten, and then the urge to take a nap gets the better of me, and I give in to it.

CHAPTER 16

I WAKE TO THE SOUND OF POUNDING ON MY HOTEL room door. Sun streams through the slotted windows, creating lined shadows across everything in the room. From the angle of the shadows, it seems that I've slept late into the morning.

I stumble over and open the door. Uncle Randall and Ethan stand there, fully showered, dressed, and ready for the day. They're dressed like twins, both in jeans and dark green T-shirts, almost like there is some dress code I am totally un-aware of. And in case I thought for a moment that they didn't make the trip, Ethan's got his familiar work boots on, laced around his ankles.

"What time is it?" I ask.

"Eleven," Ethan says. "We already had breakfast."

"And we have an appointment at noon," Uncle Randall says. "So you'll need to hurry."

I nod and close the door and dig through my bag, pulling

132

out one of the two extra pairs of jeans I've brought on the trip. Once we figure out where we're going, we can find an outfitter to get us everything and anything we might need. I run a hairbrush through my hair and pull it together into my two ponytails, fish out a blue and white striped knit cap, shove my feet in my running shoes, and I'm ready for the day.

I meet Uncle Randall and Ethan in the lobby. They're laughing and talking in some other language, but they stop the second I walk up.

"What were you guys talking about?" I ask.

"Ethan thought it would take you an hour to get ready," Uncle Randall says. "I was trying to explain to him that you never take more than ten minutes."

It's so unlike me, but I am hit with the overwhelming urge to smooth my hair and make sure it's in place. I lick my lips, wishing that I'd thought to bring along lip gloss. Maybe I should give more thought to my appearance. For the first time, I wonder if Ethan has a girlfriend, or possibly someone he'd like to be his girlfriend. I haven't thought to ask, but then again we haven't had much opportunity to talk.

I cross my arms, daring Ethan to say something.

"Nice hat," he says.

"Nice boots," I say.

"I'm glad you like them."

"When you weren't wearing them before, I figured you donated them to some homeless person."

"There is no way I will ever donate these boots," Ethan says.

"That's because no respectable donation place would take them," I say.

"Hannah ...," Uncle Randall says.

"I'm kidding. Anyway, what's for breakfast? I'm starving."

Uncle Randall hands over a plate with a scone that looks like it has bits of cranberries in it. At this point, it could have pickles, and I'd still eat it. With the flight and as much as I've slept, I'm going on fifteen hours with no food.

"Don't worry," he says. "It's veggie. I asked."

I take the scone happily, break off a giant piece, and shove it in my mouth. At this point I don't care that it looks undignified.

Mert is already waiting out front. We load into the black van, and he floors the gas pedal before I even have time to fasten my seat belt. He weaves through Istanbul, insisting on taking us on the scenic route since neither Ethan nor I have been here before. He points out the Blue Mosque, Topkapi Palace, and the Grand Bazaar, none of which form a straight line so we're driving everywhere.

I take pictures of everything and text them to Lucas. I guess he's awake because he responds to each text immediately with some obscure fact about each image I send.

"Texting your boyfriend?" Ethan says.

I tuck the phone back into my pocket. "He's not my boyfriend."

"Uh huh," Ethan says.

"What's that supposed to mean?"

"Nothing."

"He's not," I say.

"Okay, fine," Ethan says, but he still has this ridiculous smile on his face like he doesn't believe me.

We finally pull up to a three-story pink townhome with balconies and shutters covering every window. Right next door is an almost identical house except it hasn't been renovated like this one has. The entire neighborhood has similar houses, with about half remodeled and occupied and the other half that look vacant.

Uncle Randall says something to Mert that hopefully equates to "wait here for us," and we unload and walk to the front door.

"Whose house is this?" I ask.

Uncle Randall raises his hand to knock. "This is the home of—"

But before he can finish his sentence or even knock, the door flies open, and a man steps out, beaming. He doesn't have the dark hair and bushy mustache that lots of the men I've seen so far in Istanbul do, nor does he have a Mediterranean complexion, instead having pale skin, like he spends way too much time inside. The man grabs Uncle Randall in a bear hug which Uncle Randall happily returns, and when they're finally done hugging, they laugh and slap each other on the back and say a bunch of things I can't understand but which they both seem to find funny because they laugh some more.

"Do you know him?" Ethan asks me.

Something about the man's face looks kind of familiar,

but I can't place it. "I don't think so. But I'm guessing Uncle Randall does."

"I kind of figured that out on my own," Ethan says.

Uncle Randall seems to remember that he's not alone because he steps back so he can introduce us.

"Tobin, may I introduce you to my beautiful, intelligent, witty, and clever niece Hannah Hawkins? Hannah, this is Doctor Tobin Carter."

My face warms at Uncle Randall's introduction, which seems to be laid on a little thick. I'm sure I hear Ethan stifle a laugh next to me.

Doctor Carter steps forward and clasps my hand, but then this doesn't seem to be enough because he pulls me into a hug, giving me a kiss on either cheek.

"Hannah Hawkins, what a pleasure it is to meet you," Tobin says when he steps back from the hug.

"It's nice to meet you, too, Doctor Carter," I say.

"Doctor Carter," he says and laughs. "Tobin. Please. I feel as though I know you. Your uncle has been bragging about you since before you were born."

My face, which must be bright red, gets even warmer.

Uncle Randall clears his throat and motions to Ethan. "And our traveling companion is Ethan Oliver, longtime friend of the family."

Tobin's eyes widen. "Oliver? As in ...," he says, looking to Uncle Randall.

Uncle Randall nods. "One and the same."

Which means that Tobin very likely knew all of our parents back when we were little. And then it comes to me. This is the man from the photo with my dad, Ethan's dad, and Uncle Randall in Peru. The picture with the Deluge Segment. It all snaps into place why we're here in Turkey. Tobin is the expert Uncle Randall was talking about.

Tobin clasps Ethan's hand and tells him what an honor it is to meet him. Ethan keeps fumbling over words, like maybe he's trying to speak Turkish and English at the same time, but he manages to get out a polite thank you amid the jumble.

"Tobin and I went to graduate school together at Harvard," Uncle Randall finally says, saving Ethan. "Only other student there who could come close to my skills in linguistics."

Tobin grins. "Come close to your skills? You possibly have that backwards? If I remember correctly, it was you who nearly came close to my level of expertise. Perhaps if you keep studying, you can still get there someday."

Uncle Randall laughs. "One can only hope."

"Now please come in," Tobin says, "and meet my beautiful children."

Beautiful children is the understatement of the year. It turns out that Tobin has two teenagers, a daughter, Sena, who is sixteen, and a son, Deniz, who is seventeen. Their existence makes me think human selective breeding could be involved. Sena is probably five foot ten, has the longest legs I've ever seen which I can tell because she's wearing tight black leggings, skin as smooth as black ice and very visible because she's wearing a short-sleeved shirt that shows off a good amount of her midriff, and a toothpaste model smile. From the second we step into their family room, Ethan can't take his eyes off her. Deniz has the same amazing olive complexion, deep hazel eyes that flirt with me from the moment they meet mine, and brown hair that falls over his forehead. His smile matches his sister's, and it seems like it's directed right at me.

"I know what you're thinking," Tobin says.

He has no idea what I'm thinking. Or at least I hope that he doesn't.

"What's that?" I ask, pulling my eyes away from Deniz because I realize that I've been staring at him way too long. I almost want to take a picture of the two of them and text it to Lucas back home because if humans can be art, then Sena and Deniz are it.

"You're thinking that they got their good looks from me," Tobin says.

"I didn't want to say anything," I say, relieved that my innermost thoughts aren't given away. Though Tobin is a handsome guy, I guess, for being old like Uncle Randall, his kids look like they should be on the cover of magazines.

"I'm kidding," Tobin says, "You should see their mother. She is a beauty."

"Where is Beril anyway?" Uncle Randall asks.

"At the market," Tobin says. "She was hoping we would be able to convince you to stay for dinner. Stay the night."

"We're at the Sultan Grande Hotel," Uncle Randall says.

Tobin looks aghast. "The Sultan Grande Hotel. That's a rat trap. A place for scammers. You know they found a dead body in the trash bin there last month. There is no way in good conscience that I can have you stay there even one night." And he says something to Deniz in Turkish who then nods and leaves the room.

"What did you say?" I ask, cursing myself for not learning even a small amount of Turkish. I could have studied it on the plane at a bare minimum.

Uncle Randall looks to Ethan to see if he understood.

"He said to go get our bags," Ethan says.

"Looks like you have a protégé," Tobin says.

"It seems so," Uncle Randall says, and a brief moment of—jealously?—runs through me. Uncle Randall and Ethan seem to have a ton in common, making me feel like an outsider.

We make small talk, mostly about the dead body in the trash bin, until Deniz returns. Tobin's wife, Beril, gets back, and she insists on making us "just a snack" for lunch. Just a snack turns out to be hummus and bread and fresh vegetables and cheese, and I'm so hungry that I'm more than thrilled. She's even brought dessert, helva, which Sena says is a local favorite. It crumbles and melts in my mouth, and Ethan and I each have two pieces. If Lucas were here, he'd probably have four. Maybe Chef Lilly can learn how to make it.

Only after lunch do we get down to what we really came here for.

"You seemed a bit cryptic in your messages," Tobin finally

says, shifting our conversation.

Uncle Randall tilts his head in acknowledgment. "I couldn't be sure who might be listening in."

"And what is it that we are going to talk about that you would not want anyone else to hear?" Tobin asks.

Uncle Randall looks to me to answer. He seems to trust Tobin, and I've never doubted Uncle Randall's judgment before.

"The Code of Enoch," I say almost in a whisper as if I'm afraid the walls themselves are listening. The graffiti message from the hotel returns to me. *The ground has ears.*

It seems I'm right to be cautious. No sooner are the words out of my mouth than the entire mood in the room shifts. Tobin's face, which has held nearly a constant smile, grows serious. Sena and Deniz, who have been helping their mother clean up after lunch, sink into seats. And Beril, Tobin's wife, leaves the room.

"We're trying to find it," Uncle Randall says.

"We're not trying to," Ethan says. "We're going to find it."

My first reaction is to argue with him, but even I realize that this is not the time.

"And you come to me?" Tobin says. "Why? What makes you think I can help you? We gave up on that dream years ago, remember?"

Panic fills me. This could be a dead end. Worse, this could be alerting one more person—four more people, if you count the entire family—about our plans, and if they have no information for us, then it wasn't worth the risk.

"Of course we come to you," Uncle Randall says. And he waits.

"It doesn't exist," Tobin says.

Uncle Randall crosses his arms.

"It's just a fable."

"It's real," I say.

Tobin slowly shakes his head. "We never found anything about the alleged Code of Enoch. We could never confirm its existence."

I am not giving up on this. I'm also sure we wouldn't be here if Tobin didn't know more. "There are lots of things that people believe in that can't be confirmed," I say. "Noah's Ark. The Colossus of Rhodes."

"True," Tobin says. "But at least there is much evidence that points to the possibility of those. Many appear in ancient writings. The Bible. Plato's Dialogues. People search for them all the time. With the alleged Code of Enoch, there are no such records."

Uncle Randall leans close. "You vowed to uncover proof that might lead to the Code of Enoch. We need to know what you found."

Tobin spreads his hands wide. "I found nothing. And if you remember correctly, we all agreed not to continue the search."

I almost stand as anger moves through me. "I don't care what you guys agreed to in the past. We have to find this thing. We have to find my parents."

Moments of silence fill the room. Tobin doesn't blink.

Neither does Uncle Randall.

Finally Uncle Randall says, "Please, Tobin. We need to know. You moved here, to Turkey, to be closer to where the flood occurred, to look for proof. We need to know what you found."

"You found proof of the flood?" Ethan says.

Tobin's eyes flicker with a hint of excitement, like maybe he's dying to talk about this with us. After all, this man moved across the world to search for the Code of Enoch.

"There are many signs of the flood around Turkey," Tobin says, as if this is a safe topic for him to discuss. "Noah's Ark, rumored to be resting upon the top of Mount Ararat. Ancient villages sunken under the dead waters of the Black Sea. Fossils of sea creatures high above sea level. Rapid burial of plants and animals. These are the clues that people have been chasing for centuries. They look for proof that the flood really existed, and so much of that proof seems to be centrally located in this part of the world."

Chills run through me, like ancient mysteries surfacing after being hidden. But if we're going to get any farther on this, we need to show our hand.

"We figured out how to read the map," I say. I reach for Uncle Randall's bag and pull out the high-resolution image.

Tobin sucks in a breath as he looks at the symbols popping from the pages. "How did you do this?"

"My friend figured it out," I say.

Slowly Tobin shakes his head. "You shouldn't have this. This should be destroyed like we all agreed upon."

"But it's not," Uncle Randall says. He takes the image from me and sets it on the table in front of Tobin like a peace offering.

"Please help us," I say. "I just want to find my parents."

The silence returns, and I feel like Tobin is looking into my soul. If he is, all he'll find is that this is the only thing I want.

"Deniz," Tobin finally says, calling his son over.

Deniz gives me a great big smile as he passes by which I happily return. Tobin whispers something into his son's ear, and Deniz leaves the room, returning a minute later with a wooden box. He sets it on the table in front of us, next to the image of the map. He opens the lid and pulls out something about as big as his hand wrapped in cloth. He moves the box to the floor and rests the cloth there on the table instead.

"In my research, I found this." Tobin pulls away the cloth, revealing an artifact, circular and covered in symbols. It's like a small-scale version of one of the pieces of the Deluge Segment. "Your map is almost complete."

"Almost?" I say.

He holds up the artifact. "This is the final piece."

CHAPTER 17

"You found something," Uncle Randall says.

"Of course I found something," Tobin says. "You don't think I moved to Turkey, fell in love, had a couple kids, and slipped into some sedentary life, do you?"

"But you never told me," Uncle Randall says.

"Because we agreed to never speak of it again. But then your sister and her husband came back after our agreement." Tobin looks to me then. "You look so much like your mother did the last time I saw her."

"When was that?" I ask. My heart pounds. We are totally on the right path.

Tobin leans back in his chair. "Eleven years ago. They came here looking for the Code of Enoch."

They were here, in this very room possibly. I want them back.

"What did you tell them?" I ask.

Tobin shakes his head. "I told them again the same thing that I'm going to tell you now. Leave now. Return to America.

The Code of Enoch should not be sought out."

"I'm not leaving." There's about as much chance of me leaving as of all my chromosomes translocating.

"That's what your parents said, too," Tobin says. "Even still, I wasn't going to tell them anything. But when they told me of the danger, of what they intended to do to prevent it, only then did I share this with them. I too had figured out how to read the map, not long after I moved to Istanbul. But without a starting point, the map was worthless. I searched every site I could get access to. Even some I couldn't get access to. And finally I found it." He holds up the piece. "This is the secret."

"Where to begin the journey," Uncle Randall says.

Tobin nods. "The starting point."

"Which is where?" I ask.

Tobin says, "Why should I share it with you? What makes this knowledge necessary?"

Silence echoes around the room. The seconds tick by. All sorts of thoughts run around in my head. What if we've come all this way, gotten so close, only to find an enormous roadblock? What if this is the end of our journey before we've really even started? I can't let that happen.

Uncle Randall opens his mouth. "Because—"

I put up a hand to stop him. This is my plan. My dream. It is my place to convince Tobin.

"Because we have to find my parents," I say.

"Not good enough," Tobin says.

His words bump around in my brain. It is good enough.

I've been without my parents for eleven years. And if there is a hope that I can find them now, then I have to. I am not going to take no for an answer.

"It is good enough," I say, rising to my feet. "My parents gave up their lives for this thing. That's how it's been for eleven years. And maybe that was fine before, but the difference now is that I know the truth. I know what they went after. And I also know they are in danger. The whole world may be in danger."

"Danger?" Tobin says, and he looks to Uncle Randall.

Uncle Randall slowly nods his head. "It's true. There is a very good chance that we are not the only ones looking."

"Who?" Tobin says. His eyes flick to Ethan, just briefly, then back to Uncle Randall. It's such a small movement that I'm sure Ethan hasn't noticed, but Uncle Randall absolutely does.

Uncle Randall gives a small shake of his head. "Do you remember Amino Corp?"

Tobin cocks his head. "Giant pharma company there in Boston, right?"

"Exactly," Uncle Randall says. "Do you remember when they hired me?"

Understanding dawns in Tobin's eyes, and he sucks in a sharp breath. "That's right. They had a piece of the Deluge Segment. You translated for them."

"Yes," Uncle Randall says. "And the CEO, Doctor Peter Bingham, has been showing some unusual interest in the artifact lately. I worry that they may be trying to find it also."

Tobin presses a finger to his lips as he thinks, then he says,

"Haven't they been in the news recently? I feel like I read something not too long ago."

I nod. "They're about to go bankrupt. Lots of bad press. Some of the articles even talk about firing Doctor Bingham."

Tobin looks to Uncle Randall. Silent words pass between them. Silent words that I hope convey our urgency.

Finally Tobin blows out a long breath. "Sometimes events happen that we have no control over. They are fated to be. And though I have no proof of this, something deep inside me tells me that you showing up here today is not a random event. It is an event that has been coming for many years. Something that must happen."

Relief flows through me. He is going to help up. He's going to tell us where to start. I sink back into my seat, not daring to speak. I don't want to risk him changing his mind.

Tobin places his artifact in the center of our image of the map, overlaying it on other symbols. Immediately it comes together, like a puzzle. Symbols that hadn't connected before now form into mountains and valleys. But though they are now complete, they still don't give us all the answers.

"This is where you start," Tobin says.

"This will lead us to the Code?" Ethan asks, leaning forward.

Tobin narrows his eyes at Ethan. "What are you going to do if you find it?"

"We have no plans to disturb the Code of Enoch, should it still exist," Uncle Randall quickly says.

Tobin keeps his eyes locked on Ethan. "I'm not asking

you, Randall. I'm asking Ethan. What are you going to do if you find it?"

Ethan's face freezes at being called out. "I … my parents … it's just that …"

"You can't use the Code of Enoch," Tobin says.

"I won't," Ethan says.

Tobin narrows his eyes at Ethan. "I'm not playing around here. The Code of Enoch is dangerous. It should not be used. Even touching it could cause death."

"I'm not going to use it," Ethan says. "I promise."

Tobin slowly nods. "A promise that cannot be broken."

Ethan gulps but doesn't say anything.

Tobin points to two symbols in the center of his artifact. "You can read these symbols, Randall?"

Uncle Randall leans forward and puts on his reading glasses. He mutters a few words under his breath then says, "Gate."

"Gate?" I ask. "What gate?"

Uncle Randall's lips are still moving like he's sounding out words, testing theories. Ethan pulls his phone out and types something into it, then scrolls through the list of results.

"If you translate *Gate* into other languages, especially those of the surrounding areas …" Ethan pauses as he looks through the results. "You get Kars!"

Uncle Randall and Tobin both nod. "Kars."

"What do you mean, cars?" I say.

Ethan shakes his head. "You're pronouncing it wrong. It's Kars, with more distinct consonants. Kars means gate in

Georgian. It also happens to be a region in eastern Turkey."

"Okay, so gate. What's the other symbol?" I ask.

"Anahit," Uncle Randall says.

Tobin nods. "The Armenian goddess of fertility. Belief for her was strong. So strong that there was even an ancient city named for her."

I turn on my phone and type in the goddess's name. It doesn't take long to find something useful. "Ani. It's an ancient city in eastern Turkey. In the Kars district. Named after the goddess Anahit." It all fits together.

"Ani," Tobin says, confirming my Internet search. "It's a city with a long history. And its placement falls well within our flood region, making it a likely candidate for the information you need."

"Likely? Or for sure?" I don't want to waste my time going down rabbit holes.

"I haven't been there myself, so I can't say," Tobin says. "But it's what I told your parents when they came to see me. And it's what I'm telling you now. I gave them a replica of this piece, and they set off. You need to follow. You need to go to Kars, to the ruined city of Ani. That is your best hope for the answer you seek."

And like that, our path is clear.

CHAPTER 18

WE SET OUT FOR KARS EARLY THE NEXT MORNING. It's a twenty-two hour drive, and though Mert, our airport driver, keeps insisting that he will "take good care of us" and "make our journey safe beyond our wildest dreams," Tobin says that the driver is untrustworthy and that we can't bring anyone else into this. Which is also why he says we can't fly. He says that it would be too easy for someone to track our flight. Still, it's going to take us three days to get there driving which is hard to swallow when I know the flight would only be a few hours.

Tobin insists that we use his family car along with his neighbor's. He and Deniz can drive. The guys load the cars, leaving me to pack up food with Sena and her mom, Beril. Beril speaks about three words of English, which consist of mosque, dollar, and spaghetti, though it could be argued that the last word isn't truly English. But Sena tells me that it's her father's favorite food.

As for Sena, she and I have about as much in common as

150

panda bears have with my sugar gliders. They're both marsupials, but the similarities stop there. Unlike her mom, Sena is fluent in English.

"I'll be traveling to Harvard in a year for school," Sena says. "Papa's already secured my admittance."

Okay, maybe we do have one thing in common. I basically have a spot there too. With and my parents and Uncle Randall having attended, his working there, and the money we donate to Harvard each year, it's definitely going to get me some special consideration.

"Great. We'll be starting at the same time," I say, trying not to think about the way Ethan's been staring at Sena pretty much every waking moment. When he was asleep, he was probably dreaming about her, too.

Sena grabs my hand and squeezes it like we're besties. "We could room together! In the dormitories. I've always dreamed of living in a dormitory. Staying up late eating popcorn and wearing pajamas while we watch movies. Stopping at Starbucks on the way to early morning classes."

I'm with her on the Starbucks part, but I'm certainly not making plans for Sena and me to be roomies. If only Lucas could go to Harvard, but his grades just aren't there. I know Uncle Randall could pull strings and still get him on the dean's interest list, but the one time I mentioned that to Lucas, he started fuming, told me no way was he ever going to let that happen, and if I did do something like that he still wouldn't go. As much as I want him to stay around Boston, his dream is attending the Art Institute of Chicago where his alleged ancestor, Georgia O'Keeffe, went.

"I'll live at home," I say, unlatching my hand from hers as diplomatically as I can.

Sena's eyes widen with hope. Wait. She can't think I'm going to ask her to come stay with us, can she? Oh god. Uncle Randall is such good friends with her dad. I can almost see it happening. And it's not like we don't have the space at Easton Estate.

"What about Deniz? Where is he going to college?" Maybe if he were part of the equation, it would be almost bearable.

"He wants to stay here," Sena says. "Work with Papa at the museum."

So much for that thought.

Sena's mom continues making food the entire time we talk. She nods and smiles and laughs when we do.

Sena says, "Deniz and I speak in English when we don't want Mama to hear," and she winks.

"What do you not want her to hear?" Since I didn't grow up with my parents, I have no idea what kind of secrets I would keep from them. Maybe Sena has a secret modeling career she's not telling her mother about.

Sena looks out the window to where the guys are finishing up loading the cars. "There's a boy I've been seeing. Mama and Papa don't know, but I've told Deniz all about him. He doesn't go to my school. His family doesn't have money like our family does. Mama and Papa would never approve. But sometimes, I think I love him."

I'm not sure, but it looks like Sena's mother raises an

152

eyebrow. If she does, it must be a fluke because she continues packaging up our food until there is a feast in front of her. Sena and I load it into coolers, and then Sena wheels it out to the cars. I'm ready to head out after her because it's getting late.

"Thank you for everything," I say to Sena's mom even though she can't understand me. I'm hoping to at least get the sentiment across.

"Thank you, Hannah Hawkins," she says back, in accented but flawless English. "And remember that things are not always what they seem. Incorrect assumptions can get you in very big trouble."

Without another word, she kisses each of my cheeks and then hurries out front to say goodbye to her family.

Sena is so busted.

When I get to the cars, we try to figure out who is going to ride with whom. Since Tobin and Deniz are driving, that leaves Uncle Randall, Ethan, Sena, and me, so two passengers in each car.

"I'll ride with Ethan," Sena says.

I have to stop myself from rolling my eyes, but come on. That is ridiculous. I guess I'm the only one who thinks so though because nobody disagrees.

"Hannah and I will ride with Deniz," Uncle Randall says.

And so it's set.

As Sena hugs her mother goodbye, her mother whispers something into her ear. Sena's eyes get very wide, and I have to stifle my grin.

∞

We're on one road for about an hour, and then we turn onto another road we'll stay on for the next eighteen hours. Immediately we hit a giant pothole which I hope is not a harbinger for our entire trip ahead, but Deniz tells us about how the roads have really improved over the last ten years.

Deniz keeps us engaged with stories of growing up in Turkey. If either he or his sister has to come live at Easton Estate, Deniz would definitely be preferable. I'm not just saying that because he's a cute guy.

"Have you ever been to America?" I ask.

"Not yet," Deniz says. "Papa keeps promising that we'll go, but with as busy as he's been with his work, we haven't had time."

"At the museum?" Uncle Randall says. He seems to be nursing a headache, and his eyes look pretty tired. He and Tobin had stayed up late into the night drinking way too much wine and catching up. I'd fallen asleep easily, especially because they kept switching between languages, like they were practicing.

Deniz nods, keeping his eyes on the road. Though he's a pretty good driver, there are so many bumps from the mountainous terrain that we're getting bounced around like atoms in a particle collider. Still, the gorgeous landscape makes up for it.

"There have been many new discoveries in these past years," Deniz says. "People are searching caves, using advanced technology, almost to the point where they don't need to go inside to see what they might discover. They find scrolls and tablets and toys that children might have played with two thousand years ago."

"And do you help him?" Uncle Randall says.

"Only on the weekends," Deniz says. "Otherwise, I need to finish up school. But after that, I'll be able to work there nearly every day."

"Once you graduate, if you want to come visit, consider this an open invitation," Uncle Randall says.

I swear that Deniz's eyes meet mine in the rearview mirror. Or maybe I'm just hoping this. "I will take you up on that offer, Mr. Easton."

"Wonderful," Uncle Randall says.

Maybe it's a nice thing that Ethan and Sena got to ride together in the other car after all.

We ride until the sun is well across the sky. Cell coverage is pretty spotty, but when we slip into a zone where my phone syncs up, I get ten text messages from Lucas that have queued up. They all say one thing: Call me.

The first couple times I dial, it doesn't go through. But on the third time, it finally connects. Lucas answers.

"What's up?" I say.

"Hannah, we have a problem."

A hard ball forms in the pit of my stomach. "What kind of problem?"

Uncle Randall immediately looks my way. His mouth is half open, like he wants to ask. I hold up a finger, telling him to wait.

"The rubbing," Lucas says, and the sick feeling in my stomach grows.

"What about it?"

"I had it with me. I never let it out of my sight. Even when I was working. I brought it along, folded up in my pocket. And then, when I went to pull out my phone, I checked for it. It wasn't there, Hannah. It didn't fall out. I checked everywhere."

"You lost it?" I hate the words, but I have to ask, to make sure there's not some happy ending at the end of this story.

"I'm so sorry," Lucas says. "All I can think is that there was this guy who was super interested in what I was drawing, what techniques I used, that kind of thing. He must've talked to me for fifteen minutes. And there was this weird part where he reached across me to look at some of my supplies ... Hannah, I think he stole it from me."

"What did he look like?" I ask.

"I don't know. Just some white guy with dark hair. He was wearing a sweatshirt. And he had a beard. That's all I remember. I just really wanted him to leave me alone. But I think he was distracting me. God, I feel so stupid. I am so sorry."

I close my eyes and try to process the information. This is the worst.

"Did you make a copy?" I ask.

"You told me not to," Lucas says.

"I know. I was just checking. It's okay. We still have the full image here."

"Hannah, what am I supposed to do? I'm so sorry." Guilt

drips off his voice.

"It's okay," I say. "We'll figure it out."

"Can I do anything?"

I shake my head even though he can't see me. "No. Let me talk to Uncle Randall. I'll get back to you. Just don't worry about it, okay?"

"Ugh. I'll figure something out," Lucas says. "I can't believe I let you down."

"It's fine. Let me call you back later."

I hang up. Uncle Randall has figured out enough of what happened by listening to my side of the conversation.

"Someone stole it," I say. "It had to be Amino Corp. They must've hired some professional to do it."

Uncle Randall blows out a deep breath and slowly nods. "We have to assume that's what happened. And we have to assume that they'll figure out the map, just like we did."

I want to throw up. This increases the odds that my parents are in danger a million times over. Amino Corp now has all three pieces of the map.

"They still don't know where to start," Deniz says, cutting into the conversation.

"That's true," Uncle Randall says. "We have that going for us. But they'll be able to check flight records and know we've come to Turkey."

I ball up my hands in frustration. There is nothing that will keep Amino Corp from flying wherever they need to go. They'll be in Istanbul as soon as possible. They could already be there.

"It's okay," Deniz says. "I'll call home. I'll warn my mom just in case your driver has a big mouth."

The ground has ears. All I can think is that it's just a matter of time before they have the information they need.

Deniz calls home and talks to his mom. I don't understand what he says because he speaks in Turkish. But when he hangs up, he assures us that as of yet, nobody has come by to ask about us. She says that she'll go stay with her sister in a nearby town, just to be safe, in case anyone does come by. This is enough to settle my nerves back to something resembling normal. Still, I'm glad we're on our way.

Cell phone coverage seems better in the towns, but they are few and far between. I check in with Lucas, just to make sure he's not feeling too bad, and then I give him the update. Consoling him helps me feel better, and I finally relax.

It's getting late, and we come to what might be considered a large city, so I'm sure we'll spend the night here, but Deniz keeps on driving, passing through the entire city.

"We're stopping, right?" I yawn, not for effect, but because I can't stop it once the thought is in my head.

"Soon," Deniz says. "Papa knows a place not too far from here. Some distant relatives of my mother's. It's safer that way."

At this point, I am all for extra caution.

The place turns out to be well off the main road. We pull up to the base of a mountain, to a small patch of about five houses and some fields where a handful of animals graze. I don't think it could be even remotely called a town. As we drive up, it seems that every single person who lives there, which may add up to about twenty, watches us. We climb out of the cars, a fact that thrills me since I've been cramped in the backseat for hours. Tobin greets them with kisses and handshakes and then gives them some jeans and sweatshirts and other random things like vanilla and board games, and pretty soon we're being ushered in and furniture is being scooted aside to make room for us to sleep. We try to share our food, but his in-laws insist on feeding us even though I can't imagine they're overflowing with extra food.

Uncle Randall, Deniz, and I don't share the information about the stolen piece of the Deluge Segment. There are too many ears around. We can fill them in later, once we're alone.

I lay out a blanket on the kitchen floor once the fires have burned low and everyone who lives here heads to bed. I turn when I feel someone putting another blanket next to me.

"There's nowhere else to sleep," Ethan says. "Tobin insisted that Sena and Deniz sleep by him in one of the other houses."

"I'm sorry for you," I say.

"What do you mean?" he says as he folds the blanket over top himself. It's a tiny kitchen, so there's less than a foot of space between us.

"I'm sure you wanted to sleep next to Sena," I say.

Ethan rolls over onto his side so he's looking at me, propped up on one elbow, so the outline of his muscular arms shows in the dim firelight. "Why would you think that?"

"You're kidding, right?" I whisper so I don't disturb anyone else in the house. With so many people around, someone has to be in earshot.

"No, really," Ethan says.

"Because you've been flirting with her from the second you saw her."

"I have not," Ethan says.

"You have," I say. "It's so obvious."

"Please, Hannah. Just because I had to ride in the car with her? There was no polite way I could really say no. Not without totally offending her and her family."

"Whatever," I say.

"It's true. I promise," he says, though I'm not quite sure why he cares what I think.

"Oh, come on, she's gorgeous," I say.

"Let me tell you something, Hannah," Ethan says. "Sena is pretty. Anyone would think so. But trust me when I say that she is not my type."

"And what is your type?" I ask, but I want to bite my tongue the second I say it. Oh my god, it actually sounds like I am flirting with Ethan.

"Maybe a girl that's smart. And pretty. And independent. Someone who's not going to go through life making bad choices. Someone who knows how to take care of herself. That's my type of girl."

"Well good luck finding her," I say, and then I try to think of something to change the subject because I can't help but lie there and think about how many things he's just said are the traits I've strived for my entire life.

"Tell me one interesting thing about yourself," I say.

Ethan smiles. "One thing?"

I nod.

"Okay, I'm missing two permanent teeth." He points to his mouth to show me. "On either side of my front two teeth."

"Hypodontia," I say.

"What?" Ethan says.

"Hypodontia. It's when permanent teeth are missing. Lots of times, though not always, it's genetic."

"Do you have a genetics answer for everything?" he says.

"Pretty much," I say. "Everything about everything on Earth comes down to genetics."

"Hypodontia," Ethan says. "It makes it sound like a disease."

"Don't worry," I say. "It's not catching."

"I'm glad," Ethan says. "That would make it embarrassing when I kissed someone."

Awkward silence fills the space.

Ethan quickly says, "Okay, your turn. Tell me one interesting thing about you."

It's horrible that my first reaction is to say something pathetic like, "Oh, I don't know," but I bite my tongue. Still, something about talking to Ethan makes my stomach feel all fluttery.

"I'm scared of dinosaurs," I say.

Ethan busts out laughing.

"Shhhh ..."

"You're kidding," Ethan says.

I shake my head. "I'm not."

"But you do know that dinosaurs aren't real, right?"

"I know. But ever since seeing *Jurassic Park* when I was little, I've always been terrified of them."

"So the fearless Hannah Hawkins is not really fearless after all," Ethan says.

"Apparently not," I say.

"Well, fear not. I promise to protect you if we come across any dinosaurs on our adventure," Ethan says, and he smiles.

"Thanks," I say, and I close my eyes to sleep, but it takes a while because I can't stop thinking about how nice Ethan's smile is even with the missing teeth.

$$\infty$$

Everyone who lives in the micro-village is up with the sun in the morning, busy taking care of the animals, cooking, cleaning. They try to feed us breakfast before we go, but Tobin manages to convince them that we're in too much of a hurry. That we can eat while we are traveling. Tobin offers them money, but they refuse, saying that they could never take money from family. Regardless, he manages to hide some money where they will find it to help cover the costs of what they've spent on us. Then ensues much kissing on the cheeks, and we're back on the bumpy road.

We arrive at the nearest civilized city to our destination late the next day, the city of Kars, Turkey. Our final destination, Ani, is another hour away, and it's already getting dark, so Tobin finds us an obscure hotel, which rivals as one of the least hygienic places I've ever been. I can almost see the bacteria growing on the faucet. But the view is great; my window overlooks an ancient fortress, high on the plateau, towering over the city.

We finally get the opportunity to fill Ethan and Tobin in on what's happened.

"This gives me a very bad feeling," Tobin says.

"Yeah, me too," Uncle Randall says. "But Beril is safe. Nobody will know where we went."

A sudden horrible thought occurs to me. I whip around to face Ethan.

"Turn off your cell phone," I say.

"What?"

"Your cell phone. You need to turn it off."

Ethan looks at me like I'm crazy, then anger flashes on his face as he realizes what I'm saying.

"Nobody is going to track my location," Ethan says. "And just because my dad works at Amino Corp doesn't mean he's after the Code of Enoch."

I look to Uncle Randall. His mouth is set in a hard line. "If anyone was going to track it, they could have already done it."

"They're not going to," Ethan says.

I don't believe him, and I'm sure Uncle Randall doesn't either. I also don't see anything I can do about it. But I swear if the opportunity presents itself for me to grab Ethan's phone and throw it over a cliff, I am so going to do it.

Early the next morning, I'm up and showered. I can make it one day without a shower no problem, but two and my hair feels so gross that I can't stand it.

We pile back in the cars and drive the hour to Ani, which, unlike the city of Kars, is in ruins. Surrounding the ancient city are rock cliffs with caves cut deep into them. Sheep and goats wander in and out of the small caves, climbing high on the cliffs though they look like they'll fall at any second. We stop at the edge of the city, and Tobin tells us how churches and tombs are built into these caves, into the cliffs themselves. He points to the highest point in the city, what he calls Citadel Hill, and tells us that is where he thinks we should begin our search. It's a renowned archaeological site.

Unlike the city of Kars, the roads here in Ani can't even be called roads. They are nothing more than loose gravel that's been packed down by foot traffic. I worry that if Deniz looks away from the wheel for one second, we'll be over the side of a cliff and falling to our doom. But he keeps his hands solidly on the wheel, even as he continues to chit chat away until his words fall silent as the Citadel comes into view.

"This can't be the right place," I say once we get out of the car.

"And why is that?" Tobin says.

I motion at the alleged Citadel. "Because this is nothing but a pile of ruins. I mean sure, you have a couple of blocks stacked up here and there, but there's not even an inside for us to go in."

"The Kingdom of Anatolia fell many ages ago," Tobin says. "That's true. But what many don't realize is that before Anatolia came along, there were other settlements here. Cities tend to build on cities, over and over again."

"So you're saying that what we're looking for is underneath the Citadel?" Ethan says.

"That is exactly what I'm saying," Tobin says. "A gate to an extinct world. It's what I told Hannah's parents. Ani has been a settlement for all of recorded history. It is here that your parents went and here that we must go."

Still I'm not convinced. "Yeah, but look around. This place has been excavated clean. Anything to find would have already been found."

"Only if people knew what to look for," Tobin says. "Which we are going to assume they don't since as of yet, we've not yet heard of anyone discovering what we're looking for."

His logical responses make sense and help restore my optimism. We can find what no one else has because that's what we'll be looking for.

We walk to the largest remaining pile of stones, what Tobin refers to as the Citadel gateway.

"Gate," I say, "like the symbol on the map."

"Exactly," Tobin says. "Though this is the gateway for the Citadel, it is logical to believe that it served as the gateway for older structures built on this same site. See how it overlooks the entire city, providing an ideal vantage point." He points to some of the base stones that look different from those that rest on top. "And you see the way these stones are cut? It's classic masonry consistent with a Zoroastrian fire temple, which may have been on this site at one point."

I've heard of the Zoroastrian religion but never studied it. Zoroastrian fire temple sounds like something I'd definitely like to research more once this whole adventure is done.

"I'll head in first," Uncle Randall says, pulling out his flashlight.

I grab mine also and step up next to him. "I'm going with you."

The words aren't even out of my mouth when Ethan interrupts me. "I'm going, too."

"I don't think that's a good idea," Uncle Randall says. "We don't know what to expect inside."

"Which is exactly why I should go," I say.

Uncle Randall looks to Tobin for support, but Tobin shakes his head. "They're right. You shouldn't go in alone, Randall."

One look at me, and Uncle Randall knows that there is no way he is going ahead without me.

"Take this," Tobin says, and he hands the center piece of the Deluge Segment to Uncle Randall who passes it to me. I unclasp my bag and put it in, redoing the clasp so it doesn't fall out. Then I hoist my bag over my shoulder, and we walk to the threshold.

My light shines into the area above, revealing the remains of a fresco that once had been painted there. The colors are faded and chipped nearly to the point where I can't make anything out, but one item in the middle of the fresco still peeks through.

I take a couple pictures with the flash and then shine my

light so Uncle Randall and Ethan can see it also. "Is that a boat?"

"Where?" Uncle Randall says. He steps forward, placing his foot on the exact same threshold stones I just crossed, but the stones shift under his weight. He goes down, letting out a brief yell. The entire archway we've just passed under collapses. Uncle Randall is nowhere to be seen.

"Uncle Randall!" I scream, but I'm yelling through a pile of stones. All I can hear are muffled shouts from the other side.

"Uncle Randall!" I scream again and turn my phone on to call him. There's no signal. Stupid cellular reception.

"Come on. Come on. Come on," I say, shaking the cell phone like somehow that will make it better.

"It's okay, Hannah," Ethan says.

"It's not okay. He could be hurt. He could be trapped under the rocks." I stick the cell phone back in my pocket and start grabbing at the rocks. "We have to get to him."

Ethan joins me, shifting the stones, but there are so many, and some of them are huge. After five minutes of trying to make the stones budge, I sink against the wall.

"We can't get to him this way," Ethan says.

"Then what do we do?" I ask. Uncle Randall could be hurt really badly. He could be dying. I have to get back to him to make sure he's okay.

Ethan's light bounces back behind us, farther under the fresco of the boat. "Look. Do you see this?"

"What?"

He waves the flashlight round. "There's a tunnel over here."

"Where?" I hadn't seen a tunnel earlier.

"Right here. Maybe it opened up when the rocks fell. Maybe there's another way out."

There better be because otherwise, with all the rocks, Ethan and I are going to spend the next three days digging ourselves out of here.

It kills me to head in the opposite direction, away from Uncle Randall, but I know it's the only choice. We start toward the passageway, sloping downward. Small rocks and pebbles falls around us as we walk, as if maybe some sort of seismic activity is responsible for the cave-in that just happened. It's pitch black, lit only by our flashlights, and I loop my arm around Ethan's.

"I didn't know you felt that way," he says.

"Don't flatter yourself," I say. "I just don't want you to get lost."

"You think I'm going to get lost?" Ethan says.

"I don't know. Maybe."

"If you wanted to hold my hand, you could have just asked," Ethan says.

He's so infuriating. Still, I keep hold of his arm.

Ahead, our flashlights shine on what looks like two ancient columns, but between them is only blackness.

"In there?" Ethan says.

"It's the only way to go," I say, and we step inside.

A chill passes through me, and my muscles tense. I'm sure for a moment that someone else is in here waiting. Watching.

Biding their time after centuries alone in this place.

"Hello," I call, though it seems irrational.

There's no answer.

"Hello," I say again.

"It feels weird, right?" Ethan whispers.

"Yeah, really weird."

"Like someone's watching," he says.

Knowing that he feels it, too, makes me feel the slightest bit less crazy.

We've entered an underground room with rock walls and a ceiling held up by columns like the ones we've just passed through.

I would never admit it, but Ethan's presence makes everything better. It gives me hope that we'll find a way out of here. A way back to Uncle Randall.

"It's dark," he says, and we both shine our flashlights around the place.

There are no seats, no statues, nothing. But overhead, like what we passed under when we entered, is another fresco. Unlike the one near the entrance, this one is still bright with color and virtually unchipped. It shows a giant boat with multiple entry planks and animals climbing aboard by the hundreds.

"Look," I say, pointing to the fresco with my light.

Ethan's eyes find the painting and widen. "That's crazy. This room must be thousands of years old. There is no way, even without exposure to the elements, that the paint would be so well-preserved."

"It's Noah's Ark," I say. "It has to be."

"Agreed," Ethan says. "And if a painting of Noah's Ark is here ..."

"... then we must be on the right path," I finish, trying to control the excited flutters that run through my chest. This is really going to happen. We are going to find my parents.

I take pictures of everything because I don't know what we're looking for. The fresco is huge, and I take my time, making sure to get high resolution of everything. There are frescos on the walls also, of a mountain with a boat resting on top. Of a green hill with a gaping hole that reminds me of a bottomless pit. There are planets and stars and the sun. There's also a garden with luscious fruit hanging from trees. It's like every story from Genesis, the first book in the Bible, has been recorded on these walls.

"Did you see up ahead?" Ethan says, pulling his eyes away from the frescos.

I want to keep studying them because the detail rivals Michelangelo and the Sistine Chapel. Lucas would die to be here right now. If only I had cell service, I could video call him.

I look to where Ethan's light shines. Far ahead, at what looks to be the end of the room, is an altar.

"Altars were used for sacrifice," Ethan says.

"And prayer. We should check it out." I know it will take more time, but we can't miss out on this opportunity. Uncle Randall would tell me the same thing if he were here.

"We should be careful," Ethan says.

"Just stick close," I say, pulling Ethan along with me.

"Do you see the markings on the walls?" Ethan says as we walk forward. "They're the same kind of symbols as on the map pieces."

I stop for a moment and shine my light away from the altar, toward the walls. He's right. The walls are covered in partial symbols just like on the pieces of the Deluge Segment.

"Do you realize what this means?" I say. "We have to be in the right place." It's hard to control the excitement that's building inside me. I can almost see my parents walking here eleven years ago, following the same path that we follow now.

"Just slow down, Hannah," Ethan says. "It's not going anywhere, and you're going to yank my arm out of its socket."

I take a deep breath and attempt to slow my steps. We're almost to the altar. The shadows bounce around us, like hidden creatures playing in the dark. And when our lights reach behind the altar, three circular indentations are exposed on the wall.

My breath catches. "They're the same size as the pieces of the Deluge Segment," I say, shining my light on the stone wall behind the altar.

Ethan's light joins my own. "You're right. Like maybe the pieces used to be here."

"And were taken away," I say. "And if the pieces used to be here, then maybe the starting point is here."

I'm breathing hard now, unable to control the hope that is building up inside me. But with the closed-in area and the darkness, it's almost too much. My head starts to spin. I bend over and place my hands on my knees, trying to catch my breath.

"Are you okay?" Ethan asks, squatting down so he's at the same level as me.

I breathe deep, trying to get as much oxygen as I can.

"Just catching my breath," I say.

He holds onto my shoulders and looks me in the eye. "It's okay, Hannah. Inhale and exhale."

I do what he says, focusing on deep slow breaths to fill my lungs. The world gradually stops spinning around me.

"What's up?" Ethan says, still holding my shoulders, which helps me feel rooted to the world.

Another breath and then another. The world settles, and I raise myself up. "It's just that we're so close. My parents ..."

"We'll find them," he says. "But I can't have you freaking out on me."

I nod and take another breath. "I won't. I'm fine."

But inside me, there is no stopping the hope that now fills me. It bubbles to the surface, pushing away everything that I've lost in the past. I am going to bring them back from wherever they've gone.

"I'm okay," I say, more to convince myself than Ethan.

"You sure?"

I nod and focus once again on the world around me.

We step up to the altar. It's covered in symbols, and because I don't know what's important, I take pictures of everything.

"Look, Hannah," Ethan says, and he points to the exact

center of the altar. In the center is a circular depression, only a few inches across.

"It's …," I start to say.

"I know," Ethan says.

With shaking fingers, I unclasp my bag and pull out the center piece of the Deluge Segment. I place it into the depression. It almost seems to click into place, and then it starts to sink down.

Immediately light bursts from it. Light that has no explanation because there is no electricity around, but it shoots out and brings the already magnificent room to life. It's almost like the sun has somehow slithered into this dark place and is being channeled through the artifact.

"Wow," is all I manage to say.

Ethan is staring, too, but his mouth moves, almost like he's thinking out loud.

"Take pictures," he says, and we both walk around the room, taking new pictures of the light now hitting the wall because it doesn't feel random. There's a pattern here. I just don't know what it is. Concern for Uncle Randall presses at my mind, but I have to do this.

"I wish Uncle Randall was here," I say. "We have to find a way out and bring him back here."

Ethan nods. "And we should probably do that soon."

He's right. We've spent way too much time in here.

He reaches for the center piece of the Deluge Segment and pulls it free. But the second he does, the room begins to shake.

A horrible groaning sound echoes through the chamber, filling the darkness, like stones grinding upon each other.

"What did you do?" I ask.

"I just grabbed the artifact," Ethan says. "That's all."

The groaning sound deepens, and noises like giant egg-shells cracking join it.

"We need to get out of here," Ethan says, and he grabs my arm and pulls me away just as the entire altar crumbles apart, like a giant has stepped on it. Pieces of the walls around us begin to fall. The ceiling that has been solid for thousands of years cracks above us.

I shine my light forward and spot a small tunnel. "There. Behind the altar."

We don't think twice as we hurry toward it. No sooner are we both inside the tunnel than the entire room behind us collapses, eliminating our options. If we want to get out of here, we have to move forward.

The path ahead leads on, dark as ink, and I think it will never end. That somehow we are heading deep into the ground rather than toward any exit. But as we continue down it, from far ahead, a light begins to shine, getting bigger until we finally reach a small stone barrier with two goats nestled up against it. When I bump into the barrier, the goats start bleating like we've disturbed them. The least of my concerns is interrupting two goats from napping. It's so ridiculous, that I can't help but laugh.

The mountain still rumbles behind us, so between the two of us, we shove all the stones out of the way until sunlight bursts through the opening.

Once we're out in the daylight, I look at where we've just come from. "It's one of the tombs in the cliff side."

"And look at these markings," Ethan says. "Have you ever seen anything—?"

I grab his arm. "It doesn't matter. We need to get back to Uncle Randall."

We run up the rocky mountainside, slipping along the loose rocks and silt. Both Ethan and I nearly fall more than once, but we finally make it back to the top. From here, outside the mountain, the ground is silent, as if the earth rumbling had never occurred. As soon as we come into view, Deniz and Sena run up to us.

"Oh, I was so worried," Sena says, and she throws her arms around Ethan's neck.

I shoot him an I-told-you-so look as he half hugs her in return.

"What happened?" Deniz says.

"Where is Uncle Randall?" I ask, looking toward the collapsed entryway.

"He's in the car," Deniz says.

I rush to the car, but Tobin meets me halfway.

"How is he?" I ask.

"He's not good," Tobin says. Sweat covers his face even though the air is cool. "He broke his femur. We must get him back to a major city. He's getting a fever, and what supplies we packed are not enough."

"Will he be okay?"

Tobin's face is somber. "He should be fine as long as we get him proper medical attention. We need to get him back to Kars."

We pile into the vehicles and drive the hour back to Kars. I sit in the backseat with Uncle Randall, trying to keep his leg steady. He seems to slip in and out of consciousness. The small hospital in Kars doesn't look equipped to take care of him, but Tobin assures me that it will be okay until he can get a flight back to Istanbul tomorrow. The doctor on duty gives Uncle Randall something, which makes him pass out completely. He assures us that Uncle Randall will be out for a good four hours, and that we should get some rest and come back after that.

"Did you find anything in the tunnels?" Tobin asks, once we're back at the Kars hotel. We gather outside, on the pool deck, because it's the least crowded place around. The pool water is solid black with all sorts of sticks and leaves and dead insects floating in it.

With my concern over Uncle Randall, I've nearly forgotten. I plug my phone in to charge it because it's pretty much dead. Deniz squats down beside me, so close our arms are touching. I'm sure it's completely unintentional.

The pictures are gorgeous and amazing, and when we describe what happened with the light shooting out from the piece of artifact, Tobin and Deniz look like they want to run back there and dig out the chamber no matter what. As I look at each photo, I can almost imagine thousands of years ago, people walking down the tunnels that Ethan and I escaped from, retrieving the pieces of map, and then setting out, far across the earth to hide them. India. America. Peru. They placed the map pieces in parts of the world that they may have believed would never be civilized. They must have thought they would never be found, and thus the Code of Enoch was safe. But thousands of years passed, and slowly the pieces were uncovered. And human curiosity being what it is ... the Code could never be safe. It's hard to believe we are on that same journey, thousands of years later.

Tobin puts a finger to his lips. "I feel like there's more here than what we're seeing."

"I felt the same way," I say. "That's why I took so many pictures."

Tobin takes the phone and zooms in and looks at each one. But at the end of an hour of studying them, we still don't know what to do next.

"What about your boyfriend?" Ethan says.

Deniz raises his eyebrows. "You have a boyfriend?"

I glare at Ethan. "No. I don't have a boyfriend. I have a friend who's a boy. Not a boyfriend. And that's a great idea."

I create a folder and upload all the photos so I can share them with Lucas. Then I text him and ask him to look them over and let me know what he thinks.

Lucas calls me in less than a half hour.

"Hannah, you are not going to believe this," Lucas says from halfway across the world.

"You found something?" I say.

"Did I find something?!" Lucas almost yells across the phone. Everyone can hear him, but I go ahead and put him on speakerphone. "You know those pictures you sent of the light beams. I ran them through some filters and changed the—"

"I don't need the technical details," I say. If I don't stop him, Lucas will spend the next five minutes explaining his process.

"Yeah, okay," he says. "Well anyway, after I did all that, they fit together like pieces of a puzzle. There was an entire picture encoded around the room. There were concentric circles that look exactly like those weird maps with mountains. And there were roads and rivers ... and anyway, there was a whole new map there."

"To where?" I ask. I can hardly breathe.

"This is where it gets cool," Lucas says. "Are you ready?"

I've been ready for years.

"Yeah."

"Good. So I cross-referenced it across everything I could, using elimination, and I finally got it narrowed down to two possibilities."

"Two?" I say.

"Hang on. I'm not done. There was one object that I hadn't yet placed because the shape of it was totally off. But then I remembered what your uncle had said about how the Great Flood changed the way things looked. And that's when it all clicked into place. It had to be the Black Sea."

My heart pounds. "That's really close."

"So where do we go?" Ethan says. "Where do we start?"

"I'll send you a map," Lucas says. "But if I'm right—and let's face it, I probably am—then it looks like you need to go to a place named Krubera Cave. That's where your journey will start."

Tobin sucks in a breath. "Krubera! Deepest cave in the world. The bottom has yet to be found. It's in a breakaway region of Georgia. In the Gagra district of Abkhazia."

"Then that's where we need to go," I say. This is the path to my parents.

"Once your uncle is better," Tobin says.

No, not once my uncle is better. The thought of leaving Uncle Randall kills me, but there is no other choice. If I give up now, before I've even started, I may never find my parents, but someone else could. I can't risk that.

"We'll go without him," I say.

"You won't," Tobin says. "That area is highly volatile. The civil unrest has been going on for decades. It wouldn't be safe."

"It wouldn't be any safer with Uncle Randall," I say. Just the mere thought of having to wait until he's healed makes panic begin to take over. A broken leg could take months to heal. Amino Corp could find the Code. Find my parents.

"It would," Tobin says. "He's an adult."

"Hannah and I will be fine," Ethan says.

"You're not going without him," Tobin says.

"I am."

Tobin narrows his eyes at me. "You are not, Hannah Hawkins. And that is final."

Is he kidding? Who is he to tell me what to do?

"Last I heard, Uncle Randall was my guardian," I say, knowing it makes me sound ungrateful, but I'm not going to put the search for my parents on hold because of this.

"Yes, true." Tobin puts a finger to his lips. "How about this? Tomorrow, when your uncle wakes up, you can talk to him about it yourself. If he's okay with you going, then I won't stand in your way. Otherwise, we all go back to Istanbul and come back once he's healed."

Tomorrow. Uncle Randall. The words spin around in my head. The fact of the matter is that even though Uncle Randall is pretty lenient with what I'm able to do, he may actually side with Tobin on this one. It's a risk I can't take.

"Fine," I say. "Tomorrow we'll talk to Uncle Randall."

Tobin nods as though it's settled. Little does he know, it's far from settled. As far as I'm concerned, the only thing that is settled is that my path ahead is clear. I'm going to descend the deepest cave on Earth.

CHAPTER 19

I SNEAK INTO ETHAN'S ROOM AS SOON AS EVERYONE'S gone to bed, and there is this small moment when I actually kind of love him. His bag is already packed, and he's lacing his work boots.

"You knew I'd want to sneak away," I say, relieved that I don't have to try to convince him to see things my way.

"Of course, I knew," Ethan says. "I get that I don't know you very well, Hannah, but I have picked up on a couple of things, one being that you don't want other people telling you what you can and can't do."

"Is it that obvious?" I ask.

"Definitely."

"Do you think Tobin knows?" I ask, hoping that everyone else wasn't as perceptive as Ethan.

Ethan shakes his head. "I don't think so." He finishes lacing his boots and zips his bag. "So what's your plan? I don't think the local rental car place—if there actually happens to be one—is going to rent a car to some sixteen-year-old American girl."

"Or guy," I say. It's not like he'd fare any better.

"Or guy."

"There's a bus we can take," I say, turning on my phone so I can show him the bus route that should get us to the Georgian border.

"You aren't taking a bus," Deniz says, walking into the room with Sena.

My muscles tense. Deniz and Sena are going to try to stop us. Tobin probably sent them to find out what we were up to.

"We are," I say. "Look, I know he's your dad and all, but I'm—"

Deniz flashes me his toothpaste commercial smile. "We're not here to stop you, Hannah."

My brow furrows. "Then why are you here?"

Sena giggles and then covers her mouth. "Because we're going to drive you, of course. You don't think we always listen to our papa either, do you?"

In that moment, I think that Sena and I could actually be friends.

"We got this from your uncle's bag," Deniz says, and he holds up the image of the map.

I run over and give him the biggest hug I possibly can. "Oh my god. You guys are the best. You know that?" I hug Sena next even though Deniz holds on kind of extra long.

"We know," Sena says, tossing her long hair over her shoulder once I release her from the hug.

And so it's set. Ethan and I don't have to take the bus to

our destination because Deniz and Sena are going to drive us there instead.

$$\infty$$

I leave a note for Tobin to give to Uncle Randall. Deniz and Sena leave one for their dad, too, telling him that they'll only be gone for a few days. That they promise to return the family car unscathed. Never having traveled by car in these countries before, I only hope that they aren't lying.

We slip out of the hotel and pile into Tobin's car. Deniz drives us out of Kars and back north, where we'll have to pass through Georgia and into Abkhazia. The roads are deserted, and we're able to drive nearly non-stop, only stopping for gas.

Halfway through the first day, my phone rings. I answer it, dreading who I'm sure is on the other line.

"Hannah?"

"Hi, Uncle Randall." This is the call I knew would come. The only good news is that his voice sounds lucid, so I hope he's feeling better. "Where are you? Are you back in Istanbul?"

"I can't believe you went off, even after Tobin instructed you not to," Uncle Randall says.

"I need to find them," I say.

"You need to come back."

Ethan, Sena, and Deniz all listen to my half of the conversation, like they're wondering if we're going to have to turn around before we even get to Georgia.

"I'm not coming back," I say. "I'm continuing on the journey."

"I'll cut off your credit card," he says. "You won't have any money."

"Go ahead. I'll make it work." If he cuts off my funds, I'll still find a way to get to my parents.

"Hannah ..."

"I'm not coming back, Uncle Randall. I have to do this."

"But it's not safe," Uncle Randall says. His voice is laced with worry.

"I'll be okay."

"No. We were supposed to do this together," Uncle Randall says. "I wanted to be able to keep you safe."

"And you've kept me safe this far," I say. "But now I have to go on. It'll be fine. I have Ethan with me."

"Hannah, you know—" he starts, and I'm sure I know where he's going with the thought. Ethan still can't be trusted.

"It'll be fine. Deniz and Sena are driving us. I'll be careful, I promise."

"But something could happen," Uncle Randall says. "And the thing is that ... I don't know what I'd do if something happened to you, Hannah. I don't think I could take it. I've already lost my sister. That was hard enough. I can't lose you, too. I just can't." His voice cracks on the last sentence. I've never seen Uncle Randall cry before, but in that moment, I am sure that if we were in the same room, that is exactly what I'd see right now.

"Nothing is going to happen," I say, fighting tears myself. "I promise. And you know I have to do this. I have to find them."

Uncle Randall doesn't say anything for a moment, only lets

out a long sigh. "I know," he finally says. "Just please be careful. You're all I have left."

"I will. I promise. I'll check in once we get there. Just get yourself better, okay? And I'll see you soon."

"I hope so, Hannah," Uncle Randall says, and we hang up. I hope this means he's not planning on turning off my credit card. Sure, I'll figure it out if I have to, but it would be better if I didn't need to.

It turns out Sena and Deniz don't have it quite so easy. After fifteen solid minutes of fast Turkish that Ethan has no chance of keeping up with, they promise, in English, that they will get us to our destination, get us outfitted, and then come straight home. I don't envy them the trouble they will be in when they get there. But I also appreciate their help. Without them, Ethan and I would be on some rickety bus in the middle of nowhere.

Deniz communicates well enough to get us lodging while we pass through Georgia, but we're up early each day to continue on our way. The third day we have to pass through border patrol to get into Abkhazia, which delays us nearly an hour. Deniz assures us that this must be normal because Abkhazia is a disputed territory. Georgia claims it, but Abkhazia is not happy about that and declares itself an independent state. Given the civil unrest and the fact that we are four teenagers traveling alone, we have no choice but to answer the questions.

"We're here to visit the cave," is all I have to say when it's my turn getting questioned.

I've come to learn via spotty searching on the Internet as

we drive that when someone says "The Cave" in this part of the world, they can only be referring to Krubera. I've also learned that it's home to dozens of different species. There are fish and insects living there that have never seen light. They've adapted, living in the dark at temperatures of two degrees Celsius. It would be awesome to study them.

Deniz manages to have a female border patrol officer interrogating him who must think he's cute, probably since he is, because he not only sails through with the most minimal of questions, he even gets some recommendations for reliable and honest outfitters. And so after our delay at the border, we pass into Abkhazia and onward to Gagra where the spelunking outfitters are.

It's after three in the afternoon when we get there, and I would kill someone right now for a decent cup of coffee, so before hitting Deep Cave Outfitters, guaranteed to be the best for Krubera Cave exploration, we find a small-house-turned-coffee-shop that caters to tourists. They take credit, and thankfully Uncle Randall has not turned off my credit card. I treat all four of us to what may be the best cup of coffee I have ever had in my life. Then it's on to Deep Cave Outfitters.

There's one guy in the place when we walk in. He doesn't look the least bit Middle Eastern. Instead he's got shaggy hair and a beard and looks like some Colorado transplant who came here because he couldn't stay away from the lure of "the Cave." He introduces himself in perfect English as Scott, as he eyes me up and down.

"Shoe size seven, clothing size seven. Weight—"

I put up my hand. "Stop there. You're right."

Scott winks at me then turns to Ethan, spouting off his measurements with what I'm betting is equal precision. Then, after we go over the list of everything we need, which turns out to be a ton of stuff, all of which we are supposed to be able to carry on our backs, he brings up the next question.

"You got a guide yet?" Scott says.

Ethan shakes his head. "We don't need a guide."

Scott clutches his stomach and pretends to laugh heartily. "Ha ha ha. That's funny. Of course you need a guide."

"No, we're fine," I say, not laughing at his pretend humor. "No guide."

Scott puts his tablet computer down on the counter. "Okay, just so I am totally sure that you understand, Krubera Cave is the deepest known cave on the planet, and it's only been explored to twenty-two hundred meters so far. It takes twenty seven days to reach the bottom. There are more than fifty ways for a person to die during a descent, including drowning, poisonous gas inhalation, and electrocution. There are side passages that if you accidentally take, you will never find your way back from. Many of the paths are flooded, meaning you'll need scuba gear to get through them. There are descents where you will need miles of rope. And let's not even begin to talk about the rapture."

I take the bait. "What's the rapture?"

Scott leans close. "The rapture is your worst enemy down

in the depths of Krubera Cave. It's an extreme reaction to the darkness and the depth, sort of like having an anxiety attack while doing drugs. It's where your brain begins to talk to you. It says, 'Turn around. Get me out of here. Now.' It's like a basic instinct that all humans have. Experienced cavers may be able to deal with it, but you two ..."

I roll my eyes at his over-drama. "We'll be fine."

"Did I mention the part about it taking twenty-seven days to reach the bottom?" Scott says.

"You did, but we're okay," I say. I hand him my credit card to pay for our supplies.

"Right," Ethan says, backing me up. "No guide."

"You guys are nuts, you know that, right?" Scott says, swiping my card and handing it back to me. "Because I could guide you. Take you down there and back. Help you follow the path. Improve your chances of staying alive."

Exactly what we don't want is to follow the path. Because once we're in the cave, we're following the Deluge map, not some path that hundreds of people have followed before us. I'm willing to bet that they're different.

"We don't need a guide," Ethan says again, and this time, there is enough firmness in his voice that Scott doesn't ask again.

"It's your lives," he says.

That it is. And my parents' lives. Because if my parents went down into Krubera Cave eleven years ago, then that is where we are going to find them.

I ignore the little voice in my head that adds a final thought.

If they are still alive.

They have to be alive. I have to find them. Just thinking about it makes nervous excited butterflies fly around in my stomach. I wonder what they'll say when they see me. Will they recognize me? It was a long time ago. I take a deep breath. Everything is going to be okay. We know where we're going. We have a plan.

"The first two drops are rigged," Scott says. "But you'll need help with the initial descent."

"Can you help us with that?" I ask.

"I'm a guide. I don't just do descents," Scott says, like it's far below him, and how dare we even suggest it.

"How about someone else?" I say.

"There are other descents after that," Scott says. "Longer than the initial ones."

"We know," Ethan says. "We'll be fine for those. We just need help at the beginning."

Scott seems to consider this because maybe he finally realizes that we're serious about the no guide thing. "I can ask around. But in the meantime, if you change your mind about the guide ..."

"We won't," Ethan says. He grabs a protein bar from a nearby display. And then he hands something across to Scott.

I hardly have time to react before I see that it's his credit card and Scott is about to swipe it through the machine.

"Stop," I say, but it's too late. Scott swipes the card for the protein bar purchase.

Anger flashes through me. "I told you not to use your credit card," I say to Ethan.

"It's not a big deal, Hannah," Ethan says. "I told you that my parents never check my card as long as I stay under a certain amount. It's no big deal."

"It is a big deal," I say.

"It'll be fine," Ethan says.

I want to pull my hair out in frustration. "That's not good enough. It's a risk. What if they do look? What if they see where you are? And what if whoever stole the map piece finds out?"

Unspoken but there between the two of us is the fact that I think his dad is almost certainly involved, even if it's just feeding information to Amino Corp.

Ethan shrugs, which is extra infuriating. "I don't see why you're getting your panties all in a bunch, Hannah. So they find out I'm here in Abkhazia. What are they going to do? Fly out here and get me? We'll be deep in the cave by then. It won't matter."

Of course it will matter, I want to scream, because then your dad could tell Amino Corp and they could send someone to follow us. They'd know the starting point, and they'd find the Code of Enoch.

"Just don't do it again, okay," I say, though it's too late. I should make him pay for everything from this point forward.

Scott hands Ethan a receipt to sign. "Your stuff will be ready in three days."

Panic fills me. "Three days? No. We need it today. We want

to set out tomorrow."

"You're kidding, right?" Scott says. "You think it's cost effective to keep spelunking boots in every size and color here in BFE nowhere? Sure, the cave is popular, but it's not that popular. It'll be three days minimum. I recommend the Amran Hotel."

I feel like stomping my foot, but I manage to stop myself from the childish impulse. Three days feels like forever. The only plus side is that the Amran Hotel has solid Internet, and I'm able to fill Lucas in on everything.

"What about once you're below ground?" Lucas says once I've checked into my room and called him. "How are you going to stay in touch with me?"

I've been trying to figure that out.

"I think I can buy a signal booster here in Gagra," I say.

Lucas laughs. "Did you say Gagra! I can't believe you're in a place called Gagra. It sounds like something that happens after you eat something rotten."

"You'd actually love it," I say. "Lush mountains on the edge of a gorgeous beach that curves around and stretches on for miles. You could paint for years out here and never get bored. It's a total vacation hotspot." When I checked in, the hotel manager made sure I knew where all the best spas were, just on the off chance I wanted a massage or sauna treatment during my stay. Maybe I'll come back for a vacation after this is all over.

Lucas has been stopping in to check on the animals, so I ask him about Castor and Pollux and ask him to give them a special piece of fruit and to tell them that it's from me. This may seem silly, but they will recognize my name. Sugar gliders are smart.

"How long do you think this whole thing will take you?" Lucas says.

"No clue." I feel like once we're in the cave, even though we've seen the map, everything will look different. "It'll probably be at least a month. Maybe two."

"One month! Two months! You're kidding, right?" Lucas says.

"It's like an adventure," I say.

"I don't like you being on an adventure," Lucas says. "Especially going to the bottom of some freezing cave."

"We ordered the best equipment," I say. "It will be fine."

"But what about Ethan? You hardly know him."

"Ethan's not so bad," I say.

"You don't know that."

"It'll be fine."

"Just be safe, Hannah, okay? That's all I ask." Unlike normal, Lucas's voice is laced with worry. I've never heard him so serious before.

"I promise," I say. "And I appreciate the concern."

"I miss you, Hannah," Lucas says.

"I miss you, too." I blow him an air kiss and then we say goodbye and hang up.

I meet Ethan down in the lobby, but he's on the phone with his mom. He's being really evasive, giving half answers and super general descriptions in a way I'm sure would be evident to anyone.

"You don't think she's suspicious?" I say after he hangs up.

He sticks the phone back in his pocket. "I think she's busy with work. I think she's happy to not have to worry about me this summer."

"I'm sure she misses you," I say.

Ethan shrugs. "Doubt it."

He has to be wrong. His parents must care about him.

"What about your pre-programmed email?" I say. "You need to—"

He puts his hand up. "I already changed it, so don't worry."

"You sure?" I say. The last thing we need is some "Read this upon my death" email being sent to his parents.

"Yes, I told you not to worry."

I narrow my eyes at him. I'm half tempted to snag his phone and check his email myself.

"So three days," Ethan says, trying to shift the conversation. "What are we planning on doing?"

"We?" I say. Since they got us outfitted, or at least the promise of us outfitted, Sena and Deniz are on their way back to Istanbul. Although there was an extended phone conversation with their father, including much unrequited pleading on Sena's part, Tobin was unyielding. Our goodbye had included a very friendly hug from Deniz which I was more than happy to return. He also asked if it would be okay if he emailed me.

"Of course we," Ethan says. "It's not like I'm that hard to get along with, am I?"

As much as I want him to be hard to get along with, he's not at all.

"I guess we could study the cave together," I say. "And practice rappelling. And you could run with me in the mornings. It'll help get you in shape."

"What?" Ethan says. "I'm totally in shape. Have you seen these rock hard abs?" And before I know what he's doing, he pulls up his shirt and actually shows me his stomach.

I'd be lying if I said that I haven't imagined what Ethan looks like without his shirt on, but not even my very creative imagination can prepare me for reality. Ethan's abs are so well defined that it looks like I could bounce pennies off them.

I flick my eyes upward as if I am unimpressed. "Not bad. But you can still use the exercise. And we can buy you some new boots. My treat."

"What's wrong with my boots?" he says.

"Nothing except you're not really building libraries right now."

"I like these boots."

"I'm sure they were fine ... ten years ago when you got them at the thrift store. Why don't you get a new pair?"

Ethan shakes his head and laughs. "No, you don't get it. These boots are magical. These boots, beyond anything else in the entire world, have the ability to annoy my dad with a single look."

"You wear boots to annoy him?"

"Sure. He hates them."

"Couldn't you just forget to change the toilet paper roll instead? That always annoys Uncle Randall."

"Trust me, no. I am never getting rid of these boots," Ethan says. "And anyway, what about your hat?"

My hands go to my head. "What's wrong with my hat?"

"Nothing's wrong with it," Ethan says. "You just always wear it."

"You don't like it?"

"I didn't say that."

"You did," I say. "At least you implied it."

"I did no such thing," Ethan says. "I think your hat is cute."

Awkward silence ensues. I bite my lip and study him. Cute? He thinks my hat is cute?

"Bunny rabbits are cute," I finally say, narrowing my eyes so my face doesn't give anything away.

"And puppies," Ethan says, recovering quickly from the awkward silence. "Don't forget about puppies."

"Just go get ready to run, okay?"

"Yeah, good plan," Ethan says.

Ethan has no problem keeping up with me on our first run, which is seven miles, taking us around the entire town and up into the neighboring mountains. If anything, and this is really hard for me to admit, he might actually be in better shape than me. There's even one point when he jogs backwards. I kind of want to punch him.

"I'm not going too fast for you, am I?" he asks.

"Not hardly." I pick up my pace. This will only help my training.

"Because you can meet me back at the hotel if you need to fall behind," Ethan says. "I know girls don't like to sweat."

"I'll let that one slide," I say. "But one more girl comment, and I'm tripping you."

"You'll have to catch me first," Ethan says, and he takes off sprinting.

I tear off after him, and we sprint the entire half mile back to the hotel. By the time I get there, I'm breathing heavy and feel like I'm going to heave up a lung. The only consolation I have is that Ethan is doing the same.

"Shower and meet you in the coffee shop?" I say between breaths.

Ethan nods without a word, and we go our separate ways.

∞

Who knew guys could take so long to get ready? I wait at the coffee shop for fifteen minutes, and Ethan still doesn't show up. They have a small gift section, so I pick out a pack of postcards for Lucas showing some of the best views around, then I look for a travel book written in Abkhazian for Uncle Randall. I can't decide between two different ones since I don't know what either one says, so I get them both and go to the counter to pay for them and to order my drink.

"Coffee with milk," I say. This is no Starbucks, but it seems that the language of coffee is international.

"Coconut or regular?" the barista says. She's an older woman with long graying hair and a dark complexion.

"Coconut," I say, happy that I have options even here in Gagra.

"It'll be ready in a couple minutes," she says in flawless English.

"You speak English?" I say.

"Only when English speaking customers come in," she says.

"Which is how often?" I ask.

She dumps a bag of beans into the coffee grinder and hits the button. The smell is instant, and I close my eyes and sink into the scent I love.

"Not as often as you'd think," she says. "Most of the people who come are from Eastern European countries. Ukraine. Hungary. Turkey."

"My name's Hannah, by the way," I say.

"Naala," she says. I don't know what it mean, but it makes me think of a blooming flower.

"So where'd you learn English?" I ask.

Naala continues to make my drink, not even looking my way as she speaks. "My parents taught me, in secret, back when the Soviet Union was still the Soviet Union. They could have been thrown in jail if it was ever discovered."

"I'm glad it wasn't," I say.

"Me, too, Hannah," Naala says.

"So how long have you owned the coffee shop?" I ask, as

little gears begin to turn in my mind.

"Over twenty years," she says. "Of course, back then it wasn't a coffee shop. I called it a café because that was trendier. Now everyone wants coffee, no matter where they are."

"So you were here twenty years ago?" I say.

"Sure was. Living in the apartment upstairs."

"And do you remember most of the people who come through?"

"Not all of them," Naala says. "But some stand out."

I take a deep breath. "Do you remember two people that may have come through here about eleven years ago? A man and a woman, American?"

She finishes up making my drink and slides the steaming mug my way. It's like a little piece of heaven that I can't wait to sink into. I let the steam drift over my face. Maybe I do need a steam bath like the hotel manager suggested.

"That's not much to go on," Naala says.

I'm already holding my wallet because I have to pay, so I slide a picture of my parents from it and pass it over to her. "Do you recognize these people?"

Naala takes the picture and immediately sucks in a breath. "The letter."

My heart pounds. "What letter?"

She slowly shakes her head. "They were here to visit the cave. They gave me a letter to mail. I put it aside, and I forgot about it. I was cleaning out the place about a month ago, and I found it. It didn't have an address, but I looked the addressee up online and finally mailed it."

My eyes widen. "You were the one who mailed the letter."

"I did. You received it?"

"My uncle," I say, trying to stay calm. But this is huge. "My mom and dad were the ones who were here. Did you ever hear anything from them again?"

She may be able to point me right to them.

Her eyes soften. "They disappeared into the cave. I don't know if they made it out or not. I'm sorry."

I don't know what to say. My parents were here. Right here in this very same coffee shop, eleven years ago. The connection I feel with them is so strong in this moment. I want to find them so badly. Bring them back. Erase the past and rewrite my childhood with my parents in it. But no matter how much I may want that, I can never change my past. I can, however, map out my future.

"You're here looking for them?" Naala says.

A lump wells up in my throat. "Yeah. I haven't seen them in a really long time."

"The cave … it eats people," she says, I don't think to be mean, but more to let me know what I'm up against.

"I know," I say. Research has taught me that. But I'm also going to beat the odds. "I'm going to find them."

"I hope you do," Naala says.

I nod but can't bring myself to say anything else. I take my coffee and wait at a table for Ethan to arrive.

∞

The next day I'm waiting again in the coffee shop for Ethan to show up. He takes forever to get ready, but whatever soap he uses smells amazing, so I keep my complaining to a minimum. Maybe he got it at one of the local spas.

While I wait, I order my coffee and his, black coffee, dark roast. When I head back to the counter to pick up the drinks, I glance outside to see if he's on his way.

Someone is looking into the coffee shop, staring at me. It's a man with a hat pulled low over his face, but he turns away the second I see him, so I can't get a good look at him. I head out of the coffee shop, leaving our drinks on the counter and follow him. He moves between the houses and through the streets for about five minutes, looking back every so often. I duck out of the way so he won't see me each time, and finally I watch as he goes into Deep Cave Outfitters.

"What are you looking at?"

I spin around. Ethan is right behind me. I've been so focused on watching the guy that I didn't even hear him.

"Some guy," I say.

"Checking out one of the locals?" Ethan says, winking at me.

I smack his chest. "Not like that. Some guy was watching me. I was just following him."

"No one's watching you," Ethan says.

"He was," I say. "I'm sure of it."

"You realize that sounds a little paranoid," Ethan says.

"Whatever. It's true. He was watching me."

"Maybe it's because you're so good looking," Ethan says.

Silence follows.

"I mean, you know, maybe he thinks that," Ethan says, trying to dig himself out of yet another hole. And maybe that's the truth. Maybe the guy does think that. Maybe Ethan does, too.

"Yeah, okay," I say. "Our coffee is back at the shop."

We head back to the coffee shop, but I take one more glance at Deep Cave Outfitters. There is no sign of the man.

CHAPTER 20

THE NEXT DAY, SCOTT CALLS, LETTING US KNOW THAT our stuff is in. We can pick it up today and start our descent tomorrow. The last few days spent poring over artifacts and possibilities drop away from me, and all that matters is the present. This is really going to happen.

When we get to Deep Cave Outfitters, I try everything on, just to make sure it's all there.

"Everything's a perfect fit," Scott says, rolling my sleeping bag tight so that not even cave lice will be able to crawl inside.

"You made the right call," I say. "And I'm betting you would have been a pretty good guide."

Scott cocks his head and grins. "Too late to woo me now. I got another gig." He holds up a green business card with silver lettering and waves it around.

"You got hired?" I say, trying to get a look at the card.

"Just yesterday," Scott says. "Lots of money. The guy already came outfitted and everything. All I have to do is guide."

"Who is it?" I ask because all of a sudden all I can think about is the man I saw watching me. He'd come in here. He could have been the one who hired Scott. He could be here for the same reason we are.

"Can't tell you," Scott says, tucking the card into his pocket.

"Of course you can," Ethan says, backing me up. "It's not like you're a doctor and this is some patient-client confidentiality thing. You're going caving."

"True," Scott says. "But I'm also getting paid extra to keep my mouth shut."

Interesting. So whoever is going to Krubera Cave doesn't want anyone to know.

"Fine," I say. "Whatever. Did you find anyone to help with our descent?"

Scott nods. "I did. Didn't you get my text? Two local brothers, Adgur and Daur. I've worked with them before. They'll take good care of you."

"How do we get in touch with them?" If the cell service wasn't so spotty, I might have gotten the text. I bought the signal booster, but since it runs on batteries, I want to save it for once we're in the cave.

"I gave them your number," Scott says. "They'll text you today. And don't worry. They speak English, at least mostly."

"Mostly?" Ethan says. He's been trying in the last couple days to learn what he can about the Abkhazian language, but, as he's bemoaned to me each morning over coffee, very few words are borrowed from other languages so it's really hard.

"It's fine," Scott says. "They know your names. They have lots of rope. And they're strong."

I figure that's the best we can expect. We pack up all our stuff and head out of the shop. But as we're leaving, I look back over my shoulder. Scott's holding the green business card and talking on his cell phone, looking our way.

CHAPTER 21

We travel by truck to a base camp just outside the opening to Krubera Cave. Scott has definitely overestimated their language skills, but Adgur and Daur know enough English to get ideas across. They're nearly as wide at the shoulders as they are tall, have full beards, and they say that they've lowered over one hundred people into the cave before, at least fifty of whom have come back.

I don't find this last statistic overly comforting, but Adgur and Daur grin and act like it's a great thing. I'm hoping they're joking.

Once I'm in my tent, I snuggle inside my sleeping bag and test out the cellular signal booster. It's a good thing I have it because the signal is super weak otherwise. But the booster works great. I text Lucas a couple quick pictures of the view from up here.

You aren't kidding. It's gorgeous, he texts back.

Wish you were here, I text.

Me too, he says.

Next I check in with Uncle Randall. He's not happy, but he's resigned to the fact that I'm here.

Take pictures of anything that looks even remotely man-made, he texts.

I promise I will, and then I tell him that I'll try to check in at least once a day, same as I told Lucas. Then I power off the booster and fall asleep.

Adgur and Daur are up early the next morning, taking down the tent before I've finished packing up my sleeping bag.

"Is warm today," Daur says, grinning as I zip my coat up to the top and pull the knit hat far down over my ears. I can see why men grow beards with weather this cold in June.

"It's like two degrees above freezing," I say.

Daur nods. "Yes. Warm. Early in morning, too."

The early in the morning part gives me hope that it will warm up. That said, Scott made sure we brought thermal everything to prevent hypothermia.

"Who go first?" Adgur says as we stand outside the slit in the ground that he assures me is the opening to Krubera Cave. It's not even a big slit, just wide enough that I wouldn't be able to jump across it with a running start.

"Me," Ethan and I both say at the same time.

"I'm going first," I say. "No argument."

"You're not going first," Ethan says.

"Of course I am." I don't know why we have to waste time with this discussion.

"What if you fall?"

"What if? Are you planning to catch me from a two hundred foot drop? Because if you fall after I'm already down there, I'm moving out of the way so you don't squash me."

"Ha ha," Ethan says. "But I'm going first. End of story."

After two weeks of getting to know me, would Ethan seriously think I would give in that easily? It is so not the end of the story as Ethan quickly finds out. Of course, I go first.

Adgur and Daur secure the rope to the rappelling rig and then lower me into the earth, guiding the rope and making sure it doesn't go too fast so I won't start swinging wildly. The tiny opening above ground hides the truth below: Krubera Cave is like a pit hundreds of feet down to nowhere. I descend slowly, and my eyes acclimate to the new surroundings. The early morning sun shining in from above is enough to light up the walls, which are etched with layers of Earth's formation, like a geologist's utopia. I click on my headlamp and they come to life.

Once I'm sure my feet have hit solid rock, not just some temporary ledge, I radio up to let them know I'm stable, and they pull the rope back up.

I move away from my current spot so our supplies won't come tumbling down on top of me. I force myself not to worry as I wait for them to get hooked on the rope and delivered. It takes twenty solid minutes before they finally arrive, and a small wave of relief flows through me. I now have food, water, tools, and a first aid kit ... everything I could possibly need for the Hawkins Expedition. That's what I'm calling it, in honor of my parents. When I find them, we can laugh about the name, but until then, the Hawkins Expedition it is.

I unhook the supplies and again radio up. Then I wait for Ethan. He takes forever, just like getting ready in the morning. I check my watch at ten minutes. Fifteen. Twenty. There is no reason it should be taking him this long. At thirty minutes I begin to get annoyed. I call from the radio, but there's no answer. At forty-five minutes, I pull out my cell phone and turn it on, using precious battery power. I'm about to pull out the signal booster when Ethan's silhouette finally shows up, far above me.

I watch every second of his descent, and when he finally sets his feet on the ground, I grab him in an involuntary hug. I have no idea what comes over me, and I don't care. I am just so happy that he is here because being alone in this pit in the ground for the last hour has set my every nerve on end. After I hug him, I step back and shove him, hard.

"What took you so long?" I say as anger rushes through me, pushing away the relief.

He unclips himself from the rope and tugs on it three times, letting Adgur and Daur know that it's okay for them to leave. They've done their job, at least for now. They're supposed to come back and check for us every day at noon after two weeks have gone by. Even if our journey is done before then—which I hope it is—we have enough food to last.

"Sorry. My mom called," Ethan says. "She got all freaked out and started asking really weird questions."

Fine. It's not a lame excuse.

"What kind of questions?" I ask.

He laughs in a completely not funny way. "Okay, I know this is weird, but sometimes my mom says she gets feelings. And I guess she got one because she wanted me to come home. I told her I'd be home in a couple of weeks. And then she said that my dad went on a trip a couple days ago, and she had a really bad feeling about it. I guess that's why she wanted me to come home."

Ethan's dad went on a trip?

"Where did he go?" I ask. He can't have been the person I'd seen in town. Ethan would have seen him and recognized him.

Ethan shrugs. "I don't know. He travels a lot for work."

This is not good.

Okay, I'm getting worked up about nothing. He's probably just on another business trip. He can't have been here in Gagra because he wouldn't have any idea this was the starting point of the journey. We haven't told anyone. I try to convince myself of this logic because there's nothing I can do about it now anyway. All I can do is find the Code of Enoch and find my parents.

"Who's ready to start this show?" Ethan says, and he eyes my backpack.

This is it. The start of my journey. I pull the map from my backpack, sink to the ground next to Ethan, and unroll it. We photocopied the center piece since Ethan still has it and got the whole thing laminated in Gagra since the cave is so wet. The complete map looks back at us. My headlamp is bright, reflecting off the lamination. I dim it so it won't interfere.

209

"Where do we go from here?" I ask. Sure, it's a map, but we're in a dark cave in the middle of nowhere. We could branch off from the main path now or five days from now.

Ethan shifts his light so it doesn't reflect either. He doesn't say anything right away. He's busy studying the symbols that cover the map.

"Do the directions make more sense now that we're down here?" I ask, reaching across him to point at the lines and markings that make up the symbols of the map.

Ethan pulls a map of the cave from his pocket and lays it next to the Deluge Segment, adjusting his light so it's illuminated, too. Then he points to a rock sticking out from the wall, almost like a giant pencil. "I think a lot of these symbols mixed in are supposed to be landmarks. Like this symbol has to represent that rock. I mean, the symbol here says 'Finger of God' if you want to be technical, but that rock looks like a finger to me."

"Agreed."

"So let's make that our starting point. Based on that, this next series of symbols and lines is equivalent to this path on the explored cave map." He points to the topographical map of Krubera Cave, tracing his finger along the path.

"So we follow the main path, checking for landmark symbols on the Deluge map, until the directions change, and then we veer off into the unknown," I say.

"Exactly. And then each marking that we follow on our map not only tells us which direction to go, but also how long to travel in that direction, how many cross tunnels there might be, what kind of terrain we'll be crossing."

"It's a lot of information," I say. My head spins at how many symbols there are. How far we need to go. We're only at the beginning.

"But we have the information. We have the map," Ethan says.

"I know," I say. "But it almost seems impossible. Like one wrong turn and we're lost forever."

Ethan looks me directly in the eye. "I never pegged you for a quitter, Hannah."

"I'm not quitting," I say, though my voice betrays me. Now that we're here in the cave and the enormity of our journey stretches before us, I worry that I'm like a tiny fish who's sunk its teeth into a shark and now isn't sure what to do. What have I gotten myself into?

"Good," Ethan says. "Because I'd be awfully lonely going without you."

"Aw, that almost sounds like you care," I say, trying to shift my mood away from my negative thoughts. There is no turning back now.

"Don't get carried away," Ethan says.

We both laugh. Then we pack up the Deluge map, have some water, and set out.

"I feel like we should sing a song," Ethan says. "Something to start our journey."

Of the many things I am, I am not a singer. "You don't want me singing."

"And you don't want me singing either," Ethan says. "But if

I get bored enough, then I just might anyway."

"Challenge on," I say. "I'll have to make sure you don't get bored."

So I carry the conversation as we navigate the main path in Krubera Cave. There have been enough explorers coming through that there are symbols and spray paint along the walls, telling us which way to go. I'm guessing the spray paint isn't environmentally friendly, but the need to stick on the right path is important enough to let that slide.

"So this cave," I say. "You know how deep it is?"

"Explored to almost twenty-two hundred meters," Ethan says.

"Yes. But have you visualized that?"

He shakes his head which I know because his headlamp moves back and forth ahead of us against the darkness of the cave. We descend steadily, and for all the dangers I've heard about the cave, the floor we walk on right now is smooth rock. Of course it's getting colder with each step. I pull my sleeves farther over my wrists to keep the chill out.

"Imagine this," I say. "You take the Chrysler building, and you place the Washington Monument on top of that. Next you put the Empire State Building. Are you still with me?"

"Still with you," he says.

"Good. Because after that comes the Pyramids. Then the Eiffel Tower, and finally, don't think you're done just yet, you take all those and on top of that you stack the Burj Khalifa in Dubai. That's how tall twenty-two hundred meters is."

"That's tall," Ethan says.

"Yeah, and we've walked about one percent of it so far," I say. Thinking about the facts of it helps keep my mind off of how far we need to go. I can take this ten meters at a time. "Oh, and I forgot to ask, but while we're walking, if you happen to see any bugs, let me know."

"What kinds of bugs?" Ethan says, cringing, like the request horrifies him.

"Anything that doesn't look normal."

"What's normal? Cockroaches?"

"Well, yeah," I say, "but I'm thinking more along the lines of bizarre coloring. Or shapes that don't remind you of any other bugs you've seen."

"So like bright pink bugs with five hundred legs?"

I laugh. "Not quite. White bugs. Extremely large or extra-long bugs. Bugs with vestigial eyes."

"What kind of eyes?" Ethan asks.

"Vestigial," I say. "Eyes that are really small or not really there. Maybe covered by thick exoskeleton. Or only on one side of their head. That kind of thing."

"Great," Ethan says. "So what you're saying is that you think there are giant blind albino bugs that are going to leap on us at night as we're sleeping."

I don't know why it dawns on me in that moment, but it does. Aside from the random text message with Lucas or Uncle Randall, I am going to be talking to no one but Ethan for the next who-knows-how-long. We are going to be sleeping

213

side by side.

"I told you that I don't like bugs," he says, distracting me from my thoughts.

"I thought you were kidding."

"Not kidding," Ethan says.

"I hear they like guys better," I say.

"That's comforting."

"You could always stay up all night and watch for them," I say.

"Don't tempt me," Ethan says. "Because if we do spot a two-headed cockroach, then I just might."

When we stop that first evening, based on the map, we've traveled only one hundred meters. But the next thing in front of us is a giant drop, at which point our descent distance should increase exponentially.

I test out the signal booster and manage to get text messages through to both Uncle Randall and Lucas. Just a quick check in that everything's okay because I don't want to waste batteries. Then I power it off.

It's about ten degrees above freezing, but Scott's set us up with some incredible gear so that only my face is cold. The excitement of descending into the cave finally wears off. I am exhausted. Not long after I curl up into my thermal sleeping bag, I'm fast asleep.

CHAPTER 22

ENERGY BARS ARE WHAT'S FOR BREAKFAST. WE'VE packed about a million of them along with every flavor of MREs available. I'm sticking to the vegetarian ones, but Ethan was all about the BBQ Beef Sandwich, making sure he ordered that for the majority of his meals. There are enough small trickles of fresh water running through the cave that we're liberal with drinking. The last thing we want is to get dehydrated and weak.

After spending the first half of day two rappelling another hundred meters, it passes much like day one. Day three is the same. It's only on day four that things become more interesting. We reach the end of the recorded path on the map. The only way I know this is because I've been using a wax pencil and marking off every single symbol on the map that we've traveled. It's time for us to diverge.

To my left, someone has leaned a sign against the wall that says OVERNIGHT CAMP AHEAD in English.

"America's been here," I say, and I pull out my phone, turning it on long enough to snap a picture of the sign. Aside from my text check-ins, if I only use the phone when I need to document the Hawkins Expedition, it should last, especially because I did bring four extra batteries. Except I have no idea how long the journey will really be. Without a unit of measurement on the ancient map we're following, I can't be sure what we have ahead.

"What now?" Ethan says, scanning the area with his flashlight. "The symbol here is for water, which has to be this pond. But the next symbol is a door, and I don't see any doors."

I take a long sip from my canteen and scan the area, but as far as I can tell, he's right. There is nowhere else to go but along the main path.

From the direction we've just come, something echoes in the distance, like metal falling against the rocks. It's the first time we've heard actual proof that the client Scott was guiding started out. For the last three days, the only sounds I've heard besides rushing water and wind whipping through the cave are either Ethan's or my voices.

Ethan turns his head to look in the same direction I am.

"You heard it, too?" I ask.

He nods. "Sound can carry pretty far. They could still be far away."

If so, this should buy us some time to figure out where we're supposed to go. Still, I don't want to risk running into anyone else and having to make excuses as to why we've left the main trail. I search the area again, this time being more thorough. We're in a wide underground cavern, nearly circular. The walls, though made of rock, are detailed and smooth, as if water once flowed freely inside here.

"How are we supposed to find a door that nobody else has found?" Ethan says.

"Who's the negative one now?" I ask as I continue my search.

Ethan joins me, scanning the walls. "I'm not trying to be negative. I'm trying to be realistic. People who spelunk for a living have been marking out Krubera Cave for years. This is still pretty high up in the cave, in the grand scheme of things. Don't you think they would have found it by now if it were actually here?"

I don't want to give in to his thoughts, even though logically they make perfect sense.

"Maybe they didn't know what to look for," I say. "You said the symbol was door?"

"Yeah," Ethan says. "Or portal. Something we have to go through. Something we have to open."

I pull my glove off and dip my hand in the clear pool of water. At first glance, it looks perfectly normal, like the crystal pools inside natural caverns all over the world. But when I shift the light just right, I notice that there are all sorts of ridges in the stone at the bottom. They look random, and yet, if I kind of shift my eyes out of focus like I'm trying to look through them, certain parts of them take on more of a three-dimensional appearance.

"Do you see that?" I say, pointing to the 3D pattern of ridges.

"That's just the rock," Ethan says. "Natural water erosion."

"Really? You, Mr. Linguistics? You don't think they look like symbols?"

"I don't think they look like anything."

"Try to look through them," I say. "Like shift your focus."

Ethan shines his light into the pond and squints. "Maybe ..."

"Try not to blink." I'm sure I'm right.

Ethan studies the underwater symbols then shakes his head. "Text them to your boyfriend."

"He's not my boyfriend. He's my best friend." But texting them to Lucas had been my exact thought of what to do next.

"Yeah, whatever."

"It's true," I say. "Lucas and I are just friends."

"Dude's probably totally in love with you," Ethan says.

"That's ridiculous."

"I've seen the way he looks at you," Ethan says.

"He doesn't look at me any way."

"Yeah, whatever you say, Hannah."

I cross my arms and stare him down.

"Fine. Fool yourself. Anyway, just take some pictures and text him."

He is so wrong about Lucas.

I take pictures as best I can through the water, making sure to show the fact that the symbols are 3D. Then I turn on the signal booster and text Lucas. The signal has been getting weaker every day. It won't last much deeper into the cave.

What do you think of these? I text.

I have no idea what time it is back home. Here in the cave, time almost loses meaning. But Lucas texts me right back.

I'm on it, he says.

It pains me to sit there waiting because with every second that passes, the battery in the signal booster dies. And I don't have any backup batteries for it. Five minutes go by. Then ten.

Anything? I text.

He replies. Look around the room. Do you see any matching symbols?

"Check the walls," I say to Ethan, and we scan the room. If there are matching signals, I don't see them.

"There," Ethan says. "You see it. This looks like one of the symbols underwater."

I take a picture of it. Ethan spots three more, and I take pictures of those, too, and send them to Lucas.

Then we wait again.

This time we don't have to wait long at all.

Lucas texts, Remember Magic Eye? And then attaches a picture.

"Magic eye?" I say aloud.

"Oh yeah, Magic Eye," Ethan says. "I have a poster hanging on my wall at home. Those were the coolest."

I narrow my eyes at him. "Weren't they from like thirty years ago?"

"Sure," he says. "But I found it in my dad's stuff ages ago, and he said I could have it. Magic Eye is a 2D image with a 3D image hidden inside. You can come over, and I'll show you sometime."

"That almost sounds like a date," I say.

Ethan opens his mouth, like he's going to whip out some sarcastic reply, then closes it.

"Anyway," I say, trying not to smile. "If we line this image up with the bottom of the pool ..."

I lean close to the water and look for the symbols that Lucas has highlighted in the picture he sent.

"There, there, there, and there," I say, pointing to each of them. Lucas has not only highlighted them, he's written a number next to each one. One, two, three, and four.

I reach into the water to touch one of them, and it moves, almost like it's on some kind of circular sliding mechanism. I slide it until the symbol is at the top of the others but in the middle. I do the same for the second. Ethan catches on and rotates the third and then the fourth symbols into place.

The entire cavern begins to shake.

CHAPTER 23

"Okay, that did it," Ethan says.

I yank my hand out of the water, even as the pool begins to drain into a separate basin. The base of the pool splits apart like there's an earthquake and we're right in the middle of it. I barely have time to jump to the side as the crack spreads from the pool straight across the cavern floor. By the time the world stops shaking, the rift is five feet across. But unlike a crack created by a real earthquake, the edges of the split in the ground are smooth. Ethan stands on one side, and I stand on the other.

I shine my light downward, into the divide, trying to see how far it goes.

"Hang on," Ethan says. "I'll jump across to you."

"I don't think you'll need to," I say because instead of a pit of blackness looking back at me, there is a massive staircase hewn from the stones of the rock itself. It's about a ten-foot drop to the top of the staircase.

Ethan walks to the edge and looks down also, and he lets out a low whistle.

"We found it, Hannah," he says. "I can't believe it. This is the door! The portal! Your boyfriend did it again!"

I let the boyfriend comment slide because I can't believe it either. Though I don't want to admit it, up until this moment, I harbored doubts. Doubts as to whether there was a separate tunnel from the main one. Doubts as to whether my parents might still be alive. Doubts about the Code of Enoch. But this … it confirms so much. It lets me know that we are on the right path. That there is a path.

I text in all caps to Lucas. THANK YOU! YOU ARE A GENIUS! TALK LATER. Then I turn off the signal booster and shove it in my backpack.

I pull my pack off and toss it across to Ethan, then slip my gloves back on. My sleeve is still dripping from the water, and I don't want my grip to slip. Before I can over think it, I squat down, swing my legs over the side of the opening, and with a deep breath, I let go of the edge.

Even though I'm well over five feet tall, the landing makes my teeth rattle together. Ten feet may have been a bit of an underestimate.

"You okay?" Ethan calls.

"I'm fine," I say, looking upward. "Drop me our bags."

He drops me his, but then he pauses.

"Drop it," I say.

"I got it," he calls, and I realize that he's worrying about giving me the only copy of the map. And this after I just handed my bag over to him.

"Seriously?" I say. "I just trusted you. You have to trust me. It's not like I'm going ahead without you."

I can't believe he thinks I'm going to betray him, especially after all we've been through.

"Fine," Ethan says and drops my bag. It lands hard, but I catch it before it topples down the steps.

"Got it," I say, and I move them both out of his way.

I shine the light on the spot on the ground where he should land, so it will be easier for him to see where he's going, or maybe where I am—I don't want him landing on top of me.

"Here I come," he says, and then he lets go and falls, landing with a giant "ooof."

"God, that hurt," Ethan says, standing up and brushing himself off.

"Don't be such a baby," I say, pushing his pack over to him. "And just for the record, I'm not going to take off with the map, okay? I'm not that kind of person."

Ethan swings his bag onto his shoulders. "I'm not saying you are, Hannah."

"Then why did you hesitate?"

"Because ...," he stammers. "I don't know. It's just hard. I mean, my dad ... your parents ..."

"We aren't our parents," I say. "And I'm not going to steal anything."

"Fine," Ethan says. "I'm sorry."

I shoulder my own bag. "I accept your apology this time only. But do it again, and I get your energy bars for the next five days."

This is enough to ease the moment. "Not the s'mores flavored one."

"Yes, even the s'mores ones."

"You're brutal, Hannah."

We stand on a stone platform about five feet across, just the width of the gap above us. I scan the area with my light. On the wall behind us are the same four symbols, perfectly aligned, exactly like we'd assembled above in the lake. We rotate the concentric circles that the symbols are part of, separating them back out, and the crack in the cavern floor begins to close above us.

"Move, Hannah," Ethan says, pulling me from the platform, because the ceiling is getting lower and lower as the split closes.

We hurry down a bunch of uneven steps until we reach another platform. When I look back, there is no sign of where we've come from.

"I wondered what those things that looked like steps were on the Deluge Segment," he says. "And now I get it."

"So we're on the right path?" I'm unable to keep a huge smile from creeping onto my face. We found a secret path. Our destination seems so close.

He grins along with me. "We're totally on the right path. But one thing."

"What?"

"Let me see the map."

I dig it out and hand it over to him. His finger moves from one symbol to a different one next to it. "If I'm reading this symbol right, it's a really big number."

I stare at him. "And that's important why?"

He slowly shakes his head as he hands the map back to me. "Because I think it's the number of steps we need to go down."

I roll the map and return it to my bag. "How many can there possibly be? I've climbed to the top of the Eiffel Tower, the Washington Monument, and the Empire State Building."

"I guess we'll find out," Ethan says.

We descend to the next platform, and then the next. And then the next and the next and the next, and pretty soon I am regretting my words. When I shine my light far ahead of me, all I can see are more steps. They're endless. The walls around us are rough stone, as is the ceiling. And even though we've been in the cave for four days so far, now that we are descending so quickly, I'm struck with the thought that there are tons upon tons of rock now over my head. Memories of Scott telling us about the rapture return to me. But I'm not alone. And I refuse to panic.

My legs ache with each movement, but I'm not about to complain to Ethan. I can do anything he can do.

"Can we stop?" he says, after we've been walking for close to an hour.

The air around us is cool, but not cold, and it's fresh, though I'm not sure how that's possible seeing as how this tunnel's been blocked off for ages.

I almost snap out a sarcastic response, calling him a weenie and telling him to suck it up, but my legs hurt too badly, and more than anything, I want to rest, too.

"I guess we can take a small break." I drop to the ground when we hit the next platform, inhaling an energy bar, but I limit myself to only a few sips of water. The last thing I need, in addition to my aching legs, is to have my stomach start cramping up.

"Have you noticed how much warmer it's getting?" Ethan says.

We've both shed our outer coat layer and unzipped our jacket liners, too.

I pull out the mobile thermometer Scott had insisted we'd need and set it on the ground so it can get a solid reading. Scott said it was so we could tell what the hypothermia risk was, but at the rate things are going, I'll be down to my tank top by tomorrow.

"It's up thirty degrees," I say as the thermometer settles.

Ethan picks it up to double check. "That's like spring in Boston. But it doesn't make sense. Where do you think the heat is coming from?"

I take off a glove and press my hand to the rock wall. It's hot to the touch. When I pull it back, it's covered in a greenish residue. "There's some kind of moss covering the rocks. Thermogenic I'm guessing."

"What does that mean, Science Girl?"

I brush the moss off my hand and put my glove back on. "It

means that the moss is producing heat. Some plants do it to help with pollination."

"You're saying you think the moss growing on the rocks has raised the temperature thirty degrees?" Ethan says.

"Sure. Each plant on its own doesn't account for much, but cover the entire wall in it, and you have yourself a regular sauna."

Ethan pulls his jacket liner fully off and begins to roll it in a ball. "Well whatever the reason, it's better than the cold, except now I'm sweating. These steps are a workout."

I pull my jacket liner off also and instantly feel better. "I think we've gone down a million so far."

"I've counted almost two thousand," Ethan says.

"You've been counting?"

Ethan nods as he tucks his coat into his backpack. "Numbers are just another form of linguistics. We've been following a pattern in case you didn't notice. Sixteen steps then thirty-two then eight then thirty-two again then four then thirty-two two more times. It's been repeating pretty much the entire time."

"So it's binary."

"What? Like ones and zeros?" Ethan says.

"Yeah, like powers of two. Two. Four. Eight. Sixteen. Thirty-two. You get the idea. Whoever built this place had an advanced understanding of the world around them."

"Who do you think built these steps?" Ethan says. "And don't say God because I'm not buying that."

"I wasn't going to say God," I say. "I'm not sure what I was going to say, actually. Uncle Randall and Tobin told us those stories about the flood survivors. Noah. Utnapishtim, Manu. But one person couldn't have done all this. It's too much. Too hard. How would they have done it?"

"Carved one stone at a time?" Ethan says.

I shake my head. "There's too many. You said we've walked close to two thousand steps so far, and I'm not seeing an end in sight." I kind of inadvertently groan after I say it because my legs hurt so badly.

"You're not ready to stop for the day, are you?" Ethan says.

My legs scream at me to say yes, that we stop here for the night. But that won't help me find my parents. According to my watch, it's only two in the afternoon.

I pull myself to my feet, trying to make it look effortless, which doesn't go over very well because I'm grimacing.

Ethan laughs.

"Yeah, I know," I say. "But we have to keep going."

And so we do. We manage another hour. And then another. And then there is some mutual, unspoken agreement that passes between us because we both sink to the ground at the next platform, and neither of us suggests getting up again that day.

I turn on the signal booster, but the signal comes up blank. Inside this secret tunnel, there is no hope of us getting a message out. Which means that if we need help from either Lucas or Uncle Randall, we are out of luck. We are now totally on our own.

CHAPTER 24

WE DESCEND THE STAIRS FOR TWO MORE DAYS. OUR pace has slowed, and though Ethan is still muttering numbers under his breath like he's keeping track, my mind is too numb to even think about it. I have no clue how deep in the earth we are, but it's way more than the Eiffel Tower or the Empire State Building.

"You know what just occurred to me?" Ethan says.

"What?" I ask.

"When we're done, once we find the Code of Enoch, we have to climb back up these."

I stop walking and fix him with my look of death. "Never mention that again. Because if you do, I will kill you right here."

"Whoa, anger issues," Ethan says.

"My legs hurt too bad to be angry," I say.

"Just don't trip me, okay?"

I try to come up with a witty response, but my mind has entered a dull place where I can't think of anything except the next step in front of me—which means that when I go to take that next step and my foot doesn't descend at all, I fall over and land on my side.

"Hannah, are you okay?" Ethan says.

"I think I found the bottom," I say. "Be careful. The last step is a doozy."

It's such a stupid thing to say, but I can't stop myself as giddy laughter takes over. Ethan falls to the ground beside me, and we lie there laughing until tears stream down our faces. I shine the light around just to be sure, and I can't believe it. There are no more stairs.

All the exhaustion I had from coming down the staircase vanishes. Around me is a chamber unlike any I have ever seen. The area we're in is vast and cavernous, with stalactites and stalagmites that rival those I've seen in both Carlsbad Caverns and Mammoth Caves. My light shines out, falling upon seven arches carved into the walls, each with what looks like a tunnel extending beyond it. It's like a *Choose Your Own Adventure*, where whichever path we pick will determine our fate. Possible gold and riches in the form of the Code of Enoch lie through one of those arches, and grisly death lies beyond the others.

"Let's see what the map says," I say, digging it out. With the steps, we haven't needed it. There was only one way to go. But now there are seven.

"What does it say about this chamber?" I ask.

Ethan studies the map and then stares at the tunnels, his head slightly tilted as if he's contemplating a problem.

"What's wrong?" I ask.

"All the next symbol says is 'Golden Archway,' but none of these are golden."

Nothing in the chamber is golden. Sure, it's carved, obviously manmade, but everything is the gray color of stone.

"So it doesn't talk about making a choice?"

He shakes his head. "No. Just 'Golden Archway.'"

I study the symbols on the map, looking for something that he's missed. The stairs are there, along with the horrible number for how many we descended. There's the archway symbol he's talking about, but nothing else.

"We should complain to the map maker," Ethan says.

I press my fingers to my temples. There has to be something to tell us which way to go. Some kind of clue. If only I could text Lucas. He'd be able to figure it out. But he's not here.

What would Lucas do in this situation?

I stare at the symbol on the map, waiting for something to pop out at me. But nothing does. My eyes drift to the letters that surround the Deluge Segment that tell about the artifact we're seeking. Nothing there either. Along the edge of the map are the notches. They're not lined up since Lucas flipped the images around and rotated them, using the golden ratio as a guide. My eyes move back to the center piece, the part Tobin filled in. But that doesn't help either.

"Wait …," I say. Almost out of my peripheral vision, the notches on the edges blend together. I hold my head still but let my eyes drift over to them. "These." I run my finger over the notches.

"What about them?"

It's there. I can't believe I didn't see it earlier.

"You see the pattern they're in? There were five notches on each of the three pieces, right? That means fifteen total notches. And you see how even though they're not lined up, most of them are near one other?"

Ethan's eyes widen. "Oh, yeah. Except this one." He points to the second from the right. "It has three notches."

"Exactly," I say. "Lucas used the golden ratio to align them. And I'm willing to bet the one with the three notches is our tunnel."

Ethan walks over to the second tunnel from the right. He runs his hands along the sides of the tunnel, squatting down until he's near the ground.

"What does this look like to you, Hannah?"

I walk over to join him. Ethan points to a carving near the base of the rock. I recognize it immediately.

"It's the DNA symbol from the map," I say. "It's the same symbol."

"Yeah, and look at this," Ethan says, pointing to another carving.

Three notches have been carved into the wall. Three notches just like on the map. We check the other entryways but don't find the same DNA symbol or the notches. This has to be the way we're supposed to go. This is our golden archway.

We don't die when we walk through which I take as a good

sign that we've chosen correctly. Unlike the walls of the stairwell, the tunnel has been carved into a perfect arch, stretching before us. It's also covered with the thermogenic moss. Along it, I find the first insect I've seen since we started down the steps.

"Albino bugs!" I say, reaching out for one.

"Don't touch them," Ethan says, yanking my hand back. "They're huge! And they could be poisonous."

"They're not poisonous. At least I don't think they are," I say, placing my hand flat on the wall ahead of us. Slowly, one of the insects crawls onto the back of my hand. It's ten times the size of a normal beetle from back home, covering almost the entire back of my glove. "Pretty sure it's a *Catops Cavicis*, except it's albino unlike the normal species."

"Look at those teeth," Ethan says. "Does it bite?"

"Probably," I say. "Most beetles do. But only if you provoke them."

"So don't provoke this one," Ethan says. "Put it back."

"It's fine," I say. "What I'd really like to do is take it back with us."

"We're not here for our bug collections, Hannah," Ethan says. "And anyway, it's freaky with its giant crunchy white shell and weird little antennae. Just put it back where it came from."

"You are such a wimp." I move my hand back to the wall to release the beetle.

"It looks like it came from here," Ethan says, shining his flashlight into a crack in the wall.

"Stop!" I say, but it's too late.

Hundreds of the giant beetles pour from the wall, dropping to the floor and scampering across our boots before we have time to jump out of the way.

I flick the beetle off my hand. The bugs keeps coming.

"I told you that you shouldn't have messed with them," Ethan says, stepping back.

But he's stepping the wrong way, back in the direction we came.

"This way," I say, grabbing for his hand. The bugs are crawling up my legs. They're everywhere. Biting through my clothes.

Ethan jumps over the insects, crushing them under his feet, and then we run down the passageway, swiping the beetles from our legs. The bugs pour after us, coming out of new cracks along the tunnel. We reach the end of the passageway, but it's blocked by a small river of water, about five feet across. Neither Ethan nor I hesitate as we jump across it. We land and brush the last of the bugs off our legs, flicking them into the water.

"Do they swim?" Ethan says.

I shake my head. "Only some kinds of water beetles swim which I don't think these are."

"You don't think?" He shakes some more off, swatting around his ankles where his boots meet his pants.

"That's why I wanted to take one back with me," I say. "To study it."

"Yeah, well you can forget that idea," Ethan says. "Man,

their bites hurt."

"I told you they don't like being provoked," I said.

"How did I provoke them? By looking at them?"

"You shined your light on them," I say. "Remember that they've never seen light. They have no idea what it is."

"Well, sorry for trying to help you see better," Ethan says.

"I'm not saying you did anything wrong," I say. "Only saying that you provoked them."

"So did you," he says. "You picked one up. They probably viewed that as some kind of act of war."

I glare at him because his statement is ludicrous.

"Fine. I provoked them. But warn me next time," Ethan says.

"I tried to."

"Try earlier," he says.

"I'll do my best."

The horde of albino beetles stays on the other side of the river, and Ethan and I have no need to go back, at least not right now. We'll figure out how to deal with them when we return this way. If we return this way. Maybe there's a different path without the insects. For now, we keep moving forward.

Instead of being in an open room with many choices, like we were before, there is only one path that lays ahead of us.

"Check out these markings," Ethan says, shining his light on a bunch of carved symbols.

"More DNA?" I ask.

"It looks like it," he says.

We find two more sets of the DNA carvings along with the

three notches as we follow the path ahead. When we come to an intersection, our very first, Ethan and I study the map and agree that we need to go left at a giant rock with two protrusions on the top. The symbol on the map means "Devil's Rock."

As we turn, drawn on the rock wall of the cave, is the infinity symbol.

"It's like on the piece of the rubbing I found. My mom put it there. And she must've put this one here." I brush at it with my fingers. "It's drawn with rubbing wax."

"Something your parents would have had," Ethan says.

"And something that wouldn't have been around thousands of years ago when this place was built."

It has to be a symbol drawn by Mom, like a message left for anyone who might come looking for her. I can't begin to imagine what she'll say when she finds out that someone is me.

CHAPTER 25

WE TRAVEL FOR FOUR MORE DAYS, FOLLOWING THE map. All the while, we are moving lower into the earth, continuing to descend. Each day that passes, my suspicions of Ethan wane. Though I would never admit it to him, him being here, with me, has made the entire journey tolerable. He's smart and funny and protective, but not in some overpowering way that would drive me crazy.

We share our food and water. We tell stupid stories about our lives. And at night, I pull my sleeping bag close to his because here in the dark, I have reached the point where I have to know he is here. I have to believe that I am not alone. Because alone on this journey I am pretty sure I would go out of my mind.

That fourth night since the steps, I wake with a start. I click on my flashlight, sure I've heard something. Aside from dripping water and some occasional rocks falling, we haven't heard anything since we've entered the secret passage. Even the wind has settled down to a whisper in this place.

Next to me, Ethan breathes deeply, fast asleep.

I shake him gently. "Wake up," I whisper.

He doesn't move.

"Wake up," I say, shaking him a little harder.

"What is it?" he mumbles, not opening his eyes.

I shine the light in his face.

He winces. "Turn off the light, Hannah."

"I heard something," I say.

Ethan blinks his eyes a couple times and then finally opens them. "It was probably some rocks."

"It wasn't rocks. It sounded more metallic. I think someone's down here with us."

"No one's down here with us, Hannah. We sealed the entrance to the secret tunnel."

"They could have found it." It could be Scott with the group he's guiding.

"Go back to sleep," Ethan says. "You didn't hear anything because there is nothing around to hear."

Annoyance flashes through me. "I'm telling you that I heard something. Someone is down here with us."

Ethan shakes his head. "There is no one down here with us. You must've imagined it."

"I didn't imagine anything," I say. "Now get up. We need to look around."

Ethan slowly lets his eyes close again. "I'm not getting up. It's the middle of the night. It's probably just the beetles, plotting their revenge."

"It's not the beetles," I say.

"You're imagining things." He lays back down, rolls onto his side, and is breathing deeply before I can even process the annoying fact that he's disregarding my suspicions.

I lay back down next to him, and I silently click off my light. But I don't fall back asleep. Instead, I sit there, in the dark, listening. I hear dripping water and small rocks and stuff like that, but nothing metallic like I'd heard before. Still, something had woken me. I know it. I've become so used to the dark that my ears have probably become supernaturally superior to what they were before. I listen for at least another hour, but I don't hear anything else suspicious. And I begin to wonder if maybe Ethan is right. Maybe it was my imagination. Sleep finally comes.

My watch alarm is set for seven o'clock, not that it matters in this place. Seven o'clock looks the same as noon. I rub my eyes to help wake up. Ethan is still sleeping. I turn the lantern back on and then make every noise possible until he wakes.

"How'd you sleep?" he asks.

I glare at him in reply.

We pack our stuff, and like every morning, I check my bag to make sure the map is still there.

It's gone.

"You took it," I say, not really seeing the humor, but maybe he was just trying to have fun.

"Took what?" he says.

"The map. It's not in my bag."

"You must've put it in a different pocket," he says. "Because I don't have it."

"You do. I always keep it in this front pocket." I pat the large zip pocket on my backpack.

"Except today," he says. "When you moved it."

"Just check your stuff, okay?" I say. He could have borrowed it and then forgotten.

So he checks his stuff, and so do I because maybe I did accidentally put it somewhere else after we settled in for the night. I check every pocket in my backpack and clothes, but after fifteen minutes of searching all of our stuff, we can't find the map anywhere. I even look through his stuff just to make sure. It's missing.

Realization floods through me, mixed with a rising panic. It's like a bad nightmare where I can't wake up. "Someone stole it."

"It could have dropped out," Ethan says.

I shake my head and clutch the straps of my bag to try to control my hands because they're shaking. "We both know that's not true. We were both looking at it last night after dinner. It was here with us, and now it's not."

"But it's the only logical thing that could have happened," Ethan says. "You lost it."

I glare at him. I didn't lose the map. And now we're out of

luck. We have no idea which way to go. It's not like either of us memorized the map.

"We need to turn back," Ethan says, like it's all so clear.

"Did a rock fall on your head? Because for a second there, it sounded like you said we were going to turn back," I say.

"We have to, Hannah."

"And why is that?" I ask.

"Because we have no idea which way we're supposed to go."

"And?"

"And that's not enough?" Ethan says. "We're God knows how many thousands of feet below the earth's surface. If we keep going, we're only going to get lost."

I shake my head. "I'm not giving up. I refuse to give up." I start packing my stuff so I can make a point. Ethan watches me until my backpack is completely put together.

"So what's your plan?" Ethan says.

"We keep going forward," I say. "We follow our instincts."

"Instincts?" Ethan says. "What's that supposed to mean?"

"I don't know," I say. "But I do know that we are not turning back, which leaves one option only."

"Moving forward," Ethan says.

"Right answer. Now pack your stuff so we can get moving."

I manage to keep my false optimism for the first hour until we come to an intersection. Ahead are two choices, right or left. Right or left. It seems like such a small decision, but if we make the wrong turn here, we could be off the path forever. I look for the three notches but don't see them anywhere.

241

"We should mark which way we're going," I say, pulling a small can of spray paint from my bag.

"And which way is that?" Ethan says.

I look on the ground for some kind of sign or carving but don't find any. I try to be confident. I've always been a confident person. Always known exactly what to do. But here, this, it's too much.

"I don't know." Stupid tears of frustration form at the corners of my eyes. I wipe them away, hoping Ethan hasn't seen them. He's looking right at me, but if he notices, he doesn't say anything. This is so unlike me. I have to be able to figure something out.

"Look for signs of recent activity," I say, squatting down so I can examine the dirt.

"There is no recent activity," Ethan says. "We're the only ones here."

He still doesn't believe me.

"I didn't lose it," I say. "I told you that. I heard someone last night. They stole it while we were sleeping."

Ethan takes my shoulders. "Hannah, do you have any idea how ridiculous that sounds? We're—oh, I don't know—fifteen hundred meters below ground in a secret passageway, and you think someone else is here with us. No one knows about the secret tunnel. Nobody could be following us."

It all comes together then, so clearly. The missing map. The way Ethan kept trying to use his credit card. How he kept looking over his shoulder at the airport.

"Don't pretend you don't know," I say.

"I don't know," Ethan says. "At this point, I think you're crazy."

"I'm not crazy, and you know it," I say. "And you also know exactly who's looking for the Code of Enoch. You're helping them."

Ethan raises his voice, louder than I've ever heard him do before now. "I'm not helping anyone, and I don't appreciate you throwing your guilty accusations my way."

I study his face, looking for hints that he's deceiving me. And though there seems to be a permanent look on his face like he's trying to prove something, if he's also hiding deception, then he's a master of it because his eyes plead with me to believe him.

"Do you swear that you don't know what's going on?" I say.

"I swear it, Hannah," Ethan says.

"This has to be Amino Corp," I say. "They stole the copy of my piece from Lucas, they got a copy of yours from your dad, and then they had all three pieces."

"My dad wouldn't have given it to them."

"Are you sure?" I say.

Ethan bites his lip and doesn't reply. My question hangs there in the air between us. He knows his father had wanted the Code of Enoch before, to save his brother. He also knows his father had a renewed interest in it.

"Fine," Ethan says. "Let's say this is Amino Corp, and they did have the map. How did they get through the secret tunnel?"

"They figured it out, the same way we did. Maybe they know how to read Magic Eye."

"Okay, fine, maybe," Ethan says. "But why steal our map then if they already have a complete map?"

A complete map. When he says it, my thoughts click into place.

"They stole the map because they didn't have the center piece," I say. "They had the other three pieces, but not that one. And we had it on ours before we laminated it."

Ethan shakes his head. "But why would they need it? We already used it to find Kars and the Gate."

"I don't know. But they must've needed it. And now they're ahead of us, and we have no map, and we're totally out of luck." Saying it aloud makes it that much more real. I try not to cry, but I feel like I've lost everything.

Ethan puts a hand on my shoulder and looks in my eyes. "They're ahead of us. So what we need to do is find them. They'll leave a trail, and we'll follow it. It'll be okay."

I close my eyes and force away my tears. It will be okay. And at his words I feel like we really are allies. We were meant to be on this journey together.

"Do you see any signs as to which way they went?" Ethan says.

I shine a light down and study the dirt. Both paths have small markings, like animal footprints, though aside from the mammoth insects, we haven't seen any animals. Aside from the animal trails, the dirt that covers the ground of the path on the left seems a small bit different in color.

"It's a little darker," I say. "Almost like it was more recently upturned."

Ethan squats down next to me, so our shoulders are touching. I try to ignore this small detail.

"I see what you mean," he says. "So we go left?"

I shrug because I'm not really sure. It's not like I'm some professional tracker. "It's as good a choice as any."

So we set off left. I use the spray paint to make a small arrow showing which way we came from and which way we went. We use this same logic for the next four turns, but after a couple hours, the growing, unsettling feeling inside me cannot stay contained any more.

"Does it seem like we're heading upward?" I say. The muscles in my legs tighten, but the twinge isn't in my glutes and hamstrings like it was when we were walking downhill. Instead, it's on the top of my thighs.

"Yeah, it does," Ethan says. "But we've followed the signs. The dirt has definitely been moved recently."

"I know," I say. "But what if they left us a false trail?"

"You think they did that?" he says.

"There's no way to know," I say. "But I suggest we continue on this path for just a little bit longer. If they did leave a false trail, then it should disappear."

Sure enough, after another hour, the trail we've been following vanishes.

"So now, not only are we on the wrong path, they're even farther ahead," I say. If my parents are at our destination, then I need to find a way to get there first. To warn them that someone else is coming. The whole thing is a mess. Instead of keeping them from danger, I've placed them in even more. I turn to head back.

"Wait a second, Hannah. There's something in here." He's continued on down the tunnel, but he takes a turn and his light blinks out, leaving me alone.

"What are you doing?" I call, but he doesn't answer.

I hurry down the path, making sure to not trip on any loose stones, and when I reach the end of the path, there are again two choices. I'm pretty sure he turned right, so that's what I do.

There's another immediate turn, then I see Ethan. Relief pours through me.

"Don't run off like that," I say, smacking him in the chest. He could've gotten lost forever.

"Hannah, look."

Ethan's light shines out across a chamber carved into the stone. The ceiling is held aloft with large simple columns, and in the walls are alcoves, cut symmetrically, spaced every five feet or so.

"There's something in these alcoves," Ethan says, walking toward the nearest one.

"Something like dead bodies?" I say because this is reminding me way too much of the catacombs under Paris that I'd seen when I visited with Uncle Randall.

He shakes his head. "Not dead bodies. Jars."

Ethan rests his flashlight on the ground and reaches out for one of the large jars that rests against the wall inside. They're each about half my height, are the same brown as the dirt and walls around them, and are sealed with a lid.

Ethan places both hands on the lid of the jar.

"You don't know what's inside," I say.

"I think I do," Ethan says, and he lifts the jar.

For someone who'd been so freaked out by the insects earlier, Ethan shows no fear as he reaches his hand inside the clay jar all the way to his elbow.

"We need to get back on track," I say.

"Hang on. Almost got it," he says, and then he pulls his hand back out of the jar. Except his hand is no longer empty. He's now holding a large scroll that looks like it may be made of some kind of thick cloth.

I back up to give him room and shine my light for him as he spreads the scroll onto the floor of the chamber.

"How did you know what was in there?" Worry for my parents still presses on my mind, but at the same time, Tobin's words float back to me. Sometimes events are fated to be. Us finding these scrolls, this room, is one of them.

Ethan doesn't look up as he answers. His eyes are locked on the scroll. "The Dead Sea Scrolls. This is exactly how they were found."

I know about the Dead Sea Scrolls. Uncle Randall and I even visited the caves they'd been discovered in because Uncle Randall was writing a paper on them. "Some shepherd found them after almost two thousand years."

Ethan nods. "That's the story. And I'm not saying I believe this or anything, but some people question why they'd never been found before. Some of your ultra-religious people theo-rize that they hadn't been there the whole time, or if they had, that somehow the caves had been cloaked from view. And that they were only found because God decided that they needed to be found. That humanity needed them."

"Do you believe that?" I ask. To me it sounds way too much like some religious miracle.

"No," Ethan says. "There were tons of caves and no electric-ity for lots of years, so no flashlights to go exploring. They were discovered then because that's when everything came together perfectly."

"So what do these scrolls say? Can you read them?" Crazy waves of excitement run through me.

Ethan traces his finger along the scroll, hovering it just above, like he's afraid he'll mess something up if he actually touches it.

"This one is written in some sort of variant of Hebrew I think. Except there are some weird random symbols mixed in," he says. "But I'm pretty sure it tells the story of Noah's Ark."

I open the next jar and bring the scroll inside it to him, lay-ing it down by the first. "How about this one?"

Even I can tell that the language isn't the same. I recognize them as the same letters Uncle Randall wrote my name in on my birthday present.

"This one is in a cuneiform script, similar to Sumerian," Ethan says. "It's about Gilgamesh and his quest for immor-tality. He went to talk to Utnapishtim who was supposed to be immortal. If you remember from what your Uncle said, Utnapishtim was the alleged flood survivor in Sumerian myth."

"I remember," I say. "He was immortal. Noah lived a really long time, too. Everyone who was mentioned in any of the stories seems to have had their lives extended."

"And those stories seem to be recorded here," Ethan says.

I know time is ticking away, but I also believe that we've come to this room for a reason. We pull more scrolls from the jars and study them. What Ethan can't read, we decipher by sketches and pictographs. All the flood stories I've ever heard are recounted along with so many others from civilizations I've hardly even heard of. Africa itself has fifteen different versions of how the earth was flooded. The Americas have twelve. The Middle East has more than any, totaling twenty-two different accounts for how the flood came to be.

"It's hard to think that the flood never happened," I say.

"It's impossible," Ethan says. "This is unreal. If we could bring these things back and study them, do you even realize all the information that's here?"

I'd be lying if I said that the thought hadn't occurred to me. This kind of knowledge could change the world. I turn on my phone and use precious battery power to take pictures of all the scrolls. I can't wait to show these to Uncle Randall.

"Is there anything about the Code of Enoch?" I ask as I continue taking pictures. We've covered about half the jars in the room, but there are still plenty.

Ethan is one step ahead of me. He's already spreading out

the next scroll on the floor. I've set up every lantern we have and lit two glow sticks so we can see better.

"This one is about Noah, too," Ethan says. "But it's after the flood."

"And? What's it say?"

"Give me a second to try to translate," Ethan says because I'm basically breathing down his neck. I hold my breath and wait, looking for words that seem familiar.

"Okay, I think it's the same text that was written around the edges of the Deluge Segment. Maybe not word for word, but I think it's generally the same. Noah re-created life on Earth. Then he needed to protect the Code. With the help of his sons, he found the hiding spot deep in the earth and took the Code there for safekeeping. His sons were then supposed to make a map to this secret location and hide it, just in case the Code was ever needed again. Don't quote me word for word, but it's something like that."

"So his sons placed the map in that hidden chamber under the mountain in Ani," I say. "But maybe then someone came after it, and they realized that they didn't hide it well enough, and that's when the sons of Noah scattered the pieces of the map around the world."

"Wow," Ethan says, sitting back and resting on his hands. "Just wow."

"I know," I say, taking pictures of this latest scroll and then joining him.

The enormity of what we're looking for is almost

overwhelming.

"If the story from the Deluge Segment is here on this scroll, don't you think there's a chance that they put a copy of the map in these jars?" I ask.

"Yeah," Ethan says. "I think there's a really good chance. If they didn't intend to destroy the map in the first place, then I'm guessing that they also made a copy before they hid the pieces."

It's a shining beacon of hope in the deep darkness of Krubera Cave.

Hours go by as we search through the scrolls. We go through them again and again. But no matter how hard we look, the map doesn't seem to be included.

Ethan closes his eyes and presses his fingertips to them. "I can't read these anymore, Hannah. My eyeballs are aching so bad, I'm pretty sure they're going to fall out."

"If that happens, I promise to pick them up for you since you won't be able to see. Just don't step on them because then you're out of luck."

"Thanks," Ethan says. "It's good to know that I can count on you."

"Take a break," I say. "It's been hours since you've eaten anything. Or had any water. Which is weird. Have you noticed how this room has no water at all?"

"That's probably why they picked it to store their writings," Ethan says.

Our canteens still have enough water, but even if they do run out, we passed water out in the main tunnel before we entered this place.

I grab us each an MRE, me the vegetarian spaghetti and Ethan the BBQ beef sandwich, because even though we're watching how much we eat, no way is an energy bar going to cut it. I inhale mine which I realize after the fact, but Ethan isn't busy judging me. He's too busy making sure he's gotten every morsel he can from the inside of the meal pouch.

"What time is it anyway?" he asks as he tucks the MRE trash back into his bag. The trash is much lighter than the MREs themselves, so our backpacks have at least gone down in weight.

"Dark thirty," I say, laughing at my own stupid joke. "No, it's about seven at night."

"We're not going anywhere tonight," he says.

I'm not about to disagree. I lie back, next to Ethan, not bothering to get inside my sleeping bag because it's a balmy seventy degrees here in the chamber, and I close my eyes.

"Do you really think your parents are going to be there?" Ethan asks.

I think of the infinity symbol, written on the wall with rubbing wax, marking where they'd been. I remember Naala from the coffee shop saying my parents had been in Gagra. All signs are pointing to it.

"I have to believe they are," I say. "They've been this way."

"But even if they had, that was what? Eleven years ago?" Ethan says. "How would they still be alive? What would they eat?"

These thoughts have run through my head many times, especially at night as I'm trying to fall asleep. No matter what answer I come up with, it's not rational, and I know it.

"Maybe they've been eating the insects and moss," I say. "Maybe there is something they can grow in the soil."

"Like mushrooms," Ethan says.

For a second I think he's teasing me about something that isn't funny, but there's no sarcasm in his voice. "Yeah, like mushrooms. Or truffles, or other things that don't need light. There could be some kind of subterranean river with fish."

"There could be," Ethan says.

"What about you?" I say. "You still think there is some way you're going to bring the Code of Enoch back? You still think it's a good idea?"

Ethan shifts so he's on his side, and even though the lanterns are low and it's hard to see him in the dark, I do the same.

"I don't know, Hannah. I mean, if I'm completely honest, that's why I set out on this journey. I was sure if I brought the Code of Enoch back to my dad, then he'd be proud of me. But all these stories we've been reading about how it was hidden away because of the damage it could do ... I don't know. There are so many stories, and they can't all be wrong."

"So you're not going to try to take it," I say.

Ethan's quiet, and I hear him breathing in the dark.

"Let's put it this way," he finally says. "I'm not promising anything. We haven't even found it. But when we do, I'm going to give it serious thought."

Unspoken are my concerns about what I'll do if Ethan does try to take it. Or what about Amino Corp? How am I supposed to stop them? It's not like I packed a gun for the journey.

"You want to know something weird?" Ethan says.

"Definitely."

"When I first saw you there in the lecture hall at Harvard, I thought that we would never be friends, and it made me really sad. I couldn't understand it. And now that we're here, together, well, I kind of feel like ..." His voice trails off.

"You kind of feel like what?" I say. My voice wavers in the dark.

"I kind of feel like that it doesn't really matter what happens. That maybe this journey was something we both needed to do, for ourselves. And even if we turned around today— never found the Code of Enoch—that would be okay because I'd know that I'd been wrong on that first day."

I don't have a response. I should think up something to say, to fill the silence, but there are so many thoughts, and I can't bring them together. Ethan reaches out, in the dark, and puts his arm around me, pulling me close. I put my arm around him, too, and we lay back down, staying like that until I drift off to sleep.

CHAPTER 26

ETHAN AND I BOTH WAKE AT THE SAME TIME TO THE sound of my watch alarm. We're still together, nestled in the dark.

"Good morning," he says.

"Good morning," I say, and even though my breath probably smells like camel dung, before I think about what I'm doing, I move my face forward, closing the distance between us, finding his lips in the dark with my own. He doesn't hesitate to respond, and we kiss there in the chamber with the ancient scrolls around us. Ethan's hands move up my back, into my neckline. He runs his fingers through my hair. I trace my hands over the tight muscles of his back, and I don't let our lips separate because now that they're together, I realize how much it was meant to be. We're both still dressed in our clunky hiking boots, but we've shed our jackets and are just down to our thermal undershirts.

Ethan moves closer, rolling me so I'm on my back, but one

of the lids from the jars crunches underneath me.

"Oops," I say, and then I start giggling, which is totally undignified, but I don't care.

"It's okay," Ethan says. "There are plenty of others." And then we kiss for a while longer until I remember that we can't spend the rest of our lives here in this underground chamber though after our journey so far, the thought is tempting.

I pull back from the kiss though it's the last thing I want to do.

"Best good morning ever," Ethan says, and he leans forward and kisses me again. It should feel like so much changes in that moment, but instead it feels like this is how things were meant to be.

Ethan lights the closest lantern, filling the chamber again with light. Around us sit all the scrolls we've looked through. We've made sure to keep them neat and in order so that when we leave, we can put them back in the jars they came out of.

"They remind me of the Old Testament," Ethan says. "Do you know that people talk about a secret code hidden in the Bible? They call it the Bible Code."

"I think Uncle Randall has mentioned it. Wasn't it like random symbols were scattered in but they turned out not to be random at all?"

The realization hits us both at the same time.

"Wait, random symbols," he says. "You don't think ...?"

"It has to be," I say. "Because there is no way they'd have all this other information stored here and not have the map."

"It's the extra symbols," he says, shifting the light to the nearest

256

scroll, pointing to the random symbols that are interspersed between the foreign letters. "I wondered why they were here, but that must be it. These aren't letters. These are map symbols."

We start at the beginning, near the entrance to the room, and pull out the pieces of the map from each of the scrolls. Every single scroll, no matter what language it was written in, has the same type of random symbols on it. And as these symbols start coming together, confidence builds inside me. We're recreating the map. The only problem is that it's late in the day when we finally finish.

"We should still go now," I say because Amino Corp has almost a two day lead on us by now.

"We're tired," Ethan says.

I roll my unused sleeping bag back up. "I don't care. They could have slowed down once they thought they got us off path."

"Good point," Ethan says, and we finish packing our stuff into the bags. We can't leave the scrolls like they are, so we each start at one side of the room and put them back, replacing all the lids except the one I crushed. I scoot its remains to the base of the jar, hoping maybe this makes it okay.

"You should be more careful," Ethan says. I love the joking tone in his voice.

"I'll remember that next time," I say.

As if the promise of next time isn't enough, Ethan covers the distance between us and our lips meet again.

"No one I'd rather be under the world with besides you," Ethan says after we've kissed.

"I'm glad I agreed to let you come along," I say as we start walking.

"If I remember right, I didn't give you much choice." Ethan reaches out and laces his gloved fingers with mine.

We backtrack to the original place where we strayed from the path. Our spray paint arrow is still clear, and this time, at the place where we went the wrong way, we head right because that's what the landmark on the map tells us to do and because we know what's down to the left. We leave the jars and scrolls far behind.

We talk as we go, and it's as if some wall has been torn down between us. I tell Ethan all about growing up in Easton Estate, about the scavenger hunts Uncle Randall always left for me. I describe the trips we'd been on.

"You never traveled much, did you?" I say.

"Not my parents' thing," Ethan says.

"But you guys have money. You could have."

"Not really," Ethan says. "When Caden was alive, we used to do a lot more as a family. Still, we were never one of those families that sent out Christmas cards each year with an updated family photo taken in some exotic place. But then, once Caden died, things changed. My dad started spending more and more time at work. My mom changed jobs, so even though she tried to be around, she was still so busy trying to prove herself. And in forensics, when there's crime evidence, no matter what time it is, she can be called in."

"I'm sorry," I say.

"What are you sorry about?" Ethan asks. "Your parents vanished when you were five. It's not like that's been the perfect childhood."

The hole in my heart where my parents reside throbs.

"I really hope we find them," I say.

"I really hope so, too."

The trail we follow looks completely undisturbed for the first hour, but then after that, it is more than obvious that others have come this way. There are fresh footprints, bright paint, discarded supplies. There's even a cavern where it looks like they may have camped for a while. I only hope this is the case. If so, that means then maybe they aren't that far ahead of us.

"I can't believe we fell for it," I say. "They must've left the false trail and then made sure to cover up the real one. I feel like such an idiot."

"Why? Because you're human?" Ethan says. "News flash. Everyone makes mistakes, Hannah. If you didn't make any mistakes, then you might as well be a robot."

"Maybe I am, and you just don't know it," I say.

Ethan laughs. "You do a pretty good human impression."

We push on well past our normal stopping time, hoping to make up the time we've lost. We're also nearing the end of the map. I can hardly keep from running. But when we reach the end, in the middle of the second day, our well-laid plans change. We've been hearing water for the last few hours, and we suddenly find out why.

We enter a room filled with thick mist. Only five feet into

the room, a river crosses the path in front of us. White water rushes through it, with rocks and a current so strong, not even Olympic swimmers would be able to make it across.

"Oh, this is not good," Ethan says.

Hope slips from me as I look through the mist at the rapids. The river is only about twenty meters across, but with the rushing water, it might as well be an eternity. Then I see what's on the other side. Someone has rigged hooks into the walls and ceiling and strung rope through it. Someone who must be an expert at this kind of thing. Someone like Scott. But if there was any hope we could use the same rigging to get across, the rope has all been pulled to the opposite shore, completely out of our reach. And we're out of rope.

"You see that?" I say. "They crossed, and they left us stranded." I throw my pack down in frustration and sink to the soft dirt floor.

Ethan walks up and down the shore, looking for somewhere to cross, but I don't hold out much hope when he comes back only minutes later and shakes his head.

"What's the last symbol?" I ask. It may have the clue we need to get across.

"'Bridge of Noah' I think," Ethan says.

"'Bridge of Noah?'" I shake my head. "But there is no bridge."

"Yeah, but that doesn't make any sense," Ethan says. "If we really do need to get across the river, which at this point it seems pretty obvious that we do, then there must be a bridge. It's not like whoever built this place had high-tech gear for spelunking."

"Maybe it's an invisible bridge?" I say, not that I'm planning on stepping out across the water to check.

"Maybe. Or maybe there are hidden symbols like before. A secret door. Or something. I don't know."

His words make sense. There does have to be a way. We'd had to figure out how to get into the secret tunnel. This might be the same sort of thing. And if Scott and Amino Corp had to put all this rigging in place, that would have taken a lot of time. They might not be that far ahead of us.

I jump to my feet. "Look everywhere."

Ethan smiles. "That's my girl."

I punch at his shoulder, but this quickly results in him pulling me in for a kiss. And as much as I want to lose myself in the kiss, I know that can't happen.

"Later," I say and push away. Then we move separate ways in the thick mist and scour the walls and the floor.

It's almost impossible to see because there's so much moisture in the air, but I don't give up. I look everywhere. I find nothing.

"I don't get it," Ethan says because his search came up empty also. "We're missing something." He sinks to a rock near the edge of the river, then grimaces and stands.

"What?"

"This rock has a giant hole in it." He turns to look at it, then his body freezes. "Hannah, come here."

Hope fills his voice. I rush over and look through the mist

at the rock. It's like any of the others lining the shore and scattered about the water except that this one looks completely hand carved and has a circular depression in the center of it.

"Look familiar?" Ethan says.

Holy mother, does it ever. It's exactly like the depression in the altar back in Turkey.

Ethan runs back to his pack and unzips it, digging through until he finds the center piece of the Deluge Segment. He rushes back to shore and places the artifact in the depression.

Nothing happens.

I reach forward and press down. An audible click fills the air, and then the rocks in the water begin moving, causing even more mist to escape. They push the water aside and create whirlpools and jetties. They move like they're on some sort of mechanical conveyor belt, turning and shifting until a path appears straight across the water where no path had been before. The Bridge of Noah. We found it.

"You did it!" I scream, not caring who hears. It's magical and mystical and unbelievable. This is the path to my parents.

Water splashes against the rocks as we hurry across. I'm careful so I don't slip. I can't tell how deep the water is, and I don't want to find out. As we move through the thick fog, each step feels like a victory, and within minutes, we're both safely on the other side. I almost feel my parents calling for me. I'm so close. There is no way I'm going to lose them now.

Then I look through the fog to the ground. Sure enough there are fresh footprints everywhere.

CHAPTER 27

THE FOOTPRINTS ARE DEEP, LIKE THEY'VE BEEN MADE with heavy boots, and we follow them in the dirt. Ahead is a corridor only wide enough for one person to pass at a time. I shine my flashlight down it to see what's ahead. The walls look wet and the ground moist, and the light reflects off the fog, back at us. It's where we need to go.

We set out down the dark tunnel. Our flashlights seem to be getting weaker by the second, and it's impossible to know how far we have to go. Five minutes in and my flashlight finally goes out. I shake it to get the batteries to make contact a little better, but the light only flickers a tiny bit then finally goes out. The thick fog probably messed with the batteries.

"Stay close," I say since Ethan's flashlight is still on. But five minutes later, his dies, too. We're cast into utter darkness.

I reach forward and grab his arm, or at least where his arm should be, but I come up empty.

"Ethan?" I say.

"Just a second," he says. "Let me get out a—"

His words stop as something weird begins to happen. My eyes start to adjust to the dark, which can't be the case because in pure blackness like we've been traveling in so far, there is no light, not even the smallest amount, to provide contrast. But here, now, there must be because when I wave my hand in front of my face, I see the contrast in blackness. I do it again to make sure I'm not imagining things. There is no doubt. Each second that passes, I am able to see more. Which means ...

There has to be a light up ahead.

I grab hold of his arm now that I can see it. I have no clue what's up ahead. The lights could be coming from Amino Corp. They could have set up camp. They could be waiting for us.

"No more lights," I say.

I can barely see him nod in acknowledgment.

I take a deep breath, and we move forward cautiously. I use my free hand to feel the moss-covered wall to my left. We take one step after another. Maybe they won't be expecting us. We can sneak up on them. And then what?

That's the part I don't know. But being cautious may give us the advantage.

The light is growing stronger. Not only can I make out the contrast of shapes in the dark, colors begin to materialize. The orange of my thermal top. The gray of the walls, streaked with crystals running through them. We continue forward silently. The path curves to the right, and when we round the bend, ahead of us is an opening, glowing from whatever light is beyond.

We step forward together, peering around the opening, prepared for anything and nothing.

Ahead of us is a world flush with plant and animal life. A vast ocean stretches beyond that. I can see everything perfectly, as if there is some hidden light source nearby providing the illumination, like an underground sun.

As my eyes fully adjust, the world around me begins to sink in. Plants with odd-shaped leaves and colors that I've never seen in nature stretch on stalks far above like trees. Animals with bizarre colors and features graze through the flowers and grass, hardly casting a glance in our direction, as if they're entirely used to our presence here. Birds fill the sky. It's like a geneticist's dream. There are so many new species. So many things that don't exist in our world above.

I run my hands over the colorful petals of a nearby flower. It turns in my direction, like an instinct to seek out warmth. I walk forward, and the flowers seem to follow me, turning their blossoms toward me. There are petals of violet and cyan and yellows brighter than daffodils. Some are nearly as tall as me, and most bend to me as I walk.

"It's like they're sentient," Ethan says, placing his hand near mine as the flowers caress it.

I lean forward and inhale the array of scents that fill the air with an exquisite perfume. Though the flowers reach even toward my face, they don't threaten me.

"Maybe they are," I say. "I mean there are lots of species of plants that have instincts. Like Venus Flytraps closing over their prey. Or Morning Glories opening to the sun each morning, or closing as the sun goes down. But these plants ... their reactions are different. Beyond instinct. Like their DNA has been infused with something more like an animal. Something that makes them aware of the world around them."

"God, that's weird," Ethan says. "You don't think they'll hurt us?"

"I don't think so. But keep close, just in case."

In response, he pulls me close. His lips find mine, and I give myself just a moment, there in the meadow of flowers. I want to lose myself. I almost do. I feel so connected to him in this moment, like we belong in this place together. Like we're part of nature.

"You think the flowers are watching?" he mumbles as his lips trail down my neck. Shivers run up my spine and reach every nerve in my body.

I barely open my eyes. Most of the flowers are still angled our way. "Whoa. Yeah, that's a little freaky." It's like we have an audience of millions.

He runs his hands through my hair and nibbles at my ear. "They're only flowers."

I gently push him away. "Still, let's keep it G-rated for now."

"For now?" Ethan says, raising his eyebrows in suggestion.

I smack him lightly on the shoulder. "Don't get your hopes up."

"Too late," Ethan says.

We walk, hand in hand, through the meadow and onto

the sandy beach. The ocean stretches as far as I can see. What looks like a sky is far above, but it's made of stone like the steep walls far off to either side. Instead of making me feel closed in, compared to the cramped corridors we've navigated through for the past days, it's like a new world down here, hidden underneath the earth.

"The river we crossed must feed into this ocean," I say.

Ethan nods. "Meaning that if we had jumped in and let the current carry us, we might have ended up here."

"Might have," I say. "Or might have died." The rocks were deadly.

"How do you think this place gets light?" Ethan says.

I've been thinking about this exact issue from the second I walked through the opening and realized that the light leading me wasn't created from any kind of flashlight or electricity, and there's certainly no sun down here. I bend down and scoop up a handful of the grainy sand, and then I rub it between my hands, letting most of it slip through and fall back to the beach. When I'm done, I turn my hands palm up to Ethan.

"They're glowing," he says.

I nod. "It's the same principle as fireflies or glowworms. Light without heat, created by chemical reactions within small animals."

"So you have mushed up fireflies on your hands?" he says.

"Something like that," I say, rubbing it on his shoulder. "But these are smaller. Like algae. Alone, it wouldn't seem like much, but billions and billions of these creatures, and it could light up this entire world."

"That's incredible," Ethan says.

"I know. Even though I get the whole science of it, the evolution that had to occur to create this place boggles my mind," I say.

"Unless it wasn't evolution," Ethan says.

"You think this is proof?"

He nods. "An entire ecosystem created by the Code of Enoch. What if whoever brought the Code down here designed this, so what we're seeing is the possibilities of what can be done?"

I spin in a slow circle, taking in the world around us, from the plants to the ocean to the strange creatures that watch us. If Ethan's right, if the Code of Enoch really is responsible for everything I see around me, then its power goes beyond anything I could have even imagined.

"It's unbelievable," I say. "I've studied science my entire life, and this defies anything I've ever seen."

"And yet it's here," Ethan says.

We walk from the shoreline toward the trees. Some have grown so large, that what I know of trees' lifespans, I'd have to guess that they're thousands of years old, thick and twisted and strong.

"Uncle Randall would love to have seen this. And Lucas. This is the kind of place he'd sit and paint forever." I pull my phone from the bag so I can take a picture because they are never going to believe it. But when I try to turn the phone on, it's totally dead, probably from all the moisture in the air. I only hope the memory is still intact.

"You'll have to tell them about it when you get back," Ethan says.

"I'll never do it justice."

"Try," Ethan says. "Just for a second." He steps behind me, wrapping his arms around me. I cross my arms over his. "Close your eyes, Hannah. Breathe deep."

I close my eyes and take a deep breath of the salty warm air around us. It's like a mix between a beach and a rainforest.

"Listen to the birds and the wind," Ethan says. "Pick out the scents. Think about how it makes you feel."

Though it seems impossible, the world feels almost more alive with my eyes closed. I take another breath and then another, relaxing against Ethan's chest, trying to capture this moment and keep it with me always. Here, this place, it's filled with freedom. Possibilities. The belief that anything is possible. This … this is what I'll bring back to Uncle Randall and Lucas. I let the moment sink into my soul.

"Did you get it?" Ethan asks.

I take one last breath and open my eyes, turning to face him. "It's like a miracle … this whole place."

"I know," Ethan says. "And maybe this is the corniest thing I've ever said in my life, but I'm so happy I can share it with you."

I squeeze his hand, and then I let it go because as much as I would love for this to be our sole purpose for being here, I have to find my parents. We have to press on.

The trees are spaced apart, leaving plenty of room for us to roam side by side between them, almost like someone has planned out trails to follow, like a scenic walk. The farther we go into the trees, the more noticeable this becomes. The path bends and turns, and where it does, flowers grow and roots cut up out of the ground, providing natural benches. The ground here is made of soft grass that depresses slightly under our steps. We move deeper into the forest, until when I look back, I can hardly see the ocean. Then we come to a clearing in the trees.

It's filled with graves.

CHAPTER 28

My heart races as a mixture of emotions floods through me. "People have been here."

"People are buried here," Ethan says.

People like my parents? I can't voice the thought that, of the handful of graves before us, two of them could contain Mom and Dad. But my thoughts are too strong. I sink to the ground and can't stop from shaking. I've tried to be so strong. I was so strong, but then Uncle Randall did the unthinkable. He gave me hope. Hope that they were still alive, and it was a hope I held on to. But now, looking out at the graves, the dread that fills my stomach threatens to destroy every bit of optimism inside me.

"It's okay, Hannah," Ethan says, squatting down next to me and putting his arms around me.

"They could be dead," I say, forcing my words out amid my fear.

"But they could also be alive," Ethan says.

This can't be happening. I can't let them have died. Not when I've gotten this close.

"I hate to be the logical voice in all this. You always do that so well," Ethan says. "But somebody actually had to dig these graves. Whoever's buried here, they can't be the last ones."

My shaking stops briefly as I let his words sink in. Of course, he's right. Why am I jumping to the worst conclusion possible? I can't let go of my hope that easily.

"We should see if the gravestones say anything." I wrap my arms around my stomach almost like they'll help hold me together if I find something I don't want to.

Ethan and I stand, but before I walk forward to read the stones, I press my head against his chest. "Thank you for being here with me," I say.

He grabs my hand and squeezes it.

We walk forward, through the tall grass that skirts the graveyard. Ghostly whispers seem to come from the forest of trees around us, whispering words I can't understand. But it's only the wind. In the center of the clearing, the grass is low, almost like it's been manicured that way. There are only about ten or twelve graves in all. I close my eyes and summon up my confidence before it slips away again. I can do this. I have to. I dare to unwrap my arms from around me, and we squat down next to the first grave.

The stone is worn, so the symbols are nearly impossible to read. Ethan traces his fingers over them, though, almost like he's reading braille. The wind continues to move through the trees, like voices of the dead.

"Pretty sure it's some variant of Hebrew, like the first scroll we found," Ethan says. "But it's hard to make out." He closes his eyes, almost as if that will help him concentrate. His fingers trace the lines. "I think ..." His words trail off.

"What do you think?" I ask.

He shakes his head. "I know this is going to sound crazy, but I think it says Noah."

He points to a few worn symbols that remind me of the writing we saw on some of the scrolls.

נח

The awe that fills his voice reflects the astonishment that runs through me. "Noah is buried here?" I say.

"Maybe, Hannah. I don't know. I told you that sounds crazy."

The wind seems to whisper its agreement, rustling the leaves of the trees and sending chills through me.

I shake my head. "Maybe not. What about these others? Can you read them?"

He does the same thing as with the first gravestone, feeling the symbols and letters when they're worn down too much. Utnapishtim. Ziudsura. Deucalion. Manu. They're all here, buried in the ground of this world that shouldn't exist.

"The flood heroes are here," I say. "The ones from the stories."

"It's hard to believe," Ethan says. "Even seeing it here."

We've looked at nearly all of them, but there are still two graves left. My stomach clenches when I realize that these two are newer than any of the others.

"I can't look," I say. Any confidence I may have had slips away.

Ethan steps to the graves. I watch his face, see his lips move as he reads them. I wait for some sign in his face that he's about to deliver bad news. But it never comes.

"These aren't your parents, Hannah," Ethan says.

Relief floods me. If my parents are here, then they aren't dead. Or at least not buried here.

"Who's buried here?" I ask. "They look pretty recent."

Ethan shakes his head. "I don't recognize the names."

Okay, good. That's good. It's not my parents. Which means that if they are here, they could still be alive. And they could be in trouble.

We continue walking, down the path. The forest continues beyond the clearing as deep as my eyes can see. But in the middle of it, stretching far above into the sky, is one tree that for some reason has grown beyond all the others.

It's where we're supposed to go.

We pass through the clearing and on toward the tree, but as it gets closer, my eyes don't want to believe what I'm seeing. One impossibility seems to build onto the next here. "It must be thousands of years old."

The tree looks like it's some type of olive tree. The trunk itself must be thirty feet wide, with gnarled gray bark and branches that twist and shoot into the air above like an out-of-control chia plant. Patched between the branches are wooden shingles.

"It's a house," Ethan says.

"So where's the door?" I say.

Birds chirp in the woods around us, but as we get closer to the massive tree, their song begins to sound more frantic, almost like a warning. Ethan must sense it, too, because he tugs on my arm to stop me.

"We need to be careful," he whispers.

I know he's right, but I also know that each step we take, we're getting closer to the end of this mystery. If my parents are here, this is where they'll be.

"I'll be careful," I whisper back. "I promise."

"Let me go first," he says.

"You're kidding, right?"

His face flashes with ... anger? "Hannah, why can't you let anyone else do anything for you? Why do you always have to be the one to go first? To never accept help from others?"

"Because I don't need help from others," I say.

"It's okay to need help," Ethan says.

"I know it is," I say. "But I'm still not letting you go first. These are my parents."

Ethan presses his fingers to his eyebrows in frustration. "Fine, but stay close."

Together we continue the rest of the way to the giant olive tree, and we skirt around it slowly. On the complete opposite side is an arched opening, revealing a hollowed-out interior. Dumped around the arched opening is camping and hiking gear like Ethan and I carry. It's state-of-the-art, just like we have. There are two large packs, so big that I almost don't see our outfitter Scott motionless on the ground next to them.

I rush over to where Scott lies on the grass and squat down next to him.

"Scott?" I say, shaking him.

He doesn't move. And though I've never seen a dead body, I've been around dying animals enough to know that it's too late for Scott. His body is limp, and his neck is turned at a funny angle. Panic hits me. We'd just seen him alive, not two weeks ago. Whoever hired him has killed him.

CHAPTER 29

"HE'S DEAD," I SAY TO ETHAN AS HE JOINS ME. My
hands hover above Scott because I can't bring myself to
believe that he's really gone. That someone would have killed
him. But this also means that whoever got here ahead of us will
absolutely kill for the Code of Enoch.

"He could have fallen," Ethan says, but his voice sounds
weak, like even he doesn't believe it.

"Oh god, my parents." If they're inside, they're in serious
trouble. I pull my pack off and quietly set it on the ground.

"Just wait, Hannah," Ethan says. "We need to be careful."

"We need to get inside," I say. Before he can even try to talk
me out of it, I step around the backpacks and into the arched
opening of the olive tree.

The inside has been carved out nearly completely, creating a huge open space. The interior of the tree, like the world
outside it, glows from the bioluminescent life forms, and moss
covers the walls here, too, providing warmth. There is no one

around, as if whoever does live here has vanished. But just at the edge of my hearing, voices begin to drift my way.

"Can you hear what they're saying?" Ethan whispers as he comes up beside me.

I'm overwhelmed with thankfulness that he is here. That I'm not alone. "I can't tell. It sounds like arguing."

At first glance, the carved-out tree seems devoid of anything. But then I notice, at the edges of the tree, a staircase spiraling down, into the earth below. I nod in the direction of the top of the steps, and we tiptoe over.

I place a finger to my lips, to let him know we need to be quiet. At this point, surprise may be the only thing on our side. It's not like we've brought weapons along to fight.

I sneak down, one step at a time, cursing our giant caving boots. Each footfall of ours sounds like a wooly mammoth. The steps spiral around the perimeter of the tree though a wall prevents me from seeing what's below. It's only after we've made a complete turn of the tree, that I realize what we've walked into. By then it is too late.

Three people stand in a large underground room. One wears hiking gear and must have been the one who hired Scott to lead him down here. The one who killed Scott. The one who will kill us if we aren't smart. My eyes shift to the other two, and I recognize them immediately.

"Mom? Dad?" I say before I can stop myself. Every bit of me wants to run across the room, warn them about the danger they're in.

At my words, all eyes shift my way. My parents' eyes fill with panic. But they don't say anything. Instead they shift their gaze to Ethan as he joins me at the bottom of the steps. But instead of looking at my parents, Ethan stares at the man who must be here on behalf of Amino Corp.

"Dad?" Ethan says.

His voice echoes the denial that floods my mind. His father can't be the one who is here. He may have been interested in the Code of Enoch, may have tried to gather all the pieces for his boss, Doctor Bingham, but is he the kind of person who would kill for it?

"You shouldn't be here, Ethan," the man who, now that I see him, I recognize as an older version of the man I saw in the old photos. "Neither of you should be here. You weren't supposed to make it this far. I left the false path, hoping you would turn back. I pulled the rigging across the river."

"You killed Scott," I say. I still can't believe it. "How could you do that?"

Ethan's dad's eyes widen. "I didn't kill him. I swear. It was an accident. I tried to help."

"What kind of accident?" I say. "Because as near as I can tell, his neck's been snapped."

"He was climbing the tree, trying to look inside," Ethan's dad says. "But the tree. It came alive. It threw him to the ground. I swear it did."

I want to believe him. If the tree is like everything else around here, almost sentient, then maybe it's possible. But still ... his eyes dart back and forth between Ethan and me.

"Oh god, Hannah, you can't be here. You have to leave," Mom says. She stays where she is, next to Dad, shifting backward just the smallest amount. Her slight movement is enough that I can see something behind her. A stone tablet.

The Code of Enoch.

The world seems to freeze around me, and for a moment, it's just me and the tablet alone in this room. It calls me. It tells me all the wonderful things it is capable of doing. Of creating. It makes me believe anything is possible.

The world returns. This must be the Code. What we are looking for. And even in the tense situation, so many thoughts flow through me in that moment. I've found my parents. They are alive. Protecting the Code of Enoch. Which is real. Except everything that Ethan and I have done to find it has led his father here, too. Whatever happens, this is all our fault.

"Hannah, your mother's right," Dad says, and his face is pained and filled with love all at the same time. "You need to leave."

Oh, how I've missed that face. I want nothing more than to rush over and hug them both. To tell them how much I love them. I want them returned to me now. I want them to reverse time and make them never leave me in the first place.

"I came to find you," I say weakly.

Mom's face is ashen. "You shouldn't have. It's too dangerous."

Ethan's dad looks to Mom. "It's not too dangerous. And it's been hidden long enough. You two stopped me before, something I will never as long as I live forgive you for. Because of you Caden died. But this time you won't get in the way of bringing the Code back to the real world where it belongs, not hidden away in some fantasyland doing no one any good at all. This time I will make things right. In the hands of a company like Amino Corp, this thing could save millions of lives. People don't have to die like Caden did."

Mom's eyes fill with tears. "Stephen, no matter how much you want it to, it won't bring back Caden. It can't do that. And I'm so sorry."

Mom's tears only fuel Ethan's dad's anger. "Don't you think I know that? Of course it won't bring him back. But it can prevent so many others from having to suffer like he did. Like we've suffered since he died. Our son. You ripped our son from us. You may as well have killed him yourself."

"Dad, Caden got sick," Ethan says. "That happens."

Ethan's dad is so angry that he's shaking. "He could have been healed except they stood in our way. You would have a brother right now if they hadn't stopped me before. Instead, he's dead."

Ethan opens his mouth like he's going to say something, but then he closes it as if he changes his mind. My heart breaks at the fact that the Olivers lost their son, but my parents did what they felt was right for the world, not just for Caden.

Finally, Ethan says, "Could it really have healed him?"

Mr. Oliver levels his eyes on my parents. "Yes. It really could have. And even though our son will never smile again, we can still use the Code to heal others. To save so many. Cancer. AIDS. Ebola. These things will become a remnant of the past. Sickness will be only a memory. We can repair DNA strands, we can regrow organs. All these things are possible and more."

His words are hard to ignore. Something with that power could truly change the world.

"Can it really do all that?" I ask my parents because I have to know. Ethan's face has shifted, and his eyes look to the Code of Enoch almost greedily, now with hopes of taking it with him. Mine have, too, if I have to be honest.

Dad runs a hand through his hair. "Yes, it can do all that. Everything Ethan's dad says is possible. It created this world around us. These plants, the animals, the fish that swim in the sea. It could cure every disease known to man. It could make old age a thing of the past. All these things and more, the Code of Enoch is capable of."

"Which is why it can never be returned to humanity," Mom says, her eyes still fixed on me as if she refuses to look away. I can't look away from my parents either. I can't believe that they're really here.

"That makes no sense," Mr. Oliver says. He grits his teeth and flexes his fingers, and it's only then that I see him reaching for something tucked into the waistband of his pants.

He's got a gun.

I don't shout out because he hasn't reached for it yet. Maybe we can still get out of this peacefully.

"You know it makes sense, Stephen," Mom says. "Imagine

that power in the hands of mortals. Yes, diseases could be cured, but as many and more new diseases could be created. Entire races could be wiped out, simply by customizing a disease specifically for their DNA type. Biological warfare would escalate to a scale we could never imagine. People could be killed with a thought. The Code of Enoch in the wrong hands would bring the end of the world."

Mr. Oliver's eyes are wide. "So we never let it fall into the wrong hands. We protect it."

"We can't protect it," Dad says. "Not out there. Imagine Hitler getting his hands on the Code of Enoch. Stalin. Leaders throughout history. They would see the potential in moments, and once they started using it, it could never be stopped. It's why we have to keep it here. Protect it here. Why it's been that way forever. And why it has to stay that way."

Silence fills the room, and I think—hope—that my parents' words are making sense to those around me. They're definitely bringing me back to the reality of the danger in front of us. Ethan ... I can't read his face. But there is no understanding on his dad's face. Nothing except the desire for the Code.

Mr. Oliver lunges for me then before I know what's happening. Before I can do anything to stop him. He grabs me with one of his arms and pulls his gun out with the other. Mom shrieks as he puts the gun to my head.

I don't move. I don't dare because one wrong move and he could pull the trigger.

"Let her go, Stephen," Dad says. His face is filled with horror.

"This is lunacy."

Mr. Oliver shakes his head. "This is reality. Nobody moves unless I tell them to, or I will kill her. I will pull the trigger."

His breath is hot on my neck. His hand that holds my body and head is clammy from sweat.

"Dad, let her go," Ethan says. His voice shakes, and though he's only a couple feet away, if he tries to grab me, his dad could kill me.

"No, Ethan. I'm not going to let her go. And here is what's going to happen. You are going to walk over to the Code of Enoch. You are going to pick it up. If Hannah's parents try to stop you, if they interfere in any way at all, then I will pull the trigger. I'll kill Hannah first, and then I will kill them."

"We can't let you have it," Dad says, even though there is this part of me that wants him to say something, anything, to make everything all better. My heart pounds in my ears. My vision is tunneling. I get it then, in that moment. Ethan's dad is truly beyond help. The death of his child has done something to him. Pushed him over an edge. I need to get away. Get the gun from him.

"Dad, no, I won't do it," Ethan says. "I'm not going to get it. Don't you see? Hannah's parents are right. Look at you. Look at what you're doing just to get the Code of Enoch now, here. What do you think people will do once it's back in the world?"

My heart melts in that moment, knowing that Ethan is siding with me, not his dad. But I can't move to meet his eye without risking my life.

"Put the gun down, Stephen," Dad says. "Just put it down, nice and slow, and we'll resolve this all."

Mr. Oliver shakes his head. "I can't do that. I've been looking for the Code of Enoch for too long to let it slip away. It's too close. I am going to take it. Finally, after all this time."

"And I'm not going to let you," Dad says, and then without warning, he lunges for Ethan's dad.

Mr. Oliver isn't expecting this, but he recovers from his surprise quickly. He takes the gun from my head and points it at Dad instead. I elbow him hard in the side, and he lets me go. I twist out of his grasp and grab for the gun.

I'm too late. The gun goes off.

CHAPTER 30

THE WORLD SHATTERS AROUND ME AS DAD FALLS TO THE ground. I hear someone scream. Maybe it's me. I rush over to Dad, not caring that Mr. Oliver still has the gun, still aims it at me.

"No, Dad, no." I fall to the ground beside Dad and try to press my hands over the giant hole in his chest, but blood pours from it, out of him.

He can't die. Can't die. This can't be happening.

His head falls to the side. His face drains of color. At the moment when I've finally found him, finally had him return to my life, Dad is dead.

I look to Mom. Horror fills her face, and her eyes brim with tears.

"What did you do?" Mom shouts. Her hands are clenched into fists, and she wants to run to Dad. But she stays by the Code of Enoch though it looks like it is killing her to do so.

"That was an accident," Mr. Oliver says. "I didn't mean to do that. But as long as you do what I want, nothing else will happen." He motions with the gun. "Ethan, get me the Code before something else happens that we'll all regret."

Fury fills Ethan's eyes. He spins around to face his dad. "No, Dad, I'm not going to do it. I'm not going to blindly follow you while you destroy the world around you. I can't believe how stupid you're being. Do you see what you've done? You've killed someone."

Mr. Oliver looks incredulous. "I said it was an accident. He was trying to stop me. How can you not see that I'm doing this for both of us? For all of us? For your mother. For Caden."

"Caden is dead!" Ethan says. "He's dead! He's not coming back. He never will."

"Get me the Code now," Ethan's dad says. His eyes don't focus. He's not thinking straight. Anger and hatred have driven him to a place I'm not sure he'll ever be able to claw his way out of.

Tears roll down my face. I blink them out of my eyes.

"It's not for you, Dad," Ethan says. "It's not for anyone. Why can't you see that? We have to destroy it." And then before anyone can stop him, he rushes to the Code of Enoch.

Mom screams at him and reaches for him, but he shoves her aside. She falls to the ground, landing hard. Then Ethan grabs for the Code, as if he's going to pick it up and throw it across the room.

Lightning streaks from the Code, straight into Ethan's chest. Every muscle in my body tenses as a horrible silence fills the room punctuated only by the crackling of the lightning. Then Ethan falls to the ground.

Smoke begins to curl from his chest. Ethan's eyes go wide, as if he's only just realizing that he's been hurt. The smoke wisps around him, forming a spiral, almost like it represents his life leaving him, seeping away.

Mr. Oliver's eyes land on Ethan, there on the ground, and confusion and anger flicker across his face. He looks to Ethan, to the Code, then back to Ethan, then back to the Code again. And horror fills me completely. What he's done hasn't even registered on him. First Dad and now his own son. There is no end to Mr. Oliver's obsession.

I rush to Ethan's side, no longer afraid. No longer caring. Why had we even come on this journey in the first place? Why hadn't I just let this stay as it was, my parents missing, but alive? The Code of Enoch nothing but a fable that could have been forgotten. Then Ethan's dad would have never known where to go.

"Please be okay," I say, grabbing Ethan's hand. His eyes are having a hard time focusing. He opens his mouth, like he's trying to say something, but no words come out.

I turn my head, just enough that I can see Mom, rushing back to the Code of Enoch. I mouth a single word. *Please.*

Mom's eyes are filled with grief, but she understands. She places her hands on the Code of Enoch and closes her eyes. Where before lightning streaked out of the artifact, the room now explodes with light. Explodes out of her, as if somehow she's channeling it through her body.

Warmth fills me, so deep, so bright that I can't keep my eyes open. I squeeze Ethan's hand, and I let the light and warmth consume me. I think of trees and flowers and of happy times, playing with my parents when I was a child, walking through our menagerie, watering the plants in the greenhouse. I remember Dad reading to me, late at night, teaching me Latin names for the world of plants and animals around us. And then I think back to when my parents vanished. When Uncle Randall moved into Easton Estate to take care of me. How I hated that my parents were gone, dead I thought. I knew I had to make them proud. Make them happy. It became my passion, as if I had to prove myself to them even though they weren't there to see. And now, with the light and the warmth around me, I realize that the need to prove myself vanished long ago and that I became my own person.

I squeeze Ethan's hand harder.

He squeezes back, strong.

The warmth fades, and when I open my eyes, the light coming from both Mom and the Code of Enoch diminishes. Ethan's eyes meet mine, and he smiles, a smile filled with life. There is no sign of the smoke. No sign of his impending death. The Code has healed him.

I lean over and kiss him and then rush back to Dad. Unlike the life that has been returned to Ethan, Dad is still dead.

"It can't bring the dead back to life," Mom says, and tears stream down her face. "It's why we have the graveyard outside.

To bury the protectors once they've passed on."

I dare a glance back in Mr. Oliver's direction, horrified at what he will do next, but a complete transformation has come over him. His face is void of anger and hatred, as if the Code has removed it from him completely. Healed him along with Ethan and me.

He lets out a wail that fills the chamber around us, then throws his gun to the ground and rushes to his son. "Oh, Ethan, what have I done?"

Ethan's sitting up now, and Mr. Oliver grabs him in a hug that Ethan returns. And it's in this moment that it dawns on me that there is nothing separating Mom and me now. I rush over to her because she refuses to leave the Code of Enoch. She pulls me into a hug so fierce that I worry it will crush my ribs, yet I don't care.

"I've missed you every day, Hannah," Mom says. "God, how I've missed you. Watching you grow up. Seeing everything you've now become. We never intended to leave you. We came here to destroy it. But when we got here, we learned that it couldn't be destroyed. You saw what happened when Ethan tried. And then the protector passed on, leaving us with no choice. We had to stay and protect it. One of us was going to return, but our map was destroyed in the water. We had no way out."

"I understand, Mom," I say, and just being able to say that simple word, Mom, and knowing that she is here to listen to me, lets me know that everything will be okay.

CHAPTER 31

MR. OLIVER AND ETHAN CARRY DAD OUTSIDE. THEY DIG graves for both him and Scott, and we bury them there in the clearing in the middle of the forest. We fashion two simple stones, just like the others. Mom kneels by Dad's grave and presses her hands to the soil. Her lips move, but I can't hear her words. I don't think I'm meant to. He's all she's had for the last eleven years, and now he's gone. Though I feel like a hole has been ripped in my heart, I don't think it can even compare to what she must be feeling. But her moment at the graveside is brief. She stands and walks back toward the tree, resting her hand on my shoulder for a fleeting, comforting moment as she does so.

I wait for everyone else to leave, and then I kneel by Dad's grave. I stay there with him, telling him all the things I would tell him if he was still alive, pretending he still is, just for this moment.

"I don't know what's going to happen now, Dad," I say. "I can't leave Mom here. But I don't want to stay here either. Maybe I should. Maybe that's what I'm meant to do."

I don't bother wiping the tears from my face because there is no one around to see them.

"But I also don't want to leave Uncle Randall. Or Lucas. Or Ethan," I say to Dad. "I know that's silly. Ethan and I have only been hanging out for a little while, but I feel like he's meant to be a part of my life. And I don't know what I'm supposed to do."

Dad doesn't answer, but the birds sing around me. The voices in the wind whisper in the trees like the dead are talking to me. I only hope that I am able to make everything work out.

I walk back to the tree and down the steps to where Mom stands by the Code of Enoch.

"I can't leave it, Hannah," she says once I enter the room. "It has to have a protector."

I close my eyes. Take a deep breath. I've been practicing the line, and each time I say it, it gets easier to accept.

"I'll stay here with you," I say.

Anger flashes in Mom's eyes. "Absolutely not."

"I will. It's the only way."

"It's unacceptable," Mom says. "There is no way you are staying here when you have such a wonderful life ahead of you out there."

"But I can't leave you." The thought of leaving Mom, of never seeing her again now that I know she's alive, is too much.

Her eyes brim with tears. "You have to, Hannah."

Ethan comes up beside me and takes my hand. "I don't want you to stay here either which I know is totally selfish. But not now. Not when ..." His words trail off, but I think I know where they were going because they're the same words that are running through my mind.

"I have to," I say.

"What if you don't?" Mr. Oliver says, speaking for the first time since I've come back into the room.

"What other choice is there?" I say. "I am not going to leave my mom."

Ethan's dad takes a deep breath and lets it out before speaking. "I've had the last eleven years with my son, and I didn't appreciate a single minute of them. All I could think of was what I had lost. What could have been if only I'd found the Code. My mind was a fog of hatred. I had eleven years, and I never lived one moment of them. Whereas you, Hannah, you lost as much as I did back then, and yet you went on with your life. You moved forward, and for that I hated you. I hated your family for what I thought they had done to me when none of it was their fault. My life, or the lack of how I've lived it, is my own fault. I'm done blaming others."

"Dad ...," Ethan begins, but his dad puts his hand up to stop him.

"As we buried Robert, and as I saw everything that is out there, everything that is possible, I came to a decision. There is only one thing that makes sense for everyone. One thing that will work."

"I stay here, as I have been," Mom says, "and you take Ethan and Hannah back to the surface."

Mr. Oliver shakes his head. "I stay here, protect the Code

293

of Enoch with my life, not only as payment for the wrong I've done but because it's the right thing to do. It's what must be done. What I have to do. And in turn, you take Ethan and Hannah back to the surface. You live the life you missed. It's a life without Robert, for which I will be eternally sorry. I can't change that now, but I can do this."

Silence fills the room. There it is, right in front of me. A perfect solution. A solution I want so much.

But Mom slowly shakes her head. "I can't let you do that."

"You don't have much choice," Mr. Oliver says.

"I do," Mom says. "I am the protector."

Mr. Oliver nods. "True. But look inside your heart. What does it tell you that you need to do, Laura? What is the best path we can all take from here? If I return to the world above, I return a failure. A murderer. As much as I want it to have been, Scott's death was no accident. Neither was Robert's. I was insane with my desire for the Code, but those were still my actions. I can never bring myself back from that up there, no matter how hard I try, no matter what I do. But here, now, I can do something real. Something that will matter forever. Something that will maybe, partially, make up for what I've done."

Ethan's face is a mask of indecision. This is his dad we're talking about, and yet everything Mr. Oliver says makes sense. It is the perfect solution … for me and Mom at least.

I look to Mom. How much I want her to say yes. I implore her with my eyes. And in response, without a single backward glance, she steps away from the Code of Enoch forever.

294

CHAPTER 32

"YOU CAN NEVER LEAVE THIS PLACE," MOM SAYS AS MR. Oliver steps up to the Code of Enoch. "We'll take all the copies of the map with us."

The Code is quiet now, so unlike before when it had come to life and healed Ethan. Almost like he knows what I'm thinking, Ethan presses his hands against his chest where the lightning had struck.

"I understand," Ethan's dad says, and then his eyes shift to his son.

I feel like I should have no part in the words that pass between them. Mom and I step away as they talk, but their words still drift over to us.

"I am so sorry," he says.

"Dad, it's—" Ethan starts.

"It's okay?" Mr. Oliver says. "No. It's not. But I can't change what I've done. I can only do what's right now. The decision is made, and I am so happy about it. Relieved. I feel like it's the only thing I've ever done right in my life."

Ethan says something, but his voice catches in his throat, and then Mr. Oliver grabs his son in a giant hug.

"Please tell your mother that I love her," Mr. Oliver says. "And know that I love you, too. I've always been proud of you, even though you may never have felt that way. I'll miss not seeing you grow up."

"The Code of Enoch will keep you young," Mom says, seeing that their conversation is coming to an end. "Nearly immortal."

Mr. Oliver runs a hand through his thinning hair. "I wondered why you didn't look any older than you had the last time I saw you."

Mom nods. "It's why the flood heroes were rumored to have such long lives."

"They say Noah lived until he was over nine hundred," I say.

"And that was before he brought the Code here," Mom says. "It's kept us young, nourished, healthy."

"I'll be younger than you someday, Ethan," Mr. Oliver says.

"We'll come back and visit," Ethan says.

I know he's joking, but both Mom and Mr. Oliver shake their heads.

"No one can ever come back here," Mom says. "When we get back, we have to hide the pieces of the Deluge Segment. Better this time."

We retrieve our stolen copy of the map from Scott's backpack along with Mr. Oliver's copy. We also make sure we have the map we decoded from the scrolls. Once we're out of here, we'll destroy everything.

"I found the copy of the Deluge Segment you hid in the Canopic jar," I say.

Mom puts her hand to her head. "Why did I ever make that copy?"

"Because this had to happen," I say. Fate has brought all this together.

"Amy will hide our piece," Mr. Oliver says. "And please, Ethan, bring our families together again. Your mother and Hannah's mother used to be best friends. I know Amy misses her terribly. She never got over everything that happened."

Mom and I say our final goodbyes and then we leave the tree, giving Ethan and his father a few more minutes before we start back. And though there are a million things I want to talk to Mom about, I find, in those moments that pass, all I want to do is have her wrap her arms around me and tell me that she loves me.

∞

Ethan, Mom, and I walk away from the massive olive tree, back through the clearing where we've buried Dad. Mom pauses, only briefly, and says a few words over his grave, and then we continue on, into the meadow by the ocean.

"Your father and I loved this place so much," she says as we walk through the flowers. "We spent weeks out here. We sailed on the ocean. We communed with the animals. We created new species, testing the limits of the Code. It was everything

297

we'd ever worked for. Truly unbelievable."

"It's almost a shame, isn't it?" I say because even though I can logically see that it can never be in our world, being a scientist, it's also hard to let it go.

Mom sighs deeply. "A tragic shame, but we have no choice. We have to leave it behind."

And that's exactly what we do. We have enough supplies from the extra packs such that we are ready for the journey, or at least as ready as we'll ever be. We head back through the tunnel, away from the light of this impossible world. We cross the river and pull the circular center artifact from where we placed it. The stones in the river separate, once again making the river impossible to cross. The Bridge of Noah vanishes. Then we find our way back.

We tell Mom about the room with the scrolls, but we all agree that there is no point in returning to it. We're not going to pilfer from it. The stories need to remain where they are. Bringing them to light will only keep the mystery of the Code of Enoch alive. Even though we plan to hide the map pieces, the rumors of the Code itself may always exist. And we all know that as technology improves, with radar and sonar and underground mapping, this place could still be discovered.

Mom is quiet at first, and I realize it's because she's containing her sorrow at losing Dad. My heart aches when I think about him. I loved him, and I miss him—even more now that I've seen him. His death has left a hole that will never be filled. And yet, even with his death, I've gained a parent this day, something I never thought would happen as long as I lived. I am going to make the most of the happiness that thought brings me and not dwell on what cannot be anymore.

Having Mom along definitely puts a crimp in any romantic moments between Ethan and me. But one evening, after we've settled, Mom heads down the tunnel to fill our water bottles. I'm alone in the dark with Ethan, and almost like our minds are working together toward one goal, he presses me up against the rock wall of the cavern. My lips find his, and the next thing I know, we're kissing. Every wonderful emotion I've ever felt explodes through me. I trace my hands under the back of his shirt, feeling his muscles harden at my touch. His hands run through my hair, down my side. He kisses the nape of my neck, sending chills through my entire body. I pull him so close that there isn't any space between us because I have to feel him against me. To know that he is real, and that he is not going away.

"Hannah, I—," he starts saying as he's kissing me, but I press my mouth against his to stop any words he might say because even the thought of what the words might be scares me. I'm not ready to move too fast. I don't want to ruin anything we might have ahead of us. But, that said, I also have no intention of letting him go anywhere.

Our kisses stop at the sound of Mom clearing her throat ... loudly. Her flashlight points on the ground in front of her but lights up the room enough that I'm sure she saw us.

Ethan and I step apart.

"Did you find water?" I ask as I try to calm my heart, which is wild and beating out of control.

Mom smiles, though sadness pulls at the sides of her eyes. "Yeah, I found water. I filled all three canteens. I double checked our supplies. I tried to spend as much time away as I could. But you'll have to remember that I'm still your mom. I couldn't stay away any longer."

How much I love her in that moment. And how happy I am to have a mom who cares.

CHAPTER 33

It takes ten days, all uphill including the endless days of steps. My legs have become so strong that they make me think my flesh has dissolved and been replaced by steel cables running under my skin. The steps keep going even though multiple times I'm sure we've reached the end. I'm convinced it will never come. That we're on some kind of stair-stepper to nowhere. But finally we reach the top.

"Are we ready for the real world?" Mom asks.

Popcorn. Chocolate. Lucas. He's going to think I fell off the face of the earth.

"Totally ready," I say, squeezing Ethan's hand.

Ethan and I align the four symbols, and the world splits in half above us. Mom and I hoist Ethan out first who helps Mom up next and then me. Then we rotate the symbols apart so they are no longer lined up. The crack in the cavern floor rejoins, the small lake refills with water, and the underground world is sealed away forever.

We rest there for the evening because all of our heads are still spinning from the endless staircase. But the next day we head on, and it's not long before we hear voices other than our own for the first time in days.

Four spelunkers have set up camp and sit around in a circle talking a language which I'm guessing Ethan knows because he walks up and starts talking to them and laughing like they're all having a good old time while Mom and I stand there watching.

Ethan keeps motioning back in the direction we've come from, and the cavers, two guys and two girls, are shaking their heads in confusion. Finally, Ethan comes back over to us.

"They're Ukrainian," Ethan says. "They said they were sent on a search mission. That some spelunkers disappeared a little over three weeks ago and nobody who'd been this way since had seen them."

"So what did you tell them?" I ask. We haven't thought this far. The last thing we want is people exploring Krubera, looking for missing cavers.

Ethan shakes his head. "I couldn't say that my dad was dead, Hannah. I know maybe I should, but I can't bring myself to do it. So I told them that the three of us were fine. That we descended together. And that we hadn't seen anyone else."

"It's okay, Ethan," Mom says. "The secret will be safe. You're the only one who would go looking for your father, and you already know he's okay. Some people may look for Scott. People will buzz about the story for a couple months. Maybe a year. They'll send scouting parties. But pretty soon that will stop. They'll start coming up with stories to explain why they can't find them. Someone will say that they saw them exit the cave. That they aren't lost. And then all but legends will fade away."

Like the legends of my parents and their descent. They'd disappeared into the cave and moved from reality into myth.

Ethan speaks with the Ukrainian spelunkers for a while longer who offer to phone Adgur and Daur for us because they've wired a phone line. Then we continue on, moving uphill, toward our destination. Gradually our eyes begin to adjust to the dark again as we reach the point where light seeps in to the cave. After two more days, we finally reach the wide opening at the bottom of the descent shaft.

Mom breaths deep, smelling the air of the world above her. "It's been so long ..." Her words trail off, as if there is no real way to express what she wants to say.

According to my watch, it's late afternoon, but the Ukrainians had promised to call ahead. Still there is no sign of Adgur and Daur. I'm getting ready to insist that we hook ourselves to the ropes and begin climbing because I don't want to spend one more minute in this cave than I have to when a rope drops for us along with a note from Adgur and Daur written in spotty but readable English.

We come for you. Hook to rope and we pull you up.
—Adgur and Daur

The Ukrainian spelunkers had gotten our message through!

I hook myself to the line, double securing it and also grabbing the safety rope just in the event this one fails, and then I ascend the shaft. The sun is so bright and warm, it nearly blinds me. I close my eyes and soak it in as I near the top. Adgur and Daur begin chatting excitedly as I come into view, though I have no clue what they're saying. I open my eyelids just barely into slits to protect my eyes as the brothers reach out and help pull me up the final way, lifting me out of the small crack in the earth. One of them, Adgur maybe, slips sunglasses over my eyes. I hug him and his brother because I'm so happy to see them. So happy to be back, ready to continue my life.

But Adgur doesn't return the hug. He's tense. And as my eyes adjust to the brightness, I see why.

Doctor Bingham, President and CEO of Amino Corp stands there on the precipice of Krubera Cave. Surrounding him are four guards, all with guns pointed directly at me. Our eyes meet, and dread fills my body. This can't be happening. Not now. Not after everything we've been through. Everything we've lost.

"Hannah Hawkins," Doctor Bingham says. "I can't wait to hear about your adventure."

CHAPTER 34

I WANT TO SCREAM OUT TO ETHAN AND MOM TO WARN them, but they're too far below. They have no reason not to hook themselves to the rope and begin the ascent.

"What are you doing here?" I ask Doctor Bingham, trying not to think about the guns aimed at me. It's way easier said than done. All the guards have to do is pull the trigger.

Adgur and Daur eye him and the guards warily. They can't have helped these criminals ... unless Doctor Bingham paid them off. Or threatened them.

"Do you have any idea how long I've been working to get the Code of Enoch?" Doctor Bingham says. "Do you have any idea what this means to me?"

I have to stall. It's my only option until I come up with a plan.

"What does it mean to you?" I ask slowly, trying to keep my breathing under control.

Doctor Bingham laughs. "It means my life. It means my job. It means everything."

"There is no Code of Enoch," I say.

"But there is," Doctor Bingham says. "And when I bring it back to Amino Corp, there is no way they'll be able to fire me."

This is something I can latch on to.

"They were going to fire you?" I ask, hoping I sound like I haven't heard this rumor.

He nods. "The Board of Directors. They said I was ruining the company. They had the nerve to say that I never would have gotten the job in the first place if it weren't for nepotism. Then they gave me a month. That's when I knew that I had to renew my search for the Code. It would be the answer to everything. I'd bring it back to them, show them its power, and they'd beg me to stay."

Oh my god. Doctor Bingham has completely gone rogue. Amino Corp isn't behind this. It's been him, alone, this entire time. And with someone like him running Amino Corp, it's no wonder they want to get rid of him. But even if he is rogue and out of control, that doesn't change the fact that I'm in the middle of nowhere with four guns pointed at me. I have to get him to stand down.

"We don't have the Code," I say. "It doesn't exist. It's just a rumor. It's not real."

Doctor Bingham smiles at me like I'm a silly little girl. "But I know that's a lie. I've been in close contact with Stephen Oliver. He always wanted the Code. He was the perfect person to pull over to my side to help me. When I originally got the idea, I remembered how much he'd wanted it before. So I mentioned it to him and said I had a lead. You should have seen him. His eyes lit up like I'd offered him a billion dollars. He was more than eager to help.

"We had two pieces of the map. We only needed the final piece and the location to start the journey. Once I realized that you had it, I had your copy of the piece stolen. Then we tracked Ethan's credit card usage. It was so simple. As soon as we figured out where you two were, I put Stephen on a private jet straight here to go after you. He hired the guide, and they set off. We stayed in touch constantly until a couple of weeks ago."

My hands are shaking, but I can't let him know that I'm scared. I put on my best you're-full-of-crap look. "There's no cell signal in the cave. You're lying." Unless Ethan's dad had a signal booster also. My stomach turns at the thought.

Even as we speak, Adgur and Daur are already pulling on the rope, helping bring up either Mom or Ethan. I want to scream at them to stop.

"He had a signal booster, just like you did."

It confirms my worst fears. But even if this is true, Doctor Bingham still has no concrete proof of the Code. He would have lost signal the same time we did.

"Why don't you go ahead and tell me what happened after I lost contact with him?" Doctor Bingham says.

He wants to pretend he knows everything, but he's still not sure. He needs me to corroborate the story.

"He's dead," I say quickly before I have time to think out the entire story. "We found his body, washed up next to an underground river. We think he fell in and the current killed him."

Doctor Bingham doesn't buy it for a second. That much is clear. Before I have time to add any more to it, though, Adgur and Daur haul Mom out from Krubera Cave. She closes her eyes because they have to adjust just like mine did.

Doctor Bingham sees her, and his mouth opens in complete disbelief. "Laura Hawkins?"

I realize that my story has a major hole in it that I haven't thought out: the presence of Mom here, now, after being missing for so many years. I hadn't bothered to think up anything since I hadn't expected anyone to notice or care.

"Doctor Bingham?" Mom says, squinting at him. She raises her hand to block her eyes from the blinding sun.

Adgur and Daur lower the rope once more. At least Ethan isn't going to be stranded down there. What isn't so good is that two of the guards point their guns at Mom.

"Now this is a surprise," Doctor Bingham says. "How is it that you are here, now, when no one has heard from you in eleven years?"

I think fast because Mom has no idea what I've already said. "She's been living in Gagra. We reconnected with her there, and we went looking for the Code of Enoch together. But like I already told you, we didn't find it. It doesn't exist."

"I don't believe you," Doctor Bingham says. "But it doesn't matter. This is perfect. Your mother will tell me everything she knows, won't you, Laura? Especially if her daughter's life is on the line."

Mom's eyes, now adjusted, meet mine. I telepathically plead with her not to say anything. Her eyes confirm what I already know. She won't give away the secret. She's lost her husband, given up eleven years of her life to protect the Code. She knows that she has to continue that protection no matter the cost.

"It doesn't exist," Mom says. "What Hannah said is the truth. I've been living in Gagra for the last ten years, researching the cave, trying to unearth the secrets. I explored it a multitude of times. Robert died on one of our trips. But it's all been futile. There is no Code."

"I don't believe you," Doctor Bingham says.

As we all watch, Adgur and Daur help Ethan from the cave.

"Where is your father, Ethan?" Doctor Bingham says before either Mom or I can say anything.

"Don't tell him anything," I call out.

I hear one of the guns click, like it's being cocked. My blood freezes.

"Another word and you won't like how this all turns out," Doctor Bingham says. "Now tell me, Ethan, where is your father?"

Ethan's eyes haven't even had time to adjust. They're open barely to slits. But he's not an idiot. He catches on to the fact that things are definitely not as they should be.

"I haven't seen him," Ethan says, which, though a solid lie, does not in any way corroborate my story.

One of the guards points his gun at Ethan.

"Hannah told me he died," Doctor Bingham says. "In the cave. She also told me that you found the Code of Enoch."

"I didn't say that. Don't say anything!" I scream to Ethan.

Doctor Bingham walks slowly and tears Ethan's pack away from him. Then he unzips it and starts pulling things out. He's looking for the Code.

"It's not in there," I say. "I told you that we didn't find it."

"You told me it didn't exist," Doctor Bingham says. "But I think I'll find the map and go looking myself."

I have to get the pack from him. We can't have him finding the map or the center piece of the Deluge Segment. Those could bring him right back to the Code.

"Don't let him near Mom's pack!" I scream, and I run for it, hoping to deceive him. She, of the three of us, doesn't have anything of value in it.

My deception doesn't work for a second. He reaches into Ethan's bag and pulls out the circular artifact.

"Now what is this?" he says.

My mind spins. I can't think of any way out of this. I glance to Ethan, begging him for help.

"It's a key," Ethan says. "You have to hold it over the opening of the cave."

"Ethan, no!" I yell, putting as much anger and betrayal in my voice as possible.

"I'm sorry, Hannah. He's going to figure it out. Maybe if we tell him, he'll let us go."

Doctor Bingham actually smiles. He nods at the four guards

who lower their weapons. "Go on, Ethan."

Ethan sighs. "If you hold it over the opening, it casts a shadow. You have to make sure you angle it just right, and when you do, you'll see four symbols. Those unlock a secret tunnel. Those are your answer."

Doctor Bingham narrows his eyes. "Show me."

"Don't do it!" I say.

"I have to, Hannah," Ethan says. He walks toward the edge of the cave opening. I want to yank him back because he's way too close.

"Step back, Ethan," I say. This is not part of any good plan. A good plan would be us running away while Doctor Bingham looks for the alleged symbols.

"Ethan is going to show me, or I'll push him in," Doctor Bingham says. He raises a hand and rests it on Ethan's back.

Wait, what! There's no way I can wrestle a gun from one of the guards. I need to do something else.

I rush forward and grab for Ethan, but my stomach lurches as I realize how close I am to the edge of Krubera Cave. Vertigo hits, and my head spins.

"Hannah!" I hear Mom shout, and she runs for me.

"I've had enough of you, Hannah Hawkins," Doctor Bingham says, and he shoves Ethan out of the way and grabs for me instead. But he misjudges his steps and hooks his foot around the safety rope Adgur and Daur are pulling from the cave. It throws him off balance, and his arms wave in the air as he tries to find something to hold on to. But there's nothing around, except me and Ethan. The center piece of the Deluge Segment flies from his hands, falling into the mouth of the cave.

Doctor Bingham grabs for me. I shift, and he catches the strap of my pack instead. I lean out, way too close to the edge of the precipice. Things begin to slip from my pockets, falling into the cave below: my phone, my thermometer, energy bars. Ethan grabs hold of one of my arms and Adgur and Daur grab the other. But Doctor Bingham's weight is too much. Daur tries to reach with his free hand for Doctor Bingham. The straps of the pack rip as panic fills his face. It's holding on by only a thread, and then finally the straps break, and Doctor Bingham, president and CEO of Amino Corp, tumbles over the side of the crevasse and vanishes from sight as he falls into the mouth of Krubera Cave.

CHAPTER 35

ETHAN PULLS ME AWAY FROM THE EDGE OF THE CAVE.

My legs wobble as I sink to the ground and scoot backward. Mom rushes over to me, grabbing me in a hug to comfort me, but I'm shaking uncontrollably because that had been way too close.

"Another damned body retrieval," Adgur says to Daur in halting English, as if this is an everyday occurrence. "Daur, you radio the police."

At the word "police," my chest tenses, but there's no way around it. We have to face the real world. Our journey will eventually devolve into nothing but rumors. Teenagers trying to find something that didn't exist. And Doctor Bingham? I have no idea what the rumors will say about his part in all this.

With the threat of the police, the four guards take off, running, never looking back. They jump in a nearby truck and drive off, tires throwing rocks as they skid away. I don't know if Doctor Bingham hired them local or brought them from the

States. Either way, I don't think we'll be seeing them again.

While Adgur and Daur radio the authorities and begin the body retrieval, I wait for the world to settle around me.

It's a couple days before we can leave Gagra. Even though people have died and vanished in Krubera Cave before, the authorities need our statement. We all make sure that we're on exactly the same page before we talk to them, saying we stuck to the main path. That we'd never seen either Ethan's father or tour guide Scott while we were down there. The authorities nod as if this kind of thing happens all the time. But Scott was a local favorite, so there are a couple spelunking societies that want our story, too, just in case they decide to go looking for the two of them. Even if they do, they aren't going to find him. Scott and Mr. Oliver are beyond the hidden entrance. We consider trying to retrieve the center piece of the Deluge Segment, but decide that it's safer there than anywhere else. Even if someone finds it, they won't have any idea what it is.

After we've quelled as many rumors as we possibly can, it's on to Moscow, to visit the American Embassy. Since Mom has been off-grid for eleven years, she needs a new passport. Ethan's phone is trashed, and mine is lost, along with all the pictures I took along the way. So much for bringing images of the scrolls back for Uncle Randall to study.

With a not-so-quick stop into the nearest cell phone store, I'm able to buy a new one. No sooner is my new phone activated, a million messages begin to ping through. There are over a hundred texts and a full voicemail box of messages both from Lucas and Uncle Randall.

"So what's really up with this Lucas guy anyway?" Ethan asks as we sit there in a coffee shop in downtown Moscow. Mom's out seeing what she can find to wear since she's been wearing the same thing for years.

"I told you he's my best friend."

Ethan looks skeptical. "How many times did he text you? A thousand?"

"He was worried."

Ethan shakes his head. "Yeah, okay, you just keep telling yourself that. But he likes you way more than as a friend."

"He does not," I say, shaking my head because Ethan's crazy. Then I dial Lucas's number.

"Hannah!" he says, and just that like I am firmly replanted in this world.

I promise Lucas that I'm okay. That I will tell him everything when I get back, which should be in the next couple days. I tell him to make sure and let Uncle Randall know. But I don't tell Lucas about Mom. Not yet.

$$\infty$$

We left Boston in June, and now it's closing in on August as we board a private jet in Moscow for our return flight. We have to stop in London, so it takes us nearly fourteen hours to get back, but finally we land at Logan International Airport.

Three people wait for us as we leave the terminal. Lucas is there, holding Castor and Pollux in a pouch around his neck. I can't help but smile when they poke their darling heads out at the sound of my name. Ethan's mom is there also. Ethan called ahead and filled her in on most everything, so she would know what to expect. It was only fair that she knew ahead of time that her husband wasn't coming back. Ethan walks to his mom, who starts to cry, as she shakes her head and hugs her son.

Uncle Randall stands there, too, holding a crutch under his armpit because he's got a cast on his leg nearly up to his hip. When he sees Mom, disbelief flows down his face like water. He mouths her name and makes like he's going to move forward, but the crutch and cast make running out of the question. Mom runs to him and grabs her brother in a hug that makes my heart melt into a puddle.

"They missed you," Lucas says, pulling the pouch off from over his neck, returning Castor and Pollux to me.

"Thank you for taking care of them," I say, and I hug Lucas and kiss him on the cheek.

"I missed you, too, Hannah," Lucas says. "Jeez, don't do that to me again, okay? Or next time, you have to take me with you. I don't care what we have to tell my parents. Do you have any idea how many times I tried to text you?"

"Over two hundred?" I say because I'd counted on the flight back.

Lucas cringes. "Was it that many? Sorry, I didn't realize. But come on. You vanished."

"I told you exactly where I was going."

"Which may as well have been another planet," Lucas says. "No, wait, at least there are satellites out in space. We might have at least had a consistent signal that way."

I give him another hug. "Thanks for caring."

Ethan and his mom head home as does Lucas, and Mom, Uncle Randall, and I head to Easton Estate. Back in my own house—my own shower—water pours down on me. I wash away every memory of albino insects, dirt floors, and weeks without showers. Once I dry off and dress, I visit the animals, all of whom, even King Tort, act thrilled to see me. I've never appreciated Easton Estate more than I do today.

I want to give Mom her space because she hasn't been home in eleven years, but she's already waiting for me when I walk into the dining room.

"It doesn't look like anyone's touched our rooms since I left," Mom says.

I shrug, acting like it's no big deal. "We have enough space. There was no reason to." The true reason is that I wanted to hold onto my parents in that small way. Maybe it was my subconscious hope that they were still alive.

Mom's also changed clothes and showered. She motions at herself. "I'm guessing my clothes are totally out of style."

I bite my lip as I choose my words. "Well, high-waisted jeans are kind of coming back. But the polka-dots have to go."

I myself am back in my favorite pair of skinny jeans, my pink Uggs, and a black T-shirt that says TALK N Er Dy TO ME.

Mom pulls at the waist of her jeans. "I could borrow some of your clothes until we go shopping."

"Done," I say. We are about the same size now.

"You've grown so much, Hannah," Mom says. "And I missed it all."

"I'm still growing," I say. "Studies show that females continue to grow until their late teens."

Mom smiles. "Good. Because I promise you this: You may get sick of me and never want me around again, but I'm not going to miss one more minute of your life."

The next day everyone regroups at Easton Estate. Chef Lilly makes the best meal in the entire world, including Spanakopita and Lentil-Barley burgers. And even though it's only lunchtime, she makes S'mores Cake-In-A-Jar for dessert. Lucas has three servings. I sit with Ethan on one side of me and Lucas on the other in the dining room, and the three of us make the most awkward small talk because neither guy seems to be willing to accept the other. That'll have to change. They'll have to get used to each other because I have no plans of letting either one out of my life. Mom, Ethan's mom, and Uncle Randall also traipse through awkward conversations as Uncle Randall and Mrs. Oliver fill Mom in on all the discoveries and technology that's come about in the last eleven years. Mom excuses herself halfway through lunch and doesn't return until we're just finishing up. I don't think much about it except that everything must be a little overwhelming to her.

"We need to hide the other two pieces of the map," Mom says once she returns.

Uncle Randall fixes an eye on her. "Are there any more copies we should know about?"

Mom lets out a deep sigh. "I don't know why I made the copy. I wasn't supposed to. But something told me I should. I never told anyone about it, not even your father."

"I'm glad you did," I say.

"Me, too." Mom turns to Ethan's mom. "Amy, you're going to have to part with your piece."

Mrs. Oliver's eyes go wide. "It's my only link to Stephen."

Next to me, Ethan tenses up. "It doesn't matter, Mom. We have to hide it. It's the right thing to do. Dad would want us to. He would insist."

"I know," she says. "But it's still ... I just don't think I'll be able to bring myself to do it."

"I'll do it," Ethan says, and it's so nice knowing that he is totally in my camp now. That I can trust him completely.

Mom nods. "And what about the piece at Amino Corp?"

Uncle Randall runs a hand through his hair. "It won't be easy to get it, but we'll figure out a way. Maybe I can pull strings with Harvard and filter a private purchase through that way. If Amino Corp is on the edge of bankruptcy, they might be willing to part with it."

"Good," Mom says, and then she kind of wavers and sinks into a chair.

"Are you okay?" I ask, rushing over to her side.

Her face is pale, and her hands are shaking.

"I'm fine, Hannah," she says.

Ethan's mom comes over to join her. "You're not fine, Laura," she says, and their eyes meet, as if some kind of understanding passes between them.

"What?" I say.

"Your mom," Amy Oliver says.

"What about her? Somebody needs to tell me something right away because if there's something wrong with my mom, then I need to know."

Mom lets out a small laugh. "There's nothing wrong with me, Hannah. I promise. If anything, I've been healed."

"Healed from what?" I ask. Mom wasn't sick, at least not that I ever knew of.

Mom's eyes soften. "Hannah, did you ever wonder why you were an only child?"

I shrug. "I always figured that you and Dad didn't want any more kids. Or didn't have time to have any more kids."

She shakes her head. "No, we did want to have more kids. A brother or a sister for you. But I was never able to. I couldn't get pregnant again after I had you."

Things are starting to come together in my mind. "What are you saying, Mom?"

She rests a hand on her stomach. "The Code of Enoch. I think it healed me there at the end."

My eyes widen. "You're pregnant?"

She nods. "A final gift from the Code. You're going to have a baby brother or sister."

It's amazing news. Something I never could have even hoped for. I hug her, but then worry that I'm putting too much pressure on her stomach.

"It's okay," Mom says. "I feel great."

"You'll have a stomach to match mine," Uncle Randall says. "Having a broken leg can put a real damper on any type of physical activity. The only place I've walked is back and forth to the kitchen, it seems."

He pats his stomach for effect, which, now that I look at it, has paunched out just the smallest bit since we left.

"But that said," Uncle Randall goes on. "I have been doing quite a bit of reading. And studying. And you wouldn't believe what I've found." He stands up and uses the crutch to walk to his office. I help Mom up, and we all follow.

Uncle Randall hobbles to the circular table in the center of the room. It's strewn with papers and ancient books.

"What have you been up to, Randall?" Mom asks, walking over to the table. Her color is returning, and I remember that pregnant women can get nauseous during their first three months.

Uncle Randall's eyes are wide and filled with excitement. "I met with someone when we went to Turkey."

Memories of Uncle Randall and his secretive meeting return to me. I'd nearly forgotten.

"I saw you. In the hotel restaurant, meeting with some

woman. She gave you something. Some kind of package."

"You were spying on me, Hannah?" he says, narrowing his eyes.

"You were acting suspicious," I say. "What do you expect?"

"I expect you to do exactly what you did," Uncle Randall says. "Be observant, which you were. And yes, she gave me something."

He pulls a small carved wooden box from his pocket and sets it on the table but doesn't open it.

We all gather around so we can see. Light seems to emanate from the box.

"What's in it?" I say.

Uncle Randall smiles. "It's not so much what's in it as what should be in it."

"Which is what?" Ethan says. He's studying the box, trying to read the symbols.

"Which is what we need to find next," Uncle Randall says. And without another word, he opens the box.